# Where Gods Once Walked

## A Novel

# Where Gods Once Walked

## A Novel

## Christina A. Dudley

masnago press

ISBN 978-0-6452-8688-5 (paperback)
ISBN 978-0-6452-8689-2 (ebook)

A catalogue record for this book is available from the National Library of Australia.

Published by masnago press
masnagopress@gmail.com

Cover image https://bookcoverzone.com/

*For Rod, Franny and Nicky*

# PART ONE

# - 1 -

I place my foot on a metal cross bar and hoist myself up. Everyone does this in the evening, after the beach, climb the gate and trespass upon the precincts of the thermal springs at Kaiafas. Though the gate is firmly shut and locked, as business for the day is over, we want to enter and have a free bathe in the hot waters bubbling up from deep within the earth.

'Need a hand?' a voice behind me says, and suddenly he's beside me as I cling to the bars. 'Put your other foot there and then you can swing your leg over.'

He's about my age, I suppose, thirty something, thick ebony hair, and his eyes look at me quizzically. He reaches over and steadies my elbow, and I make a little jump to the ground.

'Thanks,' I say.

He walks off towards the overhanging cliff face, crunching the dry grass under his rubber sandals. I follow him and scratch my leg on a thorny bush. Ahead, seams of terracotta and pink sandstone jut out over the hot pool. We reach the stone slabs rimming the edge of the water, and I hang my bag and towel on a rusty hook banged into the rock wall. I remove my dress, adjust my bathers and look up, and he is there, standing before me, naked, his body lean and sculptured.

'You're bleeding,' he says.

Unsure where to look, I lean over, examine the scratch on my leg and rummage for a tissue in my bag.

'Don't want you leaping into that water all bloodied,' he says dryly. 'You might attract the sharks.'

'It's stopped now.' I dab it with the tissue. Sensing his gaze, I stand, look him in the eye and extend my hand. 'I'm Marina.'

He takes my hand. 'Dimitri. You Greek? You've got a Greek name.'

'No, though my parents loved Greece and so do I. Always holidayed here, so I got a Greek name. I was conceived here. In a tent in that pine forest above the beach. I'm Australian but live in London.'

'Oh, I see.'

He steps down onto a wobbly stone slab and dives into the pool. He resurfaces and cries out, 'Aaah, *polý kalá.*'

I lower myself into the hot waters.

The pool disappears within the cave under the mountain from where the hot waters flow in a continuous stream. We remain at the opening, beneath where the overhanging cliff face kisses the twilight sky, and glide about as our bodies become limp and silken, enveloped like embryos in the 35 degrees heat of the waters. A sulphurous odour wafts about, blending with the pungent perfume of eucalypts and wild sage. Within minutes the pain in my joints flows out of my pores and dissolves.

A German family bathe near us. They scoop up the pool's therapeutic mud and slap it on their faces. It's good for the skin, and the father says, '*Es ist sehr gut. Sehr gut.*'

Further within the cave, where the pool recedes into dimness, a young couple clasp in a coital embrace, oblivious to us.

Dimitri emerges from beneath the water beside me, and his nakedness and the ripples of sex emanating from inside the cave release a frisson within me.

'Have you ever been to Ceduna?' he says suddenly.

I am flummoxed by his question, but I want to know something about him first, so I say, 'How is it you speak such good English?'

'Worked in the States for two years.'

'Ah, I see. And what was it you wanted to know?'

'Have you ever been to Ceduna?'

'Never heard of it.'

As he treads water before me, he lathers his hair with mud and applies a vigorous scrubbing. His naked body drifts closer to me, a little too close, and I wish the water wasn't so clear. I paddle backwards a couple of strokes.

'Ceduna is in South Australia, on the coast,' he says. 'I went there in December a few years ago.'

'Whatever for?'

'The eclipse of the sun. Ceduna was the only place on Earth where you could see the total eclipse.'

This unexpected revelation of his amazes me. 'Are you an astronomer?'

'An amateur one. And I like to travel. The whole world gathered on the beach at Ceduna that day and gazed at the sky. Not going to happen again for a long time. Got some good shots too. The clouds cleared at just the right moment.'

He dips his head under the water and rinses off the mud. I paddle off then return when he resurfaces.

'How did you get to Ceduna?'

'Flew to Melbourne. Visited my uncle in Oakleigh, then stayed in a youth hostel in St Kilda.' He dives under the water. I have trouble following his story. Eventually I learn that he bought a Ford station wagon for $2,000 from a Polish backpacker at the youth hostel, then set off on a trip around Australia, stopping at Ceduna on the way.

'Never had any problems with that car,' he says. 'The only hitch I had on that trip was the bed bugs in the youth hostel in Perth. Never go to that hostel. Filthy. I sold the car back at the St Kilda Youth Hostel for $2,000. See! Broke even!'

Something black swishes past my head, and I dive beneath the water. I resurface and say, 'What was that?'

'Bats. These caves are full of them. A German professor travels from Munich every year to count them. Five hundred bats nest in there. They're filthy too. Carry all sorts of diseases. Come on. Time to go. It's getting cold and dark.'

I look about and realise everyone else has gone. It is dark, and I hardly know this person. The diving swallows have retreated for the night, and only the swoosh of the bats breaks the otherwise eerie silence. A breeze, slight and cool, rustles the dry grass, and a bright star hangs low in the sky, a star I've observed every evening, with its gilded reflection rippling in the sea.

I quickly change my clothes behind a lone bush, relieved to find a pullover in my bag as I am suddenly quite cold. He appears beside me. I am nervous now, indeed wary, and I shiver in the cool night air. I just want to leave quickly on my own. My car's outside the locked gates. I've climbed over them many times but never in a rush. I'm in a rush now.

'Coming?' he says.

'Sure.' I decide to make conversation. I'm getting anxious over nothing, I tell myself. He's done nothing to me. 'What's that star?' I point to the western sky.

'That's Venus. It's almost gold, isn't it? The reflection in the sea is gold.' He's also observed it. 'Venus is exceptionally close to Earth right now, as close as it's ever going to be for a very long time. Want to come up to my house and look at it through my telescope? I can cook some fish on the grill.'

For a second his invitation tweaks my curiosity, and I almost say that I'd love to, but I decline his invitation with some contrived excuse, even though the thought of grilled fish whets my appetite. 'No, thanks, perhaps another time,' I say soppily.

We reach the gates and he helps me over.

'*You* should know all about Venus and your Captain Cook,' he says. 'You know he sailed to the Pacific to observe the transit of Venus and then went on to discover Australia. Clever man, clever man.'

'That's right. Look, I really need to get going. I'm cold.'

'Where are you staying? Give me your phone number.'

I decide not to answer. I get into my car and look up at him through the unwound driver's window. I suddenly say, 'I might see you back here again. I come most evenings. Had a bad car accident once. Helps ease the aches from my injuries.' I immediately wish I hadn't told him that.

'Are you eating in the piazza tonight?'

'Maybe.' I start my car. 'See you, Dimitri. And thanks for helping me over the gate.'

# - 2 -

I stand under the shower and let the hot water penetrate my bones, then wash my hair and shave my legs. I take extra care with my personal grooming for some reason and won't admit to myself why. I put on a muted pink and green dress, with its low-cut neck and full skirt that sways when I walk, and apply a faint brush of make-up and shade my eyes. I head downstairs and stroll up the narrow road that leads to the square, a road I know well, for whenever I visit Greece when working for Lonely Planet, updating the section on The Peloponnese, I stay in Kato Samiko in the little flat above Dina and Vassilis's butcher's shop.

Outside, the air is still balmy, and the day's heat beats off the walls, creating a cocoon of warmth. It is dark, but, ahead, the street beneath the amber lighting throbs with life. A mixed aroma of fresh peaches in wooden boxes and baking spinach and cheese pies wafts about. I pause before the greengrocer and look at the scarlet tomatoes and green basil in plastic pots. Helena, the owner, stands at the doorway with her hands in her apron pocket and smiles at me.

*Tomorrow*, I gesture.

Outside another shop further up the street, tin buckets, plastic bowls, spades, rakes, forks and wicker baskets clutter the footpath. I enter the shop, and among the chaos of shelves jammed with tins of tuna and beans, batteries, balls of string, wooden implements and sacks of flour, I find a basket of tiny bottles of nail polish. I buy a pearly pink one, put it in my bag, then exit and pause at the corner and look across the square. Nearby, a French couple eat braised pork with lemon, garlic and oregano. Their wooden table wobbles, and the young man tears a piece off the menu and sticks it under the table leg. An aroma of garlic stirs pangs of hunger within me. I see Christos and Sophie, the butcher's son and daughter, eating salad and chips at a nearby table and join them.

'You're looking nice,' Christos says.

I smile at his compliment.

'Wine?'

'Thanks.'

I soon have a pile of Greek salad with feta in front of me, then souvlaki and fried balls of zucchini. We talk of the heat and jobs while a bouzouki plays next door. Townsfolk crowd the square and children run about the tables. Sophie talks to me, but I am distracted, wondering if I should have accepted Dimitri's offer to view Venus though his telescope. I, too, am a traveller and explorer, a searcher, and he's tweaked my curiosity. *Ceduna, an eclipse, bedbugs, bats, Venus, grilled fish.* All from a naked body with mud in his hair. All in less than an hour. I admit I find something compelling about him despite his frayed shorts and broken sandals. Spontaneous yet solemn. His jaw square and hands fine. I'll note it in my journal, I tell myself.

I feel a tap on my shoulder and turn and see Dimitri.

'Thought I might find you here,' he says.

I smile at him and say, 'I always eat here in the evening.'

'Care to join me?'

He's all brushed up now, handsome in his slim jeans, chalk-white t-shirt and navy canvas loafers. His thick hair is combed, and a spring scent floats about him. I introduce him to Sophie and Christos, yet they all know each other, and the butcher's children sneak glances across at me, smiling.

'You off?' Sophie says with a little laugh.

'Guess so,' I say. I leave a €20 note with her to pay for my dinner.

I follow Dimitri as he weaves past the crowded tables till we find and sit at an unoccupied one in a far corner.

'More wine?' he says.

'A little, thanks.'

'Pano,' he calls to the waiter. '*Krasì.*' He returns his attention to me. 'You're looking good. Nice dress. Different from today with your bloody leg, your bottom on the gate and your salty hair.' He smiles, and his eyes screw up.

'Thanks.'

He pours wine into my glass.

'Oooh, not too much.' I notice he pours a glass of water for himself. 'No wine for you?'

'No, I have to work tomorrow.'

Of course, it is Sunday. I am losing count of the days. 'Well, a little glass won't do any harm, will it?'

'In my job it will.'

'You work? Doing what?'

'I'm a doctor. Work in the hospital at Patras.'

'Oh, I see.' I am silent for a long time as I did not expect this. I had envisaged him as unemployed, lying about, like so many other young men in Greece. 'So … you're a doctor?'

'Yes, that's right. In Emergency … though I don't get paid for it.'

'Whyever not?'

'Government's got no money. Greece's bankrupt. Can't pay its employees. Teachers, doctors, nurses, pensioners and all the rest. I worked in Athens, but when the pay stopped, I had to move back here. Couldn't afford the rent. Here, I've the family house to live in, and my aunt down the road keeps chickens and goats and tends a vegetable garden. That way, we keep going.' He pauses, taps the table and sips his water. 'Hundreds have left Athens and returned home to the provinces.' He combs back his fringe with his fingers. 'Someone's got to look after the sick. Even if it's only the emergency stuff.'

'I see. Greece is in a terrible mess, isn't it, even though everyone round here looks pretty happy?'

'Yeah, it's OK here. Everyone looks after everyone else. Our shopkeepers give away groceries, vegetables and clothes to all the families without work.'

We sit in silence and sip our drinks, then I say, 'Well, if you've got to work tomorrow, I guess you'll be wanting to get home.'

'No, no, let's go for a little walk. Today is my day off.'

We work our way past the tables and chairs and head down the road, now quiet as the shops have closed. We come to a little church just off the square. Pale light shines through its windows, and solemn voices emanate from within. Dimitri suggests we go in for a minute, and I follow him in.

Flickering candlelight illuminates the dim, almost empty church. A robed priest with gold braids stands beside the altar and chants before an open book covered in etched gold and enamel. A heady scent of incense seems embedded in the walls around me. I find the chanting haunting yet comforting. I sit, meditative and transported into another space, and Dimitri sits

11

beside me, listening, looking ahead and occasionally closing his eyes and crossing himself. I relax in the ambience.

He reaches over and takes my hand. 'I'm just going over to light a candle for my mother,' he whispers. The pressure of his hand on mine moves me.

He returns and whispers that we can leave, and we exit and continue our walk down the road towards a bend that leads to the sea. On the bend we pass a cluster of tiny altars, each with its own ikon and candle and decorated with flowers. I see them most days. He pauses before an altar, crosses himself, pulls a candle from his pocket, lights it with a match and presses it into a bowl of sand, where it stands erect and glows.

I remain silent, feeling like an intruder.

'My mother was killed in a car accident on this bend,' he says.

Another unexpected revelation of his that again surprises and shocks me. 'Oh, I am sorry.'

'I like to keep a candle lit for her. It's been ten years now.'

'That's terrible. You never get over things like that … I know all about that.' I take his hand, thinking he needs comforting. Does he? I'm not sure as I hardly know him.

We walk on to the beach, and with sand underfoot I remove my sandals and run to the sea.

'Yay!' I yell stupidly.

We run about and splash in the shallows and look up at Venus hanging low in the sky.

'You know, if we hurry,' Dimitri says, 'we could still get up to my place to see Venus before she dips into the sea.'

'OK', I say, as if it's the most natural thing in the world.

We drive in his car up into the hills overlooking the sea, weaving past olive groves and vineyards, and then up a rough track to a house built of stone. It is cool and renovated, with a wide veranda with a panoramic view of the sea and sliding doors leading into a living room, where large paintings adorn the walls and busts—some copies of classical Greek works, others modern—rest on low tables.

I caress the smooth, marble cheeks of the sculptures, but stop and say, 'Sorry, shouldn't have touched them, I suppose.'

'Why not?' he says. 'They're made to be touched.' He leads me towards the veranda. 'Come on. Venus is going down.'

He adjusts the lens of the telescope for me, and I look through. Venus is the most amazing thing I've seen for a long time.

'It's so powerful, like a blazing sun,' I say.

I swing the telescope and look at the moon. Its craters stand out like a crazy land mass in Antarctica. Dimitri points out craters on the moon and tells me there are more than 5,000.

'Too many to name,' he says.

I point the telescope downwards. 'Wow, I can see people dancing on the beach. Hey, you could spy on anyone you like. Bad man!'

I sit on a cushioned divan and admire the ripples of gold upon the sea. Dimitri disappears, only to return carrying a tray with orange juice in green glasses and a plate of cut-up fruit. He sets the tray on a low table before me.

'My own oranges,' he says. 'Freshly squeezed.'

He sits beside me, and we sip the juice and fork up watermelon and pineapple.

'You said before that you went to the pool because you'd had a bad accident,' he says.

'I did … though I wish I hadn't mentioned it.'

He pauses. 'You OK now? I mean, are you over it now?'

'Well, as I said before, you never really get over these things, do you?'

'What do you mean?'

'Like with the death of your mother.' I wish he wouldn't ask me about … my past. 'Look, I don't really want to talk about these things now.'

'OK.' He nods.

We eat in silence until, without any inner bidding on my part, I say, 'My accident was really bad, much worse than your mother's. I … I mean, I was driving the car, and it skidded in the rain and ran off the road, and my mother was killed. I mean, I killed my mother. I can almost say it now without crying. It was an accident, oil and rain on the road, and on a bend, just like that bend where your mother was killed. My father, brother and sister never got over it.' Cicadas thrum in the trees. 'I was in hospital for months while they fixed up my legs. But I'm good now.'

'Sounds like you had a bad time. I hope they did a good job on your legs. I know a lot about legs. I specialised in orthopaedics in the States and have had plenty of practice in Emergency.' He pauses for moment. 'You sure you're OK now?'

'The scars on my legs are still there, if you look closely … though they're pretty invisible when my legs are tanned.'

'What about the wounds in here?' Dimitri points to his head.

'They're healed, but I've still got scars, so I have to be careful not to exercise my mind too much. Those scars are delicate. They're getting stronger, though.'

'Everyone's got scars. Even the gods. They're full of them. You feel immense guilt, I suppose. You said it was an accident. You can't feel guilty forever. Imagined guilt is paralysing. It grips your mind.'

'True.'

He reaches over and places his hand upon my arm, albeit briefly, before withdrawing. Distance again separates us.

I sit silent and still and don't say anything. Again he reaches over. He takes my hand and strokes it. We watch Venus slip into the inked sea, and the moon, up high now, casts a bright light over the fruit trees and olive grove. I rise, step down from the veranda and wander between the trees where nocturnal animals rustle the branches. He follows me, takes me in his arms and kisses me with urgency.

'There's more to us than just climbing over locked gates together,' he says with a touch of irony. 'Let's go back to the veranda. We can lie there and look out at the stars.'

## - 3 -

Dimitri lays cushions on the veranda, and we lie down and look up at the Milky Way. Feeble light from an amber candle in a corner flickers, so the over-arching sky is dark, close and crystal. The myriad of stars form great swathes of low-hanging white gossamer. We are in touch with the Universe, its numbing vastness beyond my understanding. I sense Dimitri's excitement at its mystery, yet I need him to describe it to me. He tells me about the constellations named by Greek astronomers, their knowledge the fruit borne of this verdant land with its sweet climate. Now it is in economic and social decline.

'Ptolemy catalogued 48 constellations in 150 AD,' Dimitri says, pointing heavenwards and picking out the brightest stars and formations. I remember never being able to find my own Southern Cross. I find searching for celestial bodies and understanding their distances daunting, almost frightening, beyond comprehension, but Dimitri talks on with avid passion.

I need to hold his hand. I reach over and take it and turn towards him. He caresses me tenderly as we lie crooked in each other's bodies. He pulls a loose cover over us. Our immersion in the hot springs that afternoon has fatigued us—it always does—and within minutes I hear his low regular breathing, and I, too, fall asleep beside him.

*   *   *

A hand on my breast wakes me, and through slit eyes I see early rays of sun flickering through the olive branches. His hand wanders over my back and down my thighs, and we kiss, lightly.

He props himself up on his elbow and says, 'I fell asleep. Sorry.'

'Why are you apologising? I did the same.'

'Too late now.' He looks at his watch.

'Too late for what?'

'Oh, it doesn't matter.' He runs his fingers through my hair. 'Something platonic on a Greek veranda, shall we say?'

'Do we have to define everything?'

'No, not at all.' He rises from the cushions. 'I need to get going. I start at seven this morning. I'll drop you off in town. Sorry, it's probably too early for you.'

'Don't worry, I'll manage. And, please, don't apologise.'

I want to tell him that something has passed between us. I am drawn to him: his enthusiasms, his platters of fresh fruit, his smooth sculptures, his brown bare feet. I want to be by his side on this veranda again, lying on the cushions and looking up at the stars.

He strokes my hand, then walks into the house.

We drive into town and pass the bend again where his mother's altar stands. The candle flickers in the morning air.

'Candle's still alight,' I say. 'That's good, isn't it?'

He says nothing.

'Let me out here, I can walk up the hill.' He stops the car. I pull the latch, then turn to him. 'Thanks ... thanks for a beautiful night.' I place my hand upon his knee, and he pulls me towards him and kisses me on my mouth.

'I like your hair,' he says. He smiles and combs his fingers through my hair.

I give a little laugh. 'Thanks for everything.'

He doesn't ask for my number, which disappoints me. As I get out, he stretches his hand through the window, then the car draws away. I walk up to the square, sit down and order a frappé and a cheese pie. It's only quarter to six, so I head back to my flat and lie down.

*　　*　　*

Two hours later the sun crosses the bed in sharp rays. I sit up quickly, almost panting, not understanding why I am lying on the bed in my dress. I shower and change, then get out maps and a list of the destinations I need to check.

I decide to head for the hills above Kaiafas, where years ago, on family holidays, we would drive to Arini and visit Costas and Anna's olive farm. Along the way I stop and draw water from a spring at the side of the road. The day is already hot, and I sit and drink the cool water from a plastic cup while looking out over the olive-clad hills. I cannot rid from my mind thoughts about what occurred yesterday and last night. His hand on my breast, the brief urgency under the trees. My ruminations wrangle. What might have been, and what was not. Or maybe it was never going to be nor ever will be. Appreciate it for what it was, a moment in time, I tell myself.

I drive up the rough, cobble-stoned road to Costas and Anna's house. I hop out and call 'Hello' round the yard where chickens peck and goats wander about and munch on dry bushes. Costas and Anna appear, and following much embracing, their son, Alexi, strides around the corner of the house and greets me.

'You see,' he says, 'we are now calling our farm the Boutique Olive Farm.'

His English has improved since we last met. Now taller and more handsome, he tells me he has returned home from Athens, where his job as a graphic designer has folded. He guides me round the old stone house and shows me the renovated bedrooms and bathrooms.

'Each one has its own view of the sea and a terrace for sitting outside,' he says. 'My dad grills the chicken over there, and my mum fries the zucchini and melanzane behind here.'

I note that they have kept the rustic farmhouse ambience of the place: the open grill, the plastic curtain leading into the kitchen and the raffia chairs.

'The house is full during the olive harvest in October and November. Visitors come from London and Hamburg for the peasant life. They sit outside here, eat our chicken and our oil, tomatoes and feta cheese. Easy!' He is trying hard to sell the place to me, but he doesn't need to. 'And then they all leave with tins of oil and olives and bunches of oregano.'

We sit under the grapevine, and I take notes: prices, amenities, high season, low season, how to get there, public transport, hire car and the walking trails in the hills. Costas brings out a plate of grilled chicken, and Anna adds her tomato and cucumber salad. I crack the chalky feta and roll olives in bread. The sky is picture blue, a heavenly canopy embracing us from above, unsullied by clouds. My hosts can only smile. I'm taken back to my childhood holidays and the perfume of basil and wild sage, and warmth envelopes my body. My earlier wrangled thoughts dissolve in the sweet breeze.

As I leave, I assure Alexi and his family that the next edition of the *Lonely Planet Guide to Greece* will include the new Boutique Olive Farm. As I drive down the hill, my phone pings, and I stop and read an email from Chloe Zimmerman at The Guardian.

*Marina*

*We are doing a series on the migrant crisis in Europe. I remember you said you'd be in Greece for a while, doing your Lonely Planet research. I wondered whether you would be interested in doing some pieces on what's happening in Greece.*

*Let me know. Cheers Chloe.*

I reply immediately for I need plans and projects.

*Of course, Chloe. Round here it's all happening in Patras. People trying to get on boats to Italy from the port. I'll get onto it and get back to you ASAP.*

*Regards Marina*

Now glad to focus on a new project, I drive back to Kato Samiko, pondering on how I might investigate the migrant issues in Patras. I'll need contacts, I reason. I can't just go in there cold. Perhaps the police or other journalists or the Consulate? No, they'll advise me to keep away. I can just hear someone telling me from behind a brown desk, 'No, don't touch it. It's too dangerous.' And if I mention the word *Guardian*, they'll immediately thrust up their hackles. I resolve to some-how contact Dimitri. I'm sure he'll know someone able to give me a head start. I'll be very business-like, of course. *Just need a couple of contacts*, I'll say.

I gather my swimming gear for a twilight swim at the pool, hoping he'll be there. I'll just climb over the gate, have my swim, ask him if he can help me, and then say I need to leave.

When I arrive at the car park, I can't see Dimitri's car. I climb over the gate, change behind the prickly bush and plunge into the warm waters. I swim near a French family and an obese Englishman of indeterminate age who tries to speak to me. I feign incomprehension and paddle away. After half an hour suddenly all turns quiet. The crickets cease their thrumming and the swallows retire. Dimitri is not coming. I'm disappointed and cold, so I get out, change, climb the gate and return to my car, its cabin still warm from the day's sun. I decide to drive up to his house. Will I find him there? Asleep? With a partner? I reason to myself that I'm just seeking his assistance with my investigation, so I set off, my mind untrammelled by "what ifs".

I pull up at the house and step onto the veranda. I knock on the open door and call out, 'Hello.'

Behind me, an elderly woman wearing a straw hat comes up the veranda steps.

'Is Dimitri here?' I say.

'No, no,' she says. 'Hospital, hospital. I'm Aunt Maria.' She has the brightest blue eyes I've ever seen.

'Ah, I see. I'm a friend. Marina. Swimming pool.' I mimic a swimming action and she seems to understand. 'Could I leave a note for him?'

I see a pen and paper on the kitchen bench and write my phone number and a note asking Dimitri to ring me when he gets home.

'It's not urgent,' I say, turning to leave. 'Thanks for that. You'll tell him I called by, won't you?'

Maria carries a bundle of eggs and nuts in her tucked-up apron. 'Wait a moment,' she says. Finding a sheet of newspaper, she wraps some nuts and eggs in a packet. 'Here, take these.' She pushes the gift into my hands. 'I tell Dimitri, I tell him.'

*       *       *

At 11 p.m. my phone rings, stirring me from my drowiness.

'Dimitri,' he says when I answer.

'Oh, sorry. It's just that …' Flustered, I sit up and compose myself, and now awake and calm, I explain my migrant assignment and ask him whether he knows of anyone in Patras who would be a suitable contact.

'I'll be in Patras tomorrow afternoon. We could meet at the hospital's Emergency entrance. Say 4 p.m. Wait just inside the door. Text me when you get there. We'll talk about it then.'

'Oh, thanks so much.'

'Till tomorrow then.' He's curt, businesslike, a tired note in his voice. I try not to think about it.

The next day I arrive at Patras Hospital before 4 p.m. as I don't want to be late. I sit in the waiting room at the entrance to Emergency. His business-like tone on the phone has put me on alert, and I text him: *Waiting in Emergency.* Half an hour passes and I become anxious. Finally, he appears, and I hardly recognise him in a hospital gown, plastic gloves and cap. As he approaches me, he orders a passing nurse to undertake some task, and I see him, in command, in control, respected.

'So … sorry,' I say. 'I hope I'm not mucking up your day.'

'Don't apologise,' he says. 'I'm glad you called. Meant to give you my number.' His gloves have a splattering of blood on them. 'I need to change. Wait here.'

Twenty minutes later we drive along the road running by the port.

'They've built a huge iron-railing fence over there with barbed wire at the top and bottom,' he says, nodding his head towards the port. 'All to stop Iraqi and Afghan men stowing away on ships to Italy or hiding themselves in the back of trucks to get on board.'

He slows and points at two bars in the fence forced apart, leaving enough space for the underfed body of a man to squeeze through. The roll of barbed wire at the foot of the fence lies cut and pulled apart. Soldiers (or are they armed police?) circle the trucks waiting in a queue to board the ferry bound for Italy. Young men and boys dart between the trucks, and a soldier hauls one from the baggage compartment of a bus. Another soldier boards a truck and pokes and bangs the cargo inside with his gun. A young man emerges, hands on his head, and the soldier drags him to his feet and marches him to the gates of the port. I suspect he'll leave to try again another day.

We continue along the road until a young man appears ahead, hobbling along with bloodied feet and aided by his companion. Dimitri slows the car and stops and says to the men, 'Need a lift to the camp?'

'Yes, doctor,' the companion says. 'It would be very good of you, thank you.'

The two men get in the back of the car, and a pungent body odour assails the cabin.

'Where are we going?' I whisper to Dimitri.

'To their camp out the back of the football stadium.'

'But they know you!'

'That's right. I, or another medic, go out there every second day. That's where we're going now.'

The men remain silent. Is it because there's a woman in the car? Are they suspicious of me? I'm not sure.

## - 4 -

Dimitri drives the four of us along the road beside the port, leaving behind the centre of the city. By the sea, construction sites lie deserted with cranes erect and forgotten and bulldozers poised mid-dig, like cardboard cut-outs against the blue sky. The workers, told the government has run out of money, have long abandoned their machines and walked away.

Dimitri steers to the left and guides the car down a dirt track which passes through a rubbish dump. The car weaves between rusty bed frames, mattresses, discarded household furniture and mountains of black plastic bags oozing refuse and releasing an overbearing stench. I wind up my window.

'Where are we going?' I whisper to Dimitri, but he remains silent, concentrating on avoiding potholes and rocks.

The rubbish clears as we near the football stadium, and Dimitri parks the car. He helps the two men out, but I back away. I don't wish to offend them, yet an instinctive self-preservation kicks in as I fear I might catch something. We walk along a narrow path through high grass and thorny bushes, and a young man with honey skin and a black beard approaches.

'Hello, Ahmed,' Dimitri says.

'Ah Doctor, it's you,' the young man says. 'And this lady?'

'A nurse, come to help.'

'Huh, come on.'

We follow him along the track and into a copse of bushes where makeshift shelters covered with plastic roofs lean against branches. Circles of ashes and empty tins, pots and plastic water bottles lie strewn about the campsite.

We arrive at a bigger shelter and Ahmed pulls back the flap. Inside, stretchers surround a piece of rough carpet covering the ground. The two young men from the back of the car sit on the edge of a stretcher, and Dimitri examines the injured foot. He pours water on it from a plastic bottle, then removes an enamel dish from his case and fills it with water and antiseptic. The men remain silent and watch Dimitri as he works at the encrustation of dirt and blood.

'Ask him how he did this,' Dimitri says to Ahmed.

Ahmed exchanges words with the young men and then says to Dimitri, 'He, Aziz, was climbing the fence down at the port.'

'He'll need a tetanus shot.' Dimitri prepares a syringe. 'Got to give him a few stitches too.'

I admire the deftness of Dimitri's fingers as he sews the wound.

Dimitri hands Ahmed a packet of antibiotics. 'Tell him to take these every day. One in the morning, one at night and finish the packet. And don't forget.' Dimitri bandages the foot. 'You gotta keep this foot clean. Put a shoe over it and don't walk on it. I'll be back next week to take the stitches out.'

The young man gets up and manages a thank you.

Dimitri pats him on the back. 'Look after yourself, Aziz.'

I look around and see a group huddled by the tent flap.

'These people need treating?' Dimitri says.

Ahmed nods.

One by one they enter and sit on a chair by the entrance. Ahmed interprets as Dimitri presses his stethoscope to chests, palpates abdomens and looks down throats and ears. He dispenses medicines and instructs Ahmed on how they are to be taken. Occasionally, he passes something to me to hold. I'm unsure if this is to keep up the pretence of my being a nurse.

After the last patient leaves, Dimitri kneels and packs his case. 'Where's Hanna?' he says to Ahmed.

'Come this way,' the young man says.

The two of them exit the shelter, and I follow as they walk along the perimeter of the bushes. We reach the last shelter in the line, and Ahmed raises the flap. We enter, and before us a young woman, draped in a full-length black chador and with olive skin as smooth as a ripe fruit, sits on the floor. Her dark eyes cast down, wary of contact, but an occasional upwards glance reveals white framing a black look of startled fear. Aziz sits beside her.

We stand inside the flap, and as Ahmed talks to her, she shrinks back and her hands move beneath the chador. Aziz says something, and Dimitri exits. Ahmed and I follow.

Dimitri turns to me and says, 'Look, she's got a baby under that chador, but she won't let us go near her to check on it. You're a woman. She might let you have a look.'

'But Dimitri—'

'Don't but me … all you've got to do is have a look. I'll tell you what to look for.'

'But I don't know anything about babies.'

'I said I'll tell you what to look for. Do what you can. It's better than nothing. Ahmed will translate for you.'

My heart pounds for fear of being responsible for a newborn life, but I manage to compose myself and open the flap. Ahmed stands at the entrance with his back to the young woman. I smile to gain her confidence, then ask her to show me her child. She acquiesces with a nod, pulls up her chador and reveals a plump baby suckling, eyes closed, at her breast. In my mind I go through a checklist: eyes, hair, head, body weight, skin, creases, feet, hands. I see nothing wrong. I ask her if I can remove the nappy. Again she nods, and I see it's a boy. She has two packets of nappies beside her as well as rugs and new baby clothes. I ask Ahmed where she got them from, and he tells me that the checkout woman at the supermarket gives him something for the baby every time he goes there. But Aziz is on his feet, standing in front of the young woman and arguing heatedly with Ahmed. I calm them down by saying with a smile, 'He's lovely. How old is he?'

'Three months,' Ahmed says. 'Born on the ground there.'

I am exhausted when I step out of the tent into a scorching sun that beats down on me. With my mouth as dry as autumn leaves, I say to Dimitri, 'He seems fine, fine and chubby. She didn't mind me looking at him.' I am pleased with myself. Proud of my achievement. 'Those two young men nearly had a stand-up fight in front of me. I don't know why. Are we going now?'

He nods, and we walk back along the track to the car.

'I need a drink,' I say.

'Sure, so do I,' Dimitri says. He pats my arm. 'You did a good job. Thank you.'

We drive down the track to the road, turn left and travel along the seafront, past abandoned villas with iron chains on their gates and past wire fences waving a myriad of plastic bags caught in their barbs, until we come to a narrow road by the water's edge. We have left the decrepitude of the city behind us and are by the water —crystal, calm and inviting.

27

'I feel like paddling in that,' I say.

We park the car and venture onto the sand. I throw off my shoes and splash about in the water. We walk up to a small bar on the beach, and Dimitri slings his arm round my waist and guides me up to the veranda which drips with an overhanging crimson bougainvillea. His hand on my waist. It seems so long ago since he touched me. I can't remember when. We sit looking at tiny waves rippling on the sand, their voices low and sweet. Dimitri raises his glass, and we drink to something, I don't know what. The wine is dry yet fruity, and we dig in at the blocks of feta cheese and anchovies and tear the bread apart.

Dimitri suddenly says, 'I feel like washing off the whole day, right now, at the springs. Don't you?'

'Mmm. Yes.'

And we walk hand in hand to his car and head back to Patras Hospital to collect my car.

# - 5 -

We drive to the springs, I in my car and Dimitri in his. When I arrive, I cannot see him and have a moment of panic. I stand by my car and wait for the thrum of his approaching vehicle. Late swallows swoop from above, like black arrows darting against the azure sky. He did say we'd meet here, didn't he? I ask myself, vulnerable, uncertain of his promises. I go over to the gate, place my foot on the crossbar and heave myself up.

'Need a push over?' Dimitri says behind me, followed by a sudden laugh.

I turn and watch him emerge from the bushes, and he slips up to me and pushes my bottom over the top of the gate.

I, too, laugh and say, 'Couldn't see you anywhere.'

'I parked over there,' he says, pointing, and I look over and see his car behind a tuft of swaying bulrushes.

As we walk hand in hand towards the water, I question my reasons for doubting him. I want this to work, and any minor impediment erodes my confidence that it will. He is light-hearted now, derobed of his doctor's demeanour, and he plunges into the water and makes a wide splash.

'Come on,' he says, and I leap in on top of him.

We laugh together, and the day's events wash off as we push slowly through the water. We dive under and embrace, submerged within the water's warm cocoon, and edge under the mountain, towards the cave and the source of the springs. The water is now warmer, and Dimitri dives under and runs his hands down my legs. He surfaces and kisses me, and over his shoulder I see the obese Englishman who circled me the other evening watching us until he glides further into the cave.

'Him again,' I say.

'Who?'

'That Pom. Ruining everything.'

We are not alone, but I wish we were.

We linger in the warmth of the waters within the cave, lightly playing under the water, his hands on my breasts and mine rising up his leg to his groin, then we swim apart, a prelude for what may come later. The Englishman continues his furtive glances at us until he disappears to the pool outside.

Later, we swim out of the cave and float under an indigo sky. The sun has dipped below the horizon, and the bleaching heat of the day has dissipated. The swallows have emptied from the heavens above, replaced by sweeping bats announcing the onset of night.

We reach my car, alone at last, and Dimitri runs his hand through my hair and kisses my eyelids.

'You're coming up for dinner, aren't you?' he says.

'If you want me to.'

'Course I do.'

I get into my car and follow him up the hill.

An inked darkness fills the house except for the dim amber of the light on the veranda. The moon hovers on the horizon, and the stars hang low.

'You want a shower?' Dimitri says when we reach the veranda. He kisses my eyelids again, all tenderness. 'You might want to wash off the sulphur.'

I follow him into the bedroom, and he rustles about in a cupboard until he finds and hands me a towel, soft and white. I step into the shower cubicle and know he will follow me. What began at sunset is now to be completed, and my uncertainties dissolve with the onset of desire.

As the water rushes over us, we become one, not two. A dim light comes from the bedroom, and he presses his taut body against mine. I am blind and grope for him. His hands, strong yet gentle, stroke me, then his lips and tongue tease me. He moves slowly, rhythmically, down my body, and I become body only, a sweet spasm rising into the air towards the stars outside, and fiercely, urgently, he presses his hardness against me and into me and moans low and sighs. We slide down and sit on the floor of the cubicle, silent under the rushing water. We curl into a symbiotic embrace, a shell being washed in waves.

Later, we step out of the shower. But he can't leave me alone, and we stand clasped in the bedroom and then lie on the bed among wet towels and silver sheets and make love again. Time stretches out in a great arc. Or does it shrink to a tiny speck? I cannot tell. All I know is that we will stay here, forever.

Time moves again when Dimitri says, 'You hungry?'

I suppose I am, but all my other senses are nullified except for those which speak to our bodies. I reply, 'Suppose so.'

He pulls on shorts and goes out onto the veranda, where he sits on the divan and looks at the stars. 'A beautiful night,' he says. I'm not sure if he's referring to us or the stars.

I put on my shirt and find a skirt in my beach bag. I join him on the divan, not wanting "us" to end. He embraces me again, urgently, as if he wants me even more than before.

31

'You're lovely,' he says, and his hands caress me until he rises and goes into the kitchen. I hear the fridge door open and the clink of glass. He returns with two thin stemmed glasses and offers me one. 'To us,' he says, and we sip the dry, fruity wine.

When we finish the wine, we move into the kitchen and cook. We peel and chop together, roll out pastry, fill squares with ricotta and spinach, roll balls of zucchini in bread crumbs and fry them in oil. We work as one, filling plates with food which we take onto the veranda, and we feed each other with mini pies, grapes and slices of peaches. Later, the events of the day come back to us as we lie back on the divan and talk about the lost people in the shacks behind the football stadium. Time has caught up with us.

'They need help, those people, don't they?' I say.

'Mmm, they've come a long way. Most all the way from Afghanistan and Iraq. Walking for months, never losing hope for a better life, and now we in Greece are landed with the burden of looking after them, and we can't afford it. This is Europe, but those countries north of the Alps won't have a bar of helping us nations on the Mediterranean deal with the problem.'

'Yes, I guess you're right.'

'That girl has taken you into her confidence. You'll help me by keeping an eye on her, won't you? Come out to the camp every now and then to check on her?'

Dimitri hugs me, and I feel the warmth of complicity and a welling of tears for some reason. It's been a long time since I felt so close to anyone. He wants me to help him, be with him, and I'm glad.

'Sure,' I say. I think of the migrant article Chloe has asked me to write for The Guardian. I need human interest, and this will be it. But part of me feels a twinge of guilt about using these people's plight to sell a newspaper. Or might it, if published, aid them by bringing their plight to the attention of the rest of the world? My thoughts wrangle, but I rein them in, not wanting to mar the loveliness of this night.

'Of course I'll help you,' I say, and I take his hand in mine, and he squeezes it.

Dimitri pours the rest of the wine, and we stretch out together on the divan. A line of light appears on the eastern horizon, above the rim of the sea.

'Is it dawn?' I say. 'Have we just had spinach pies and Prosecco for breakfast?'

'Guess so. Doesn't matter now, though, does it? Nothing matters any more. Come here.'

*    *    *

We wake together to the whir of cicadas and the sun already warm on our bodies. Dimitri has his hand on my shirt and slowly unbuttons it with deft fingers, those which I saw sewing up Aziz's foot yesterday. But this is another moment. Now. And we make love again on the divan.

Dimitri gets up and moves about in the kitchen. He returns carrying a tray with a brass pot of Turkish coffee which he pours into green cups and mixes with spoonfuls of sugar.

'That's good, very good,' I say, following a sip. The brew is syrupy. 'Not working today?'

'No, taking it off to spend with you. I know a deserted beach below the pine woods. I'll show you.'

# - 6 -

The days of July merge together, a space of angora heat, sweet breezes and the pungent odours of pines in the woods and stale salt on the beaches where we swim. Dimitri rises at dawn to go to the hospital, and I set off on my trips to fact-check for Lonely Planet: Andritsena to view the Turkish architecture, then Bassae to see the temple built to Apollo more than two thousand years ago. I sit on Dimitri's veranda to write up my notes and send articles to Chloe at The Guardian. She replies that she loves them. *Keep them coming*, she writes.

Every second day I join Dimitri and go out to the football stadium to see Hanna and treat the other migrants. I'm becoming fond of Hanna and her baby with his eyes wide open and smiling when I lean over him to change his nappy.

One day, I take him in my arms, and Hanna walks with me along a narrow track which leads away from the rubbish dump to a shaded patch of grass where we can sit and play with the baby away from the men at the camp.

The baby is thriving and almost lets out a chuckle. Hanna smiles. She's becoming confident now, but I struggle to communicate with her until, to my surprise, she says, 'You know I speak a few English.'

'Why didn't you say so,' I say.

'Aziz don't know so Ahmed come to translate for me. When doctor come I need friend in camp. I don't speak with no one. Aziz, he shut me in tent. I bit afraid of him.'

'Did you learn English at school?'

'Yes, now I practise with you.'

'Does Aziz hurt you? Beat you?'

'No.' She answers doubtfully.

I remind myself to tell Dimitri that Hanna can speak a little English and to always bring Ahmed into the tent to protect her.

Suddenly, as Hanna and I sit quietly on our patch of grass, screams of rage come from the path, and Aziz appears, shouting incomprehensibly at us. He grabs the baby from the ground, yells a spate of abuse at me and storms down the path back to the tent. Hanna, terrified and screaming, turns to me, pleading, then runs off after her child, shouting and crying.

'Come back,' I shout to them. 'You'll hurt the baby, Aziz.' But he ignores my plea.

I return to their tent and try to enter, but Aziz is beside himself and bars my entrance.

'Dimitri,' I shout, rushing towards the tent where he is treating patients. 'Aziz is in a rage. He'll hurt the baby.' I turn to Ahmed. 'What's wrong with him? He seems to be enraged for no reason. We have to check on the baby.'

We run to the tent, and Ahmed calls through the opening. Inside, Aziz screams, and Hanna and the baby cry.

'He thinks you're going to steal the baby,' Ahmed says. 'He's full of rage and fury. House bombed. Everyone dead. Mother, father, sisters, brothers. He's sick in the head.'

'Try talking to him, Ahmed,' Dimitri says. 'I'll give him an injection if I can get in there.'

For the next half hour, Ahmed talks to Aziz from outside the tent. We sit and wait, but the man inside seems possessed and talks in a torrent of words, a tide refusing to be stemmed. Finally, there is silence. Ahmed calls Hanna, and in the voice of a mouse she whispers that Aziz has fallen into a trance on the ground. We enter and find Aziz collapsed on the floor. As Dimitri administers an injection to Aziz, the baby screams, and I go over to the corner where Hanna is curled, clutching her baby.

'Does he often do this?' Dimitri says to Ahmed.

'Yes, he sometimes does this. He's a bit mad, you know,' Ahmed says.

'Now what are we going to do?' I say. 'We can't leave Hanna and the baby alone here with Aziz. He's got some sort of post-traumatic shock. He's crazy and she's in danger. You'll have to stay with her all night, Ahmed. Look after her.'

'Oh no, no, no, he'll kill me if he finds me here or I take her away.'

'We could take her to hospital.'

'Depends which doctor's in Emergency,' Dimitri says. 'Some doctor could turn her over to the police, another could turn a blind eye to her not having any papers.'

'You'll have to take her back to Emergency,' I say, 'and make sure they turn a blind eye. Ahmed can tell Hanna we're going to take her to hospital and for her not to be afraid. Explain to her that she can't stay here, alone with Aziz. It's too dangerous for her baby.'

Hanna begins to cry. She sobs and protests. I can hear it in her voice.

'Tell her I'll stay with her,' I say.

I can't understand why I make such a promise, but I've said it now. She seems to calm down. I won't be spending the night with Dimitri. My first night away from him. I feel a pang.

We travel to the hospital, and Dimitri finds Zina, a female doctor he knows, on duty. She agrees to bypass some of the questions on the admittance form and lets the mother and baby into a cubicle behind a curtain. Hanna can't stop crying, and the baby whimpers too, although Hanna lets him suckle on her breast when he wants it.

The two doctors discuss whether to give her a tranquiliser, but they decide against it. No one can communicate with Hanna. I sense her fear and won't leave her.

'You'll be OK?' Dimitri says to me.

I nod. 'Sure.' But I don't mean it.

'I'll sleep in town tonight and come straight back in the morning to see how you are. Sorry, what a mess.'

He pulls me outside the curtain and kisses me next to the wall. I wish he wouldn't leave me, but I'm stuck now.

\*　　\*　　\*

The next morning he returns as he promised, and I am grateful and love him all the more for his concern for me. He has already visited the camp and now has bad news. 'Aziz has disappeared with another man. He told Ahmed he's being smuggled to Italy on a leisure boat from the island of Zakynthos.'

'But what now?' I say. 'We can't send her back to that camp, alone. She might be raped or the baby harmed.'

'Zina says she can cover for her for another twenty-four hours, then she'll have to leave.'

Dimitri and I discuss how we can help Hanna and decide to contact social services. They advise us that if we agree to employ her, they will issue her a temporary visa. But how can we employ her when we are away all day? I call the Boutique

Olive Farm, and Alexi says he can provide her work cleaning the guest rooms and gardening but asks if we can assist him with her wages. We agree to share her upkeep, and, two days later, with her bundle of possessions wrapped in a cloth, we drive her and the baby to the farm.

# - 7 -

August arrives, and instead of travelling to the camp, I visit the farm every week to check on Hanna and her baby whom she has called Abed. Alexi has returned from Athens permanently, much to his parents' delight, for he can attend to the tourists with his improved English.

One day Alexi and I sit at the wooden table under the vine. Abed, on my lap, sucks on a breadstick while, nearby, Hanna sweeps the courtyard and wipes down tables. I can see Alexi looks despondent.

'Something wrong?' I say.

'No, nothing,' he says.

'Yes, there is.'

He pauses. 'It's Georgia.'

'Who?'

'Georgia, my fiancée.'

I now remember him mentioning her once. I'd forgotten I'd met her, a girl from a nearby village. 'You were engaged for a long time, weren't you?'

'Only five years.'

'Only? Where is she now?'

'In Athens.'

'Oh, I see. Working?'

'Yes, in a toll booth on the motorway going out of Athens. She doesn't want to come back here. She's got money and freedom, and she's fallen in love with a guy in the next booth.'

I recall Georgia as bright and intelligent, with a diploma in accounting from the local technical school. 'We'll have to look around for someone else for you. Maybe one of the girls hanging around in the square in town would be good for you.'

Alexi gives a wry laugh. 'Oh, they're all village girls. No thanks. Not my type.'

'Then we'll all come up here for lunch one day, and I'll tell Dimitri to bring some friends.'

As I drive back down the hill, I decide to travel to Olympia the next day to fact-check for Lonely Planet. I also ponder how I can continue my migrant stories for Chloe at The Guardian as she is loving the articles and paying me for them.

Next morning, Dimitri says he'll take the day off and come with me to Olympia. We set off early and arrive to find few visitors about, so we linger in the hall displaying the pediments of the Temple of Zeus, before we move on to view Praxiteles's sculpture of Hermes. Its marble has a creamy sheen, and Hermes, his hip almost unnaturally skewed, stands propped while holding the infant Dionysus. Dimitri has a miniature replica of the sculpture on a bookcase in his living room. I reach out to run my hand over the sculpture, but a nearby guard pounces on me like a Nazi policewoman, and I recoil.

I want to examine the tiny bronze sculptures that people in Ancient Greece kept in their houses, so we enter the next room, and I find a miniature statue of Zeus holding a spear, and others of dogs, horses and other animals, as well as jewellery, combs and dining implements. I sneak a few photos—though we're not supposed to—and take notes.

At the back of a glass case I point to a ten-centimetre-high bronze sculpture of a soldier with a centaur. 'That's exquisite,' I say to Dimitri. 'The headwear is so detailed. You've got a copy of that in your living room, haven't you?'

'Mmm, that's right. It's one of my favourites.' We walk around the glass case. 'You know the Mycenaeans got the copper to make bronze from Cyprus and the tin from Turkey. Pretty enterprising back then, weren't we? Trading all over the place, selling our oil and wine in the Orient while we took their minerals. We even had writing then, four thousand years ago. Don't know what's happened to us now. Can't even sell our oranges to the rest of Europe. It's not worth picking them. And to think we were a land where gods once walked.'

All is silent for we are alone in this room and can linger for as long as we like, thinking of the past and the present. Finally, I take his arm and say, 'Come on, I've got enough notes.'

At the gift shop I purchase a copy of the miniature soldier and centaur sculpture. 'I want one of these too. A pair.' I don't know what I mean by that, but he takes my hand.

We emerge from the museum into a blistering heat and scurry to a drinks stand. Though almost too tired to tour the archaeological sites, we decide we can't miss a visit to the stadium, so we walk down, enter through the arch and run like children up the track and back again. We laugh, suck on water bottles and take selfies while standing on a grass knoll with Mediterranean pines as a backdrop. Dimitri turns me round and takes another photo, his arm around my waist and him kissing me. We are glad to have the place to ourselves.

As we tramp up the road to the car park, a crowd appears ahead, led by team leaders with placards and microphones.

'What's this?' I say, followed by a moan.

With their Coca-Cola t-shirts, orange sneakers, baseball caps, big bottoms, jelly thighs and sweaty brows, a tsunami of tourists on the march surge down the road towards us. We skirt around the impending wave and reach the top, only to find dozens of buses filling the car park.

'What's going on?' I say to the car park attendant.

'Cruise ship come into Katakolo today,' he says. 'Let out three thousand passengers.'

We drive away from Olympia and wind up the hill. I look back and take more photos, and then we travel along beside an orange grove in the countryside.

'Why are you crying?' Dimitri says, turning towards me.

My tears have appeared from nowhere. 'I don't think I'll ever go back there again.'

'You never know.'

Back at his house on the hill I remove my sculpture from its bag. 'Can I put it here, next to yours?'

'Sure, they complement each other,' Dimitri says. 'Hey, look at these. Bet you haven't noticed these.' He smiles as he picks up some rings off the shelf. 'Beautiful, aren't they? Exact copies of the ones we saw today, made of gold from Cyprus. Now that's really intricate workmanship. My father had them specially made for my mother. He was a crazy collector and started this collection of sculpture. His hobby was hunting for things never seen before. He went all over archaeological sites, searching for bits of pottery and chipped frescoes. Guess I'm just continuing on from where he left off. He knew everything about Greek sculpture. I'm an amateur, compared to him.'

'And what happened to him?'

'He died of a broken heart after my mother died.'

'Oh.' I gasp. I can't think of anything to say.

'He was a doctor too, but at least he got paid back in those days. Otherwise, this house with its view wouldn't exist.'

*     *     *

On Sunday we meet Christos and Sophie at the square and eat souvlaki with them in what has now become a ritual. After we finish our watermelon and grapes, we wander over to the church. I've never attended church so often in my life as I have these past few weeks, yet I remain somewhat timorous when entering this place. Dimitri has told me Greeks are very religious and close to the church. 'Perhaps we are superstitious,' he'd said, 'or need the sort of hope religion brings.' Maybe, I'd thought at the time.

We sit in a dim amber light cast by candles. Up by the altar, a priest chants, his voice haunting, and another voice, male and hidden from view, chants in response. Is it coming from behind the gold-threaded screen above the altar or from a side chapel? I can't tell. The congregation consists of a few elderly townsfolk and a youngish woman who reprimands a group of boys beside her as they wriggle and squirm in their pew. The service ends, and the priest walks down the nave, followed by another man—the other chanter, I assume—who breaks away from the procession, steps towards the woman and the boys and hugs and kisses them.

Dimitri steps out into the nave and says, 'Tomas. I thought you'd be here tonight. This is Marina.'

We greet each other, and Tomas introduces the woman, his wife, Katerina, and the boys, their four sons, to me. As we exit the church, Dimitri and Tomas walk ahead, slapping each other on the back and sharing an animated conversation. They are obviously old friends.

# - 8 -

Dimitri suggests we find a table in the square to eat cinnamon cake and ice cream. The boys enthuse at the word ice cream and go off to choose chocolate magnums and drumsticks. We sit by a bush of pink oleanders, and Dimitri brings over a carafe of water. I compliment Tomas on his singing in the church and its haunting quality which spiralled up into the cupola above. I tell him I understand nothing about religious music, but his chanting has an undeniably surreal charm. A new moment. I remember a street singer in India emitting a similar dreamlike chant whilst crouched on his mat on a dirty pavement.

'Tomas nearly went into the priesthood, didn't you, Tomas?' Dimitri says, pouring water.

'Mmm, but I decided to do medicine instead. Glad I did now. I wouldn't have met Katerina.' He leans over and pats his wife on her head, and she gives a little giggle. 'And I wouldn't have met this guy either.' He nods towards Dimitri. 'We conquered Athens together when we were in medical school, eh, Dima?'

They smile, complicit.

'You know Tomas is a compatriot of yours, Marina.'

'Oh?'

'Born in Sydney, weren't you, Tomas?'

'Mmm. That's right.'

'Ah, I thought I heard an occasional nasal Ozzie vowel.'

'We came back to Greece when I was twelve. My dad didn't like Australia. He lectured at The University of Sydney, but they didn't have much regard for Ancient Greek and withdrew funding from the Classics department. He's much happier back here, in the midst of the real thing.' Tomas pushes his glasses up on his nose and forks up the cinnamon cake. 'I was lucky. Did Med at Athens Uni, married my girlfriend, then went off to do my PhD at Harvard.'

'Whoa, Harvard! You must be clever.'

'Not really.'

I see he's humble and studious. 'And you did your PhD in what?'

'Infectious diseases.' Tomas adjusts his glasses again.

Fotis, Tomas's twelve-year-old son, the oldest of the four, comes over to the table, and Tomas puts his arm round his son's shoulders. The boy has a shock of thick, black hair which bobs on his forehead.

'We'd better go soon,' Katerina says. 'Fotis wants to go back to the house.'

The youngest, Pano, sits on Katerina's knee. She squeezes him, sets him down and goes off to find her other two sons.

We leave our table and walk down the hill, Dimitri and I behind and holding hands.

'Nice boys,' I say. 'Good looking too. That Fotis is going to steal a heart or two.'

'Sure is. He's bright too. Top of his class. Says he's going to study the classics like his grandfather and then archaeology.'

45

We stop at the bend where the candles stand by the roadside chapel. Dimitri lights a candle and so do Tomas and Katerina. They murmur prayers, and then we walk on to the bottom of the hill.

'We'll be on the beach tomorrow,' Katerina says. 'Why don't you join us?'

'Maybe towards evening, when its cooler,' I say. 'I have some notes to write up.'

'I'll come later too,' Dimitri says.

'We'll be at the mouth of the river, where it enters the sea.' Katerina draws me towards her for a farewell kiss. As she and her family walk away, she looks back and cries out, '*Kalinýchta.*'

As Dimitri and I walk to our car, we pass a branch of the National Bank of Greece. A crowd outside talks and gestures.

'What's going on?' I say.

'They're checking tomorrow's opening hours,' Dimitri says.

'Is anything happening?' I ask anxiously. 'Is the country still solvent?' For days we've watched the Prime Minister toing and froing in Brussels, trying to persuade the European Central Bank to restructure the Greek debt, but to no avail. 'I mean, has the European Union agreed to change the terms of Greek loans?'

'We don't know yet. Maybe tomorrow.'

\*    \*    \*

Six o'clock the next day and with the sun still high in the sky, Dimitri and I amble through the pine woods. The sweet scent of sap and pine wafts about the ropy trunks and the canopy of pine needles overhead.

'Perfumes of summer, mmm,' I say. I snap a twig of pine and crush the oily needles between my fingers. 'Smell that.'

Dimitri bends, inhales and smiles. 'Mmm, intoxicating. Could get stoned on that.'

A tortoise appears on the path ahead. We pause and watch as it plods forward with its head and leathery neck outstretched. Defiant, determined and oblivious to our gaze, it soon disappears into the bushes.

The path leads us to the top of the dunes which descend to the beach, a wide curve running around the bay. Below, families have emerged from the chrysalis of afternoon sleep and erected umbrellas and laid out straw mats. I see Tomas and Katerina with their four sons. Fotis and his brother Adrian play volleyball on the sand with other boys. The ball bounces into the water, and the game continues beyond the low breakers with shouts, dives, imaginary goals and critical offsides. Katerina sits with Pano on her lap, and Christophe, the six-year-old, brings her buckets of sand and seaweed. Tomas sits on a low deckchair, wearing a straw hat and reading a newspaper.

We greet each other with cries of '*Yassou*', and Dimitri and I arrange ourselves on towels and mats.

'Peaches? Watermelon?' Katerina says, offering us a plastic plate of fruit.

'Heard the news this morning, I suppose,' Tomas says, folding the newspaper. 'The country's on the verge of bankruptcy. We're only allowed to withdraw 60 euro from a cash machine a day. The banks are closed from today, and no one knows when they will open again. Can't even do any transactions through the banks.'

Dimitri and Tomas engage in a long conversation in Greek, and I am left out of the details of what's happening. I manage to interrupt and say, 'But how am I going to get my fees from Chloe at The Guardian and my payments from Lonely Planet?'

'Hmph! Nobody knows anything,' Tomas says, looking at his newspaper. 'All I know is there were long queues at the ATMs this morning. They've probably run out of cash by now.'

My stomach releases a tremor of anxiety. No more cash in the banks? At all?

'I managed to get some cash out,' Tomas continues, 'and so did Katerina. From now on we'll just run up bills at the supermarket my cousin owns in town, so we'll be OK there. And we'll just make do with our vegetables in the garden.'

I am anxious now. I don't like my life being controlled by whimsical bank closures or benevolent supermarkets. I'm not used to it. I try to imagine something similar happening in Australia or England. I can't. The Greeks seem so ready for this—to work around the fickleness of a government with its back to the wall, to solve problems thrown at them by outside forces, to get on with living, somehow.

I lie back on my towel and look up at the sky. 'Will we be all right?' I say to Dimitri.

'Sure,' he says. 'There's an ATM at the hospital that no one knows about. I'll take money out of that whenever I'm there. You can give me your card too.'

'But I don't know how much is in my account. I mean, if the bank isn't transferring my payments, then what?'

'Well, we'll just wait and see. They can't keep the banks shut forever. And Aunt Maria's got a never-ending supply of vegetables and eggs, even a chicken now and then.' He releases a little chuckle.

I remain anxious. He strides through life, ready for anything. He'll look after me, won't he?

I take his hand for a moment, then lean up on my elbow and watch Katerina walk towards the sea. She gives a little skip as her toes hit the water. I know it's not cold. Her beautiful body has a cleanly shaped back, and she is still trim and lithe despite her four pregnancies. Her mass of curly, black hair bobs below her shoulders. She turns, smiles and shouts, 'Coming?'

We follow her in, and she swims off with smooth strokes. I, too, can swim, but she has more style and is soon out in the blue, alone in the sapphire sea. Dimitri and I play under the water and join the volleyball match for a short time. Even at seven o'clock, the water remains a warm swathe of silk. Tomas does not swim and spends the time immersed in his newspaper.

Later, with our damp towels and sandy thongs, we walk up the beach and stop at a caravan selling iced coffees and drinks. The sun is now low in the sky, a ball of burning embers, and we sip a white retsina wine as chilled as ice and relaxing. As we pick at anchovies and bread, Tomas suddenly says, 'Let's go to the pool before dinner. It's not yet eight, and they won't light up the grills till nine-thirty.'

When we reach our cars, Pano says he wants to go in our car and sit beside Dimitri. Katerina sits in the back with me, and we chat like old friends. I'm drawn to her: her affection for her children, her natural beauty and her offerings of fruit. Dimitri shows Pano the gears in the car, the hand brake and lets him hold the steering wheel. The little boy's eyes shine with pleasure when he turns to his mother and seeks her approval.

When we arrive at the pool, Dimitri says, 'Come on, little boy, I'll help you over the gate.'

He carries him to the gate and climbs over with the boy on his shoulders. We change and hang our gear on the rusty hooks and plunge into the water from the wobbly stone slabs. Dimitri plays with Pano and laughs as the boy pummels him as they splash about together. I see my lover's joy in playing with this little boy. It is a side of Dimitri that I haven't seen until now, and I am pleased.

Katerina slowly immerses herself in the water. 'It's good for me,' she says, and she slaps her face with the sulphurous mud. I follow suit and hope it will perform magic on my skin.

49

'Dimitri tells me you are writing for The Guardian about the immigrants at Patras ,' Katerina says. The drying mud cracks on her lips.

'That's right although I've finished with that there. It got a bit ugly a while back.'

'Well, there's plenty to report on in Athens. It's filling up with Syrians escaping the war over there. They're all jammed into camps outside the city, waiting for papers to get to Germany. I'm out at those camps all the time, sent by the health department. They're afraid of infectious diseases breaking out … you know, cholera, measles and all the rest.'

I tread water, float away and then return. 'It would be good to see those camps. Maybe I could visit you some time.'

'Yes, yes, do that. You must come. Stay with us.' We splash water on our faces, and Katerina laughs lightly. 'Ah, that feels good, yes, so good.'

We stand on the stone slabs and dry ourselves and pull on our underwear which struggles to slide over our sticky bodies. The swallows have left, and the first black flashes of bats emerging from the cave sweep above our heads.

Outside the gate a man and a woman stand beside their Volkswagen van, removing their swimming gear.

'Hermann! Gudrun!' Tomas shouts. He goes over and embraces the couple, then calls us over to introduce us. 'This is Hermann. He comes here every year to count the bats, don't you, Hermann? He's a Professor of Zoology at Munich University.'

# - 9 -

We drive in convoy up the hill to Alexi's olive farm. At Arini Dimitri pulls over at the clearing by the road and fills bottles with water from the gushing spring. Tomas's German friends, Hermann and Gudrun, follow us in their van, and when we arrive at the farm, we tumble out and Alexi greets us with hugs and kisses.

Tonight, Katerina is golden, her dress bronze against her honey skin as she glows under the twilight sky. Nothing about her appears contrived. With her crushed dress (perhaps pulled from a suitcase?) and her sandals' plain leather strapped over her naked feet, she has an untamed beauty that is accentuated by long waves of hair down her back and sculptured shoulders under her thin dress straps. She is trim, yet still full from motherhood. As her youngest, Pano, paws for attention, she hitches him onto her thigh and her dress rides up her leg.

'Be good now,' she says, soothing him. 'We'll be eating chips soon.' She cups his head into her shoulder.

I wear my pink and sage green dress, the one I wore ... when was it? So long ago it seems ... on a starry night on a veranda above the sea when Venus hung low over the water. Dimitri stands beside me and brushes his lips on my neck. Alexi invites us to take our places at the table, and I find myself sitting at one end with Tomas and Hermann. Katerina's three older boys settle on my side of the table, separating me from Dimitri, who sits opposite Katerina. Costas places a large dish of chips in front of the boys, and they shovel handfuls onto their plates.

'Pass some down here,' Katerina says to her sons, 'before you eat them all.'

The grilled chicken arrives, and soon everyone grasps a thigh bone in their fingers and tears away at the flesh, ravenous after a day at the beach and an energy-sapping bathe at the hot springs. Never did oregano, lemon and olive oil dressing taste so good to me.

Opposite, Hermann occasionally attempts in a polite, pro-fessorial manner to deal with the meat with his knife and fork. His German manners contrast with the Mediterranean glut-tony around the table. Only Gudrun, quietly and expertly, displays her German artifice and deftly places everything in her mouth with her fork, not letting a drip of oil dribble down her chin, rather like Chaucer's Prioress. I engage her in conver-sation by offering her food and pouring water, but she remains reserved, smiling sweetly with many pleases and thank yous. Her English is perfect, as if she has studied it with great pre-cision and holds back before uttering a word until she has the correct vocabulary in order and the right pronunciation. I glimpse a small wooden cross under her shirt and imagine her in a parsimonious Lutheran church somewhere, in contrast to my Greek friends who chant amongst their coloured ikons, incense and gold adornments. I think of Angela Merkel, a pas-tor's daughter, negotiating—at that moment, up north in chilly Brussels—debt relief for the cash-strapped Greeks. With her fringe and pastel jacket, she will be looking quizzically at Yanis Varoufakis, her leather-suited, motorbike-riding Greek interlocutor, and mulling over whether to ask the diligent Germans to put their hands in their pockets yet again for those Greek hedonists in their sun-kissed land.

Here in the balmy air, oblivious, our bacchanalian feast oscillates between my self-deprecating Anglo silliness, Greek shouting and Gudrun's correctness. She sits beside Hermann like his twin, both with straight grey hair, rimless glasses, khaki clothes and canvas sandals.

'Some more wine, Hermann?' Tomas says. He picks up a jug of cold red wine with crushed ice in it and fills Hermann's glass.

'Ah, thank you, Tomas. It's very good.' He pushes his rimless glasses up on his nose and sniffs.

I smile when I see how we sup the icy red wine with much gratitude. I smile at the thought of suburban elites in distant cities, as they chatter around their dining tables, repel at the crassness of red wine being served "not at room temperature". I imagine them enunciating in lofty tones, 'Oh, that rough peasant stuff.' We are loving it, as too the plates of fried zucchini, melanzane and stuffed vine leaves which we demolish with gusto. The boys beside me have each eaten an adult's portion of chips, yet still they tear apart chunks of bread and feta cheese.

Tomas pushes back his plate, wipes his lips and leans towards Hermann. 'And how do you catch those bats, Hermann?'

The German busies himself wiping down his plate with a piece of bread. He swallows and says, 'We go into the cave and erect a mist net across the water because the first thing the bats do at dusk is dive for the water as they are very thirsty, having not drunk all day.'

'Oh, I see. And how many bats do you catch?'

'Depends. Ten, twenty, sometimes many more. We release most of them without examining them. We look for the ones we've tagged over the years and weigh them, measure them, check the length of their wings and see where they've been feeding. We collect the data and compare it to last year's ...'

But I do not listen to Hermann as the hilarity at the other end of the table distracts me. Dimitri and Katerina laugh loudly, sharing a joke, a story. Katerina throws her head back and arches her neck, and her hair falls back from her shoulders. Dimitri jabs at a watermelon slice and feeds it to her across the table. They laugh again ... chuckling, chortling in Greek. And I'm left out. They are away in a foreign land where I'm an alien. I look on, startled, and my thoughts become feelings, and I drive them out, or try to. They have a shared history, an old story, memories, students together, studying, strolling about a campus courtyard, drinking coffee in a corner—and I'm an outsider. My thoughts and feelings intertwine like a tight ball of wire mesh in my head, and I wish they weren't. Thoughts become feelings. I have feelings. *Feelings.* I want to run up to Dimitri and hug him, but instead I look across at Gudrun, who smiles and pushes the sliced melon across the table.

'Have some,' she says.

Hermann says to Tomas, 'We've found that the bats, who used to feed in the woods now destroyed by housing construction, have lost weight and have a slower wing beat.'

'In other words, they are suffering because humans are invading their feeding grounds,' Tomas says.

'That's right. That's when it gets dangerous because mutations occur in their cells because their immune systems are under stress.'

Dimitri's laugh rings from the other end of the table, but Katerina's boys distract her as they kick a football about. She shouts something to them, and Pano climbs on Dimitri's knee. He jiggles the boy up and down and feeds him watermelon.

'Bats harbour hundreds of viruses,' Hermann says, 'and they have lived quite happily with them for thousands of years, but if one of these viruses mutates it could become a pathogen.'

'You mean, it's dangerous for us,' Tomas says. 'I've read about it in The Lancet, and it seems Ebola and SARS were caused by mutated viruses from bats. We studied it at medical school. I need to study it further. You'll send me your paper when you've concluded all your findings, won't you, Hermann?'

'It's pretty well understood now that the pathogen jumps from the bat to another animal which then passes it onto a human.'

Dimitri sits beside me, and he plops Pano on my knee. The boy jiggles up and down and gives me a smile. I smile back. A pretty boy with dark, luminous eyes, I squeeze his arm and give him the forks to play with. Hanna comes out of the kitchen and clears the plates. She smiles and looks happy. She's learnt how to cook, wait at tables and clean rooms, and Alexi pays her a wage now as well as free board and lodging.

'Where's Abed, Hanna?' I say.

'Under the table,' she says, gesturing. Abed appears, crawling around and smiling at his new found independence.

'Ah, there you are,' I say, picking him up. I have one boy on each knee, and they fit comfortably but slide off when they see the ball.

Dimitri leans towards me and says, 'Let's go, eh?'

I want to sit beside him in the car and drive off into the moonlight. I can barely say goodnight to Katerina. Why? She's done nothing wrong. Shared a joke with my ... what is he? My feelings overtake my thoughts again. My ... lover? It sounds so temporary. Something passing ... almost a fling.

Not as solid and steeped in memory as their shared student days, talking medical shop, eating on a student grant, partying at friends' houses near the university.

But Katerina hugs me and tells me I'm so good for Dimitri and she's happy to see us together. 'You will come and stay with us in Athens, won't you, Marina? There's plenty of stuff in those immigrant camps for you to write about for The Guardian. I know them all like the back of my hand.' She smiles, reflecting generous, unsullied thoughts. 'We'll see you at the beach.' The cog of wire mesh in my head seems to unravel.

We wind down the hill slowly, under a moon almost as bright as daylight. Its luminosity blocks out the stars which we normally view through Dimitri's telescope. We stop at a roadside clearing where a small monument stands surrounded by many ubiquitous crosses. We pause and read a stone tablet commemorating the loss of 40 people burnt alive in their cars as they tried to escape the flames of a wild fire. I wish Dimitri hadn't stopped here. It makes me think of my dead mother.

'Oh, no,' I say, in tears, 'let's go. I can't bear this place.' I look at Dimitri and stop. 'You know someone who died here, don't you?'

'Yes, I do. We Greeks dwell on these things. You people, you say, just move on. You're right. They won't come back.' He turns and gets into the car, and I follow. 'We have a melancholic nature, we Greeks. We have a need to nurture melancholy. I don't know why.' He leans over. 'You looked lovely tonight, sitting at that distant end of the table. You were so far away.'

I've got it all wrong. Again.

On the veranda we sit on the wicker sofa in the bright moon-light, sipping his homemade orange juice. He slides up to me, puts his mouth to my ear and whispers, 'You and I are going to have a baby together, aren't we?'

I gulp at the unexpectedness of his words. Is this what he wants? Why didn't I see it? My eyes fill with tears and a wave of emotion engulfs me. I'm glad of the semi-light.

All I can manage in response is an 'Of course', and I pull him against my breasts.

Later, when I go to the bedroom, I open the bedside table drawer, pull out my packets of contraceptive pills, go through to the kitchen and throw them in the bin.

## - 10 -

Dimitri decides that we build a new room onto the end of his house. We mark out a square where the room will be, and a silent workman levels the ground and pours a concrete slab.

We climb the hill behind the house to a pile of stones—some round, some oblong, some small, some big, some chipped, some square—and stack them into a wheelbarrow and wobble it down the hill. Now we are a couple. We have our project and we're united, as solid as the stones and as round and comfortable as their shapes. We toil next to each other, congenial as old colleagues, and I bathe in a new contentment. We are us.

'But do you know how to build stone walls?' I say.

'We all do. We all learn it, a bit from our fathers and grandfathers. I helped my pappous build that terrace wall, and my father and I built that enclosure for the wood.'

'But what about your hands? I mean, you've got surgery to do. You don't want to ruin them.'

'We'll find someone to help us. It's sort of fun, isn't it? Building something together.'

Our little pile of stones looks meagre, but we'll build it up.

We spend all afternoon filling the barrow, pushing it down the hill and unloading it with a rattle. It's Sunday, and the heat bakes the ground and the stones.

Suddenly, I think of my English literature teacher in my last year at high school. Her name pops into my head as I silently unload the stones. Mrs Gibson. Passionate about poetry, she had just read us "The Rime of the Ancient Mariner" with great theatrical verve. We all knew she performed in amateur theatricals because she had told us about it a hundred times. She always had the class in her thrall when reciting to us.

'Now,' she said, 'I am going to leave you with a little couplet from a poem by Coleridge called "Work without Hope".'

She stood centre stage before the blackboard and recited:

*'Work without hope draws nectar in a sieve,*
*And hope without an object cannot live.'*

She swept up her books. The bell rang, and stepping towards the door, she said, 'You're off into the big wide world, girls. Remember. Always have hopes and projects to drive you on.'

Now Dimitri and I have our hopes and our project.

I walk through the kitchen and see him leaning over his plans on the table, drawing lines.

'What do you think?' he says. 'We could put the windows here and a door there which opens onto the veranda.'

'All looks good to me,' I say, not wanting to dampen his enthusiasm.

We rest inside and cool off. We tip ice into the green glasses and fill them with blood orange juice and break up bread with cheese. I go into the bedroom and change into a fresh t-shirt and return sipping from my glass. Scarlet juice dribbles down my chin and onto my neck.

'Are you wanting me to lick that off?' Dimitri says, grinning. 'Mmm, your tits are round, soft. The juice is trickling down your cleavage.' He glides his finger down my front. 'Come here.' He smiles, screwing up his eyes, charming me.

'Let's do another hour of stone clearing, then we'll see …'

His phone on the table rings and he picks it up.

'Oh, no,' he says, concern in his voice. 'What happened?' He frowns in silence, as he listens to the caller. 'I see. Is he bad?' He pauses. 'Pretty? OK, I'll come and see what I can do.' He pauses again. 'In about an hour. At the hospital.' He ends the call and puts the phone down with a sigh. 'That was Zina from the hospital. Aziz returned to the camp a couple of hours ago, out of the blue. He arrived yelling, and when he couldn't find Hanna and the baby, he accused Ahmed of taking her away. He started fighting, hitting and punching Ahmed. Then he produced a knife and stabbed Ahmed in the leg. He's haemorrhaged profusely.'

'Oh, no.' I see our afternoon slip away. 'So you're going to the hospital?'

'Just for an hour. Aziz is holed up in a tent at the camp and won't come out.'

'Why doesn't someone call the police?'

'Those guys are terrified of the police. Terrified they'll all be locked up or told to move on.'

Dimitri showers, changes his clothes and returns to the veranda. I follow him down the steps as he walks to his car.

'Don't be long, will you?'

'No, of course not. We've got unfinished business here, haven't we?'

He laughs, embraces me, then gets into the car, which speeds away, leaving a cloud of dust.

\* \* \*

I check my phone for the hundredth time. It's midnight, and Dimitri hasn't answered my calls or texts. I reassure myself that he's operating and can't answer. He said he wouldn't be long, but he's been away for hours.

At three o'clock in the morning Dimitri wakes me as he slides into bed beside me.

'What happened?' I say. 'Why were you so long?'

'Shh,' he whispers. 'Ahmed's in the spare room. I had to bring him back here. If he'd gone back to the camp, Aziz would have killed him. I got to the hospital and found Ahmed with two stab wounds in his thigh. Zina had stitched him up, but he refused to go back to the camp, so I decided to go out there to see what was going on. Aziz was still holed up in a tent, as they'd said, moaning and yelling in a hysterical rage. He needed tranquillising medication, so I found a new guy who spoke English and asked him to tell Aziz I was outside. This seemed to calm him down, so I entered the tent and, with the help of my new interpreter, told Aziz I'd give him an injection to make him feel better. He kept demanding to know Hanna's whereabouts. I said I didn't know a thing about her. This set him off again, and as I approached him, he produced the knife. We tried to calm him down. I asked for the knife and told him I wasn't going to hurt him. I took a step forward and he lunged at me. I dived out of the way, but he got my leg. It all happened so quickly.'

'Oh, no.' I raise myself up on my elbow. 'Are you OK?' I turn on the lamp, see a bandage wrapped around his thigh and reach out my hand.

'No, don't touch it.' He grimaces. 'I had to return to the hospital, and I told Zina to call the police. I don't know what will happen to them. Aziz will end up in prison. It'll be the end of him. He'll never get out of prison and he'll never get to

Italy. I had to bring Ahmed back with me. He's in a terrible state. Things are getting worse and worse in that camp. There's so much fighting amongst the people there. Fighting for food, stealing money, arguing over shelter. Someone will get killed soon. I'm glad Hanna and the baby are out.'

Dimitri slumps back onto the pillow and closes his eyes.

'I'll get you some tea,' I say. Ah, yes, I think, the English comfort of a hot beverage.

'No, not just now. Let me rest.' He turns to me. 'Come here.'

# - 11 -

In the morning Dimitri removes his bandage, revealing a large dressing down the outside of his thigh.

'How many stitches are there?' I say.

'Twenty, maybe. It's not too deep. Ahmed's is worse. That guy, Aziz, had completely lost sense of everything. He was angry, very angry, and in his rage he plunged the knife much deeper into Ahmed's leg.'

We go into the kitchen, and I make two frappés for breakfast and take them and a plate of apple pies out onto the veranda. Dimitri follows me on his crutches and sits and props his leg up on the coffee table. Ahmed limps out, he, too, on crutches. He looks pale and drawn—I'm not surprised given his severe haemorrhaging—with bony arms, papery skin clinging to his face and his mouth drooping.

'Sit down, Ahmed,' I say. 'I'll get you some coffee.'

I place a frappé and a pie in front of him, and he slowly spoons the coffee into his mouth but ignores the pie.

'Aren't you hungry, Ahmed?' I say. 'Do you feel sick?'

'A little,' he says.

'Have you got antibiotics?'

'I think so.'

'Where are they?'

'I don't know.'

I turn to Dimitri. 'Have you got them?'

'No, no idea where they are. Mine are here.' He taps a box on the table.

'Ahmed, I'll check if they're in your room. Do you mind if I go and look for them amongst your things?'

'No.' His spirit, like his blood, seems drained from him.

I go to his bedroom and search for the antibiotics in the pockets of his odorous clothes. The fetor of stale tobacco, unwashed body odour and fried onions hovers about the room. I feel I'm invading his privacy as I delve into his pockets. I find the antibiotics in his jacket pocket and pull them out, along with a photo mounted in a worn leather frame. It's of a girl wearing a blouse and a long, dark skirt. For a moment I'm puzzled, then I recognise her as Hanna, but she is not wearing her chador, rather, a simple scarf revealing a hint of hair on her forehead. Smiling and happy, she is pointing at something while standing among trees. People and children appear in the background. My heart skips a beat. What does this mean? I put the photo back in the pocket and return to the veranda.

'Here, Ahmed, I found your pills,' I say. 'How many should he take, Dimitri?'

'Take two, three times a day, Ahmed,' Dimitri says, 'till you finish the packet. You don't want to get an infection. You look tired. You'd better rest this morning. We've got to build you up, you're pretty thin. Have you been eating?'

Ahmed ignores the question.

'How about a shower?' I say. 'That dressing looks waterproof, but I'll find some plastic wrap to bind around it.'

I help Ahmed to the bathroom and provide him with soap, a towel and a roll of plastic wrap. I leave a pair of clean jeans, a t-shirt, underwear and sandals in the bedroom for him.

On the veranda, Dimitri and I listen to the water gushing from the shower. Washing, I think. A forgotten luxury?

I turn to Dimitri and place my arm over the back of the sofa behind him. 'You feeling OK? You look tired.'

'Yeah, I am a bit, but my wound is slight compared to his.'

'Do you know what? I found a photo of Hanna in Ahmed's jacket pocket. I wasn't looking for anything other than the box of pills, but the photo came out in my hand. Hanna's standing in a field, or somewhere in the country, without her chador, just a scarf. She was laughing, happy.'

'What are you trying to say? That Ahmed knew Hanna before all this? When they were back in Afghanistan?'

'Maybe. But here, shrouded in a black chador in that tent in the camp in Patras, she looked like a woman still living under the Taliban rule. I thought they were escaping from all that.'

'Perhaps it wasn't Hanna in that photo.'

'I'm sure it was. I've gotten to know her well. And I've seen her so many times up at Arini. She only wears the scarf now. Of course I recognised her. In that photo she's just as she looks now, almost unveiled.'

'Yes, she divested herself of that long, black robe once we moved her to Alexi's place, didn't she? It mustn't be important to her now. Should we ask Ahmed about the photo?'

'Not just yet. Look, we hardly know anything about him. And I don't think he's up to talking to us. He doesn't look well.'

The gushing of water in the bathroom ceases, and soon Ahmed reappears on the veranda. Seeing him brushed up surprises me—his hair wet and neatly combed, his face shaved, and clean and crisp in Dimitri's white t-shirt and jeans. The warm water has brought colour to his cheeks and seems to have cleansed him, figuratively and literally, of the filth and tensions pervading the camp. He smiles and takes a jaunty step on his crutches, and a waft of lavender from my shower gel fills the air. He looks better already, and the downturn of his mouth has washed away. He sits and takes a large bite from his pie.

'Getting your appetite back, eh?' Dimitri says.

We watch him eat the rest of the pie and finish his frappé.

'Ahmed, your English is so good,' I suddenly say. 'Where did you learn it. At school?'

'I did law at Kabul University, not languages,' Ahmed says. 'I learnt English from watching American films and listening to English songs. I read English and US websites and anything I could get from those US serviceman.'

'What, you knew some of the Americans?' Dimitri says.

'Yes, I worked for them. Couldn't get a job as a lawyer as there was no work, only war, so I went to the Americans and told them I spoke English, and they took me on straight away. Translating, interpreting, going around with them, telling them how things worked in Kabul.'

Ahmed works his way through another apple pie and drinks the tea I have made. His appetite has revived.

'Why did you leave?' Dimitri says.

'In the end I was assigned to a captain. I travelled with him all day as he planned operations, talked to his counterparts in the Afghan army and gathered intelligence from his officers. He was an important man. We became friends. Frank was his name, from Milwaukee. But his job was dangerous as he was a target. I was a target too, but the pay was good. Those jihadists waged war on those who collaborated with the enemy.'

Ahmed suddenly stops talking, shuts his eyes and leans back on the couch, breathing hard.

'You OK, Ahmed?' Dimitri says. He leans over and pats the Afghan on his shoulder.

Ahmed doesn't stir, then says 'Yeah, I'm OK. Just dragging all this stuff up is … is making me tired.'

'Sure, sure. I get it. Something bad happened, is that it?'

'Mmm, yes, that's it.' Ahmed opens his eyes. 'We were going along this street in Kabul, and there was a bomb blast. Frank was killed. Thirty other people too. Suicide bomber, blood everywhere, bodies everywhere, arms and legs blown off, women and children screaming. You've got to live it to understand it—a nightmare that never leaves you, even at night. I got out with only some shrapnel in my legs. They soon fixed me in the hospital.'

'So that was it?' I say. 'The end for you in Kabul?'

'Mmm, that was it. I should have died, but my guardian angel said to me, "You've got to go now. God saved you this time, but next time you might not be so lucky."'

He slumps back and closes his eyes, worn out telling us this story. Then he opens them again and struggles as he attempts to stand. I reach over to steady him and organise his crutches.

'I'm going to lie down now,' he says. 'I'm so tired.' We watch him as he hobbles inside towards his bedroom.

'Poor bugger,' Dimitri says. 'I guess they've all got stories like that.' He, too, looks tired.

'You'd better rest,' I say. He gets up, unsteady on his crutches, and I reach over to help him. 'Hey, you're wobbling.'

'Give me a kiss, even if I am wobbling.'

We kiss, and I see the wide, blue sea over his shoulder.

'Come on,' I say. I assist him towards the veranda door. 'You know, we still haven't discovered where Hanna fits into all this.'

'We'll find out. He's beginning to open up.'

# - 12 -

As Dimitri and Ahmed recuperate, we spend our days drifting between the veranda and the kitchen. The end of August nears, but the sun's heat remains oppressive though the cool evening breeze from the hills behind softens the air. I cook and dispense glasses of squeezed orange juice and ice in the afternoon and ouzo after dinner, which Ahmed declines.

'This is a great thing, this telescope,' Ahmed says. 'One day I'll buy one. Yes, I love the stars and the heavens. They take us away from all our troubles down here on Earth.' He swings the instrument around the horizon. He has a boy's enthusiastic delight in Dimitri's toy.

'We had one of these at school, but it was stolen or lost when the place was bombed.' Ahmed pauses, turns away and hobbles to the couch. 'Lost in the war. Like everything else.' He sighs. '*C'est la vie.*'

'Hey, French too!' I say.

'Yes, I learnt that at school. I also speak Turkish and Bulgarian. You learn a bit of everything when you're on the road and living in jungles of humanity. You have to eat.'

We sit in silence, listening to thrumming cicadas and crackling in the nearby olive trees as nocturnal fauna explore the night's offerings. I stroke Dimitri's injured thigh and hold my warm hand on his wound.

'That feel better?' I say.

'Mmmm. Very much,' Dimitri says. He turns to Ahmed. 'Do you need a warm hand on your wound too, Ahmed?'

The young man gasps, blushes deeply and looks away.

Every few days Dimitri dresses his and Ahmed's wounds. I watch his surgeon's hands delicately lift the gauze pads and bathe the surrounds of the wounds. They look good, and I am pleased.

After two weeks Dimitri removes their stitches, and they move about with more freedom. Ahmed's frown turns to a smile.

Three weeks pass since the stabbings. Dimitri and I ponder whether to take Ahmed back to the camp. I am loath to do it. I also want to get to the bottom of the question of Hanna.

Ahmed pre-empts my decision to ask him about it when, one evening as he sits on the veranda slicing tomatoes and peeling cucumbers, he suddenly says, 'Where's Hanna?'

Dimitri looks at me and rolls his eyes upwards as if to say, *now what?*

'I can't tell you. Yet,' I say. 'We're obliged to keep her safe.'

'So, you know where she is.'

'Did you know Hanna back in Afghanistan?'

'Yes.'

'Why didn't you say so?'

'You never asked me.'

'How did you know her?'

'It's a long story.'

'Well, I'm a journalist. I like stories. You can tell me.'

'Hanna and I lived in the same town outside Kandahar. Our families knew each other and our parents wished us to marry. I suppose we were, what do you say, "engaged" for a long time. Our parents were professional people. My father taught science at a high school in Kandahar, and Hanna's mother and my mother taught at the town primary school. We were sort of related, cousins somehow. Then I went to university in Kabul, and Hanna stayed and studied in Kandahar. We met at weekends and during the holidays.'

Suddenly, I feel guilty about seeing the photo of Hanna.

'Ahmed,' I say, 'when I looked for your antibiotics several weeks ago, a photo fell out of your jeans pocket, and I saw that it was a picture of Hanna in a garden with fruit trees and flowers.'

Ahmed reddens. 'Yes, that was taken in our orchard … full of many fruit trees. Cherries, you know.'

'I'm so sorry. I didn't mean to pry. I picked up the photo by accident.'

'It's all right. I'm glad you know. Now you can understand why I want to find Hanna.'

'But how did she end up with Aziz? I mean, did you and Hanna leave Afghanistan together?'

'Oh, yes. You see, when the Taliban came to power, my parents lost their jobs as teachers. Only boys were allowed to continue studying at the madrasah, so my mother taught the girls in secret, hiding in our home. It was risky, but she was determined. I was working for the American captain by then, and after he was killed, great trouble came to Kandahar, for the Taliban took over. I returned to our town, only to find my house and orchard destroyed and my parents taken away. It was a time of great sadness and desperation, and I spent many, many days searching for them. Everyone in my family had

70

disappeared—my brothers, cousins, aunts and uncles—but I never knew how or to where.

'I spent many days scrambling over rubble until I came to Hanna's house. I called and called her until I heard a timid whisper echoing from a stairwell. I crept down and found her hiding in the cellar. We were sad but overjoyed. I kissed her, hugged her and wiped her tears. She cried some more, and I took her soft, wet cheeks in my hands. I had never been so intimate with her, and I could feel my mother watching over me. Hanna's head scarf was askew, and I saw her thick, black hair for the first time. I touched it lightly, only for her to straighten her scarf and cover her hair. We sat on broken chairs and talked, and she told me what had happened to her.

'She said that she was in my house with the other girls, having lessons with my mother, when those brutes, the Taliban, roared up in a truck, waving their guns and firing into the air.

'Hanna paused, sighed, bent over, put her head in her hands and said that when the Taliban screeched to a halt outside, everyone scattered to wherever they could and that she had been lucky, for she knew my parents' garden and where to hide. She saw them grab my mother and all the other girls and drag them away and shove them into the back of the truck. Someone must have informed the Taliban about their secret lessons with my mother. Hanna said the last she saw of them was when the truck disappeared in a whirl of dust.

'I asked Hanna about my father. She didn't know. Later, I heard that the Taliban went to the schools and arrested all the professors for teaching subjects forbidden by our religion.

'She told me the Taliban had also taken her parents away in the trucks. She broke down, sobbing into her hands, and I was at a loss as to how to console her. I looked through a broken wall and out into the street, but there was nothing and no one.

Just rubbles of concrete. The great burden of mourning for our families weighed me down. Anger folded over into grief and dejection. I felt mute and inert and stood there like a frozen sentinel, begging a sniper to cross the road and shoot me.

'When Hanna had recovered, she told me that because her father worked for the British Army, the Taliban deemed him a traitor and came looking for him at his house. But I hardly heard her words for there was an explosion overhead, and the building opposite collapsed into a thousand pieces. Terror and shock snuffed out my feelings of anger, and I grabbed Hanna by her hand and we rushed up the stairs.

'I told her we needed to get out as the Americans were bombing the house because they thought the Taliban were holed up in the buildings, and she couldn't believe the Taliban had taken away our parents and now the Americans were bombing our homes.

'I told her that it was something like that, but why did it matter as the war was dumb and pointless, and no one was winning or losing. It was just a futile, expensive game wrecking civility and all that goes with it. I was angry again. It was easy.

'When we reached the top of the stairs, I turned, looked deep into her eyes and saw her fear and sorrow. She was shaking, and I embraced her and kissed her at length on her lips. I had not dared do this with such forcefulness before, but the world had changed and we were different people. She responded to my kisses and relaxed into my arms, and I told her I would look after her now. She said that she knew I would and that my mother would have wanted it. Of course, Hanna was right.

'We stumbled along the passage of the house, and when we reached the remains of her living room, she told me her father had kept cash in a safe under the floor by the desk. She disappeared and returned with a screwdriver which I used to prise up the floorboards and open the safe. We found rolls of dollars and pounds as well as exquisite bracelets and rings which Hanna whispered were her mother's. I tore a hole in the lining of Hanna's jacket and stuffed the valuables in there.

'We went to the kitchen and searched the cupboards and found packets of biscuits and tinned meat.

'The sun was setting and the grey clouds were streaked with rust, and in this grey light we crept through the eerie town and found my family's orchard. A single remaining cherry tree stood erect and defiant behind the stone wall, and we slipped behind it and sheltered in a nook of bushes. I picked all the ripe cherries I could find, and we supped on the most delicious meal we would ever have.

'I told Hanna that I was going inside to search for my father's safe. He had once told me of the safe behind the stove and had given me the combination to commit to memory as he thought I might need the contents one day when he was gone.

'I found the safe and said a short prayer of thanks to God and my father. When I opened the safe, I again found rolls of dollars and pounds and jewellery which I added to the cache inside my jacket. I also found more biscuits and tins of meat in a kitchen cupboard.

'That night we slept in our nook of bushes in the garden, and I kept Hanna warm with my coat but did not defile her, for she was too precious to me.'

Ahmed leans back on the sofa and shuts his eyes, clearly tired from telling me his long story.

'Can I get you a tea?' I say.

'Yes, thank you. I'm a little tired. It is not good for me to bring back all these memories.'

'I imagine it's not. I'll be back in a minute. Do you need more antibiotics?'

'Probably.'

'I'll get them.'

Back in the kitchen I lay out cups and more cakes. The boy needs sugar, I think.

I return to the veranda and lay out the cups and pour tea from a long-spouted teapot. It has a sort of ceremony and grace about it. Dimitri, who has remained silent throughout Ahmed's story, had told me that he picked the teapot up in Turkey. The cakes are bite-size, and no one speaks as Dimitri and I eat and sip.

Ahmed's story has overwhelmed me, but the puzzle pieces are not yet in place. I still haven't heard how Aziz comes into the story. And the baby Abed? Who is his father?

A container ship passes on the horizon while Ahmed sprawls with his eyes shut. I see tears well from his closed eyes and berate myself for having opened old wounds.

We sit for a long time until Ahmed somehow straightens up, sips his tea and pops a cake into his mouth.

'I lost Hanna on our journey to Europe,' Ahmed says suddenly. 'It was a hard, dangerous journey with many terrible things happening to us. We were OK when we could pay off the people smugglers. They loved our dollars, and we could even exchange pieces of jewellery for food. We travelled across Iran, and outside Isfahan we paid five thousand dollars to a bus driver with a silver tooth to take us up into the mountains of Iran to the Turkish border, but halfway there, on a pass in the middle of a precipitous mountain range miles from anywhere, bandits waving guns and knives ambushed us. They wore chequered keffiyehs wrapped around their heads, masking their faces. The bandits ordered us passengers to line up on the roadside by the bus, and they walked along the line and jabbed the passengers one by one with a knife or a gun and demanded our money. A brigand stood before the man beside me and put a gun to his head and shouted, "Money, jewels, rings. Get it out." The passenger protested and cried and lashed out, but the bandit grabbed his collar and pulled the trigger, and the passenger fell to the road and rolled over in a heap of dust and blood.

'One of the gang grabbed Hanna and wrenched her away from my hands while holding a knife to her throat. I pulled her back, and she screamed and vomited on the road. I kicked the bandit in the shins and yelled at him, "No you don't!" He shouted at me to give him all our money or he'd take Hanna, but I told him he wouldn't and to let go of her and to keep his dirty hands off her. The bandit tried to throw a punch at me but was knocked off balance and fell to the ground. While he scrambled for his gun, I removed everything I could find in my pockets and handed it to him. I then scattered coins and jewellery all over the road, and the bandits rushed forward and scavenged and fought over it like a pack of children looking for sweets.

'The driver, seeing a chance to escape, ushered us into the bus before hurrying up the steps himself, pressing the starter and letting in the clutch. He slammed the doors shut, and with a spray of stones the bus careened down the mountainside, and the screaming passengers toppled about whilst trying to regain their seats.

'The driver managed to keep us on the road, but in the end he proved untrustworthy, for about ten kilometres from the Turkish border, he stopped the bus, got up from his seat and walked along the aisle. He drew a knife from his belt, pressed it against the cheek of a young girl and announced that the trip had ended. He told us to get our purses out as there was a supplement of a hundred dollars to pay. My hands twitched nervously, but I found the money and paid him. We staggered to our feet, and to divert the driver's attention, I placed a pearl in his pudgy hand. He squashed his fingers around the jewel and smiled. I nodded and guided Hanna down the steps, and the driver abandoned us on the road.

'I told Hanna that we needed to walk and that we were nearly there, meaning Turkey, but it would take us all day. I asked her if she could manage, and she mumbled that she didn't think so and that she could hardly stand. She staggered momentarily. I offered her my hand and told her we would get there some way.

'No sooner had I spoken these words than a taxi pulled up beside us. The driver leant out and asked if we were wanting to get to Turkey. His English was impeccable. I told him yes, and he told us to get in and he'd take us to the border and tell us which guards I needed to pay. "Just a little something," he said. I asked him how much it would cost us, and he told me just a couple of hundred dollars. I asked him if that included the taxi ride, and he smiled a bar of white teeth and said, "Yes," and to trust him as he did this everyday. We got into the back of a battered Mercedes, and he let in the clutch.

'Ten minutes later, we arrived at the border crossing at Gürbulak. The driver pulled up before the border gates and got out of the taxi. He ordered us to wait there, and he went over to the office and walked inside. A minute later, he came out of the office with a border official, who asked us to get out and show him our passports. He sneered at us and said, "Ah, Afghans," and told us it would cost us. I asked how much, and he told me two hundred dollars. I pulled Hanna to the side and whispered for her to give me some dollars and asked if she had any jewellery left. She told me she only had her grandmother's wedding ring. It was gold with an amethyst stone. I turned to the two men and handed them the dollars and the ring. Hanna's hand shook in mine. The border official put the ring on his little finger and examined it while we waited. He lingered and then said he liked it and that we could now go.

'We stepped forward to pass into Turkey, but the taxi driver caught my elbow and pointed out a truck nearby and told me the driver would take us all the way into Turkey in exchange for working for them on their farm. I stopped and asked him if they could be trusted, and he said he would introduce us, and he ushered us over the border to the truck.

'The woman driver wore a red patterned scarf and a long floral skirt below her gaberdine coat. She smiled cheerily when the taxi driver greeted her, and they talked for a while. The taxi driver then said to us that the driver would take us halfway to Istanbul, to Safranbolu, where she grew saffron and needed help with the harvest.

'I asked if she wanted money, and the taxi driver said she only wanted help and that we could sleep in the outhouses on the farm.

'She was accompanied by a man who turned out to be her husband; he, too, had sunburnt cheeks and smiling eyes. She introduced herself as Dilara and her husband as Ahmet. She pointed to the tray at the back of the truck and a piece of foam rubber we could sit on. She climbed up to the driver's seat and set the engine roaring. Her exuberance was given full sway as she sat behind the wheel, and the truck hurtled downhill while we gripped the railings and were thrown from side to side on the two-day journey from the Iranian border.

'Summer arrived, and I worked in the fields of Dilara's farm, planting the crocuses from which we would harvest the saffron. Others from Iraq, Iran and Afghanistan worked alongside us. We kept to ourselves, for every night I could hear fights and arguments from somewhere above us, where the other men slept. I had an inner distrust of everyone I didn't know. Only Dilara and Ahmet seemed as smooth as two pebbles washed on the beach. We didn't need any cajoling from Dilara as we came closer to her than the others, for she became a friend and we worked willingly for her. She taught Hanna to milk the goats, clean out the pens, nurse the kids and make cheese. Hanna's hands had never done such rough work, nor had mine. We had always been students, readers and thinkers. Hanna soon looked lovely. Her cheeks rounded and her skin glowed. She told me that she felt so much better now and that maybe the peasant life was better for her.

'Then one evening, not so many days after the long journey from Iran, it happened. The sun was setting, and its last rays beamed through the tiny window in a golden shaft. I entered the room and found Hanna standing by her bed with a towel round her waist after she'd cleansed herself of the day's dirt. Her scarf was off, and her thick hair fell down her back. Although we'd been very close for so many weeks on buses and trains and trucks, I'd hardly seen her without her scarf. But now in the confines of this room I saw parts of her body she usually kept covered. I went over and touched her bare back. Her skin was the smoothest thing I'd ever felt, and I could not remove my hand from it. I knew my mother was watching me, smiling. My hand slipped down the curve of Hanna's back, then up into her hair and she did not move. I didn't say anything, for I did not know how to express this moment of pure desire. Unbidden, I simply asked her if she minded, and she said, "No." I put my arms around her body and pressed myself into her back. My hands cupped her soft, silk breasts, yet still she did not move. I gently kissed the nape of her neck and turned her face to mine. She put her arms around me and drew me even closer to her bare body, and we kissed more deeply and urgently than we had ever done before. We folded ourselves onto the bed, and in our nakedness we released the tension, desire and love we'd harboured for so long.'

# - 13 -

'Summer brought ripeness,' Ahmed continues, 'and Hanna bloomed like the roses in Dilara's garden and smiled like I'd never seen before. Her body glowed with a patina brought on by the heat and turned amber under the sun. Her body that I got to know so well, as she did mine. We were like the turtle doves Dilara had called us weeks before, busy in our nesting, busy in our union. I could feel my mother watching over us.

'One day, Dilara sat outside the kitchen door, propped on a cane chair and plucking a chicken. I sat beside her and told her that Hanna and I were not married and that I wanted to marry her and that we were supposed to get married in Kandahar, but the war came, our parents disappeared and we had to escape. Dilara replied that she didn't think we were married and that she could tell when a woman is not … well … happy. But now she could see that Hanna was happy and that I felt guilty about it. I told her that, yes, it was something like that and how my parents wouldn't approve and nor would Hanna's.

'Dilara said that things were different now and asked if our parents had approved of our marriage plans. I told her, yes, and she said that was good and that she could easily arrange for us to marry as her brother worked in the Town Hall and could hurry it along as long as we paid some cash. She said she'd see about it when next in town.

'I thanked her. I was so grateful I could have hugged her, for it was now impossible to abstain from sharing a bed with Hanna. A great burden slipped from my mind, and I could see my mother smiling as it was what she would have wanted.

'Two weeks later, I stood on the steps at the Town Hall with Hanna by my side and holding my hand. She wore a flowing red silk dress braided in gold and my mother's wedding ring, a gold band encrusted with tiny blue topazes. I had hardly recognised her when she arrived, for Dilara had lent Hanna her own wedding dress, a gown of such sumptuousness after so many weeks on the road and among the goats. All the farm workers had gathered, in from the fields and sheds, and we walked to the farm courtyard, where Dilara and the other women had set up tables and chairs and decorated the trees and flowers. I wanted a blessing from the local mullah, so he came and raised his head towards Allah and chanted verses from the Koran, after which the guests responded and then applauded as the mullah blessed us and laid his hands on our heads. The women stepped forward and showered us with rose petals and wished us sweetness, wealth and good health.

'All day we celebrated with platters of every delicacy imaginable: keşkek in large bowls, rice pilaf, stuffed peppers and eggplant, grilled kebabs, succulent lamb off the spit, sweet biscuits and the wedding cake made by Dilara. Someone turned on music and all evening the men danced. I suspect they had a hidden booty of illicit alcohol which they consumed as they danced. I danced with Hanna, and other men wanted to dance with her. I felt a pang of jealousy as one, with a cowlick of jet black hair, edged a little too close, smiled lasciviously and seemed to take too long with her. Later, we cut the cake, the lights went out and sparklers lit the scene.

'Next day, the fields were a sea of purple as the crocuses had flowered and were ready for the harvest of the saffron. Dilara showed us how to collect the stigmas with great delicacy, for saffron is the most expensive spice on the planet, costing at least six dollars a gram, so we were warned not to lose a flake. We needed to harvest at least a kilogram of the spice, requiring thousands of hours of back-breaking work.

'As I worked in the field, I smelt alcohol on someone's nearby breath. I look up and saw the cowlicked man who had danced too long with Hanna the night before. He told me I had a pretty wife and asked if she was a good "you-know-what" in bed. He spoke Pashto but with an accent I didn't recognise—hard and through the nose. A spring of rage welled inside me, and I wanted to hit him, but something held me back, for I did not want to cause trouble. Dilara had been good to us.

'I told him to shut his mouth—it was all I could think of saying—and I moved away and went to look for Hanna. When I found her, she asked if I had come to help her, and I said, yes, and that I just wanted to make sure she was OK.

'We brought in the baskets in the evening, and Dilara fed us all with flat breads, chips, cold lamb and spiced sauces. The black-cowlick man sat opposite Hanna—too close for my comfort. I did not like him, and I stood and took Hanna back to our room.

'Each day, we worked in the fields, bending or squatting to gather the stigmas. The days were shorter now; it would have been much more arduous under a biting summer sun.

'We had been harvesting for four weeks when one afternoon Hanna came down my row and told me she was going back to our room as she didn't feel well. I told her I would be back soon.

'I found her lying on the bed and asked her what the matter was. She told me that she'd been feeling ill every morning recently. I described Hanna's symptoms to Dilara, and she said, yes, Hanna is with child, and she gave me some tea for the morning sickness.

'When I returned to Hanna, she confirmed that she'd missed her bleeding for two months. I told her how wonderful and beautiful it was that we were to have a child, and how happy I was. I hugged and kissed her all over and told her she was so clever and asked if I could feel. And I touched her stomach, but there was nothing there.

'Next day, Hanna came down my row of flowers again and told me she was going back to our room as she felt too tired.

'After I helped bring in the baskets at the end of the day, I returned to our room, but Hanna was not there. I went to the privy and knocked on the door and called out her name. There was no reply. I opened the door and found the cabin empty, so I walked over to the kitchen and asked the girls if they had seen Hanna. They told me she wasn't there. I went up and down the house stairs, round the back of the pigsty, into the goat pens and up and down the rows of harvested crocuses.

'I told Dilara that Hanna had disappeared and that I knew she wouldn't do so without telling me. My voice rose in panic. Dilara suggested Hanna may have gone to town. When I told her I would walk into town as I believe something had happened to her, Dilara said it was a long way and nearly dark. I told her I didn't care.

'I walked to town and searched everywhere. The mosque, the taverns, the shops that were still open, the mini supermarket. At times I cried, other times I panicked or was angry. At midnight I returned to the farm but found our room still empty. This time I noticed her jacket hanging on the peg on the back of the door. I delved into the lining and found money and jewels hidden there. I also found her wallet with money and documents but no passport. She wouldn't have left all her money and jewels if she planned on leaving? I reasoned. I couldn't sleep as I waited for the slightest noise to signal her return. Next morning I rose and vowed to search everywhere for her, and I told Dilara so. I carried what little money Hanna had in my pocket and told Dilara I'd ring every few days to check whether she had any news. I needed more money, so I asked Dilara if she could lend me some cash and promised to pay her back. She turned, opened the dresser drawer, pulled out a roll of notes and counted out some 50 dollar bills. She told me to look after it, and as she hugged me, she said she hoped I would find Hanna.

'I spent the first week in Safranbolu, walking the streets, looking behind every shop front and house, believing every now and then that I'd seen her, but it was just a mirage, my eyes playing tricks. Every few days I phoned Dilara, but she had no news of Hanna. During one such call, she told me that the young, black-haired Afghan man, whose name was Aziz, had also disappeared, at the same time as Hanna—where no one knew—and that others at the farm hadn't liked him very much as he was too moody and said he was an escaped Taliban.

'I knew then what had happened to Hanna. Aziz had forced her to leave with him. That's why she'd left behind her jacket with all its money and most of her clothes. I was wasting my time searching about Safranbolu. Fear and rage rumbled within me as I thought about what he could be doing to her. My only hope was to take the road to Istanbul, like Hanna and I had planned to do, and along the way search the areas in the towns where immigrants gathered. I spent two months stopping at all the towns on the road to Istanbul, searching bus stations, soup kitchens and taverns where Afghans hung out, changed money and made phone calls. People squinted at my photos and called me crazy.

'Once I thought I saw her in Istanbul, getting on the ferry that crosses the Bosporus. I called her name and then again but louder, but my voice was lost in the mass of people going to Friday prayers. I visited every mosque in the city and showed my photos to the imams and the carpet cleaners, but they smiled wanly at the crazy young man they thought I was.

'It was the wrong time to leave Istanbul for the Greek border as the winter weather was starting to bite. I had my army coat, boots and a woollen cap, yet I worried if this would be enough for sleeping outside. I knew that getting into Greece would not be easy because the Greek border officials were not as corruptible as the Turks and Iranians. All the fleeing refugees had heard of the migrants freezing to death on the mountains between the two countries. But I left anyway, as did many others with me. I didn't freeze to death, but traversing the mountains took a great toll on my mind and body. We met others who promised to smuggle us into Greece by following river beds or old goat trails. Many, many times our group tried to cross over the border, only for the Greek guards to shoot at us or push us back. I thought I would die in the cold.

'Then finally on a spring day a Greek policeman walked down the hill towards me and smiled and asked if I wanted to cross into Greece. I said, yes, and followed him, all the time fearful that we would be shot, but we reached the border safely, and he held out his hand and demanded one thousand dollars. I only had eight hundred dollars, so I gave him a gold bracelet, and he was happy.

85

'The weather was warm when I reached the Patras port, for that was my destination. I planned to smuggle myself aboard a ferry bound for Italy and walk to Germany. Iraqis and Afghans lingered near the iron railings barring entry to the wharves.

'A young Iraqi, a boy, asked me if I needed somewhere to sleep, and he told me to walk along the road until I reached the stadium, then take the path into the long grass, and I would find a camp behind the stadium. He told me to say Omar had sent me and someone would look after me.

'I arrived at the camp and saw rudimentary shelters covered with sheets of plastic slung between branches and sticks, and fires lit for cooking. Empty cans lay everywhere. An air of melancholy hung about the place as young men squatted and looked doleful and mute, all life squeezed from their beings.

'I asked one if he spoke English, and he nodded and said, "A bit." I told him Omar had sent me and that I could find a place somewhere here to sleep.

'The boy jerked a thumb towards a tent behind him, and I walked over and stuck my head inside the tent and saw only ragged clothes and knotted bedding lying on the floor. I withdrew my head and looked about the camp and saw a tent beyond the others and a man stooped over a fire. It was the curve of his back I recognised, then the black hair at the nape of his neck and his jacket. A wave of fear yet joy overwhelmed me. It was the black cowlick. Had I the luck to come all this way to find him and Hanna? I asked myself.

'A voice behind me said, "Ah, you made it. Found some space in our tent?" I looked around and saw Omar approaching.

'I asked him who the black-haired man was, and he told his name was Aziz, an Afghan, that he'd been at the camp for a month and kept to himself, and that everyone steered clear of him as there was something wrong with him in his head.

'I asked Omar what he meant, and he told me that one minute Aziz was as docile as a kitten, then the next minute he flew into a rage for no reason and screamed and howled like a wolf and waved about a pearl-handled knife he always carried. That he could stab you, just like that, for anything, even just offering him a cigarette, and that he'd already used the knife and made bad wounds. Omar supposed that bad things happened to Aziz in the war and that he was a schizo. Omar cautioned me to be careful and stay away from Aziz as some said he was a Taliban, and that they couldn't get the police involved as they would lock everyone up.

'But I only wanted to know one thing. I asked Omar if Aziz was with anyone else, and he told me Aziz had a woman with a baby in his tent, and that he wouldn't let anyone near them.

'My heart sank, but I was also overcome with relief. Hanna was in there, alive, and so was the baby. All I had to do was get her out. I just needed to sit and wait and watch for my opportunity. Aziz would need sleep, sometime, I reasoned.

'Later that day, he exited the tent and made for the makeshift latrine. He was inside for only a minute. A minute. That's all the time I had to enter the tent, see Hanna and give her a note.

'When night approached, Aziz again visited the latrine and I took my chance. I crept over to the tent, opened the flap and saw Hanna sitting, enveloped in a long, black chador. I could not see the baby.

'I whispered her name, and she turned, saw me and released a whimper of joy and terror. As I bent to embrace her, she kept repeating my name before telling me to be careful or Aziz would kill me.

'I told her I'd been looking for her for months and had almost given up hope, and she said she, too, had almost given up hope, but God had kept telling her that I'd find her.

87

'I asked her where the baby was, and she told me Aziz took him whenever he left the tent, to stop her escaping. I said, "It's a boy?" Hanna nodded, and I said, "Oh, how wonderful!" And I went to kiss her and hug her, but she pushed me away and told me to go as Aziz was a very dangerous man.

'I handed Hanna a pencil and some paper and told her to hide them and write me notes whenever she could. I pointed at a place for her to push the notes under the side of the tent. That way we could communicate.

'I backed out of the tent and could hear Aziz approach through the dry grass behind us.'

\*       \*       \*

Back on the veranda the next day Ahmed sits with his leg propped on the table. He looks pale. Dimitri pours Turkish coffee for us from a copper pot and serves pastries and Swiss chocolate he has bought from the local bakery.

'You all right, Ahmed?' I say.

'Tired,' he says. 'I didn't sleep. I kept thinking about Hanna and the baby and wondering if you'll take me to see her.'

'Well, if everything you say is true, then I can understand you want to see her, but I need to talk to her first and find out from her if what you have told me is true and whether she wants to see you. We have to look after the baby.'

'But the baby is my son!'

'For now, I believe you. We'll have an answer for you tonight.'

Ahmed's mouth is downcast. He is cross with me, but I have to protect those two up at Arini. I go over to Dimitri, kiss him and say, 'I'll be back later.'

\*       \*       \*

I travel up to the olive farm at Arini, and when I arrive I invite Hanna to sit with me under the grapevine outside the kitchen. She joins me and nurses Abed on her lap.

'Ahmed told me that you knew each other in Kandahar and were engaged to get married,' I say. 'Is that true?'

Hanna nods.

'Tell me how you escaped and what happened after.'

She repeats Ahmed's story of their journey to Turkey, the saffron harvest, the discovery of her pregnancy and their wedding feast.

'Were you wearing a ring at the wedding?'

'Yes, Ahmed gave me his mother's wedding ring.'

'Do you still have it?'

She stands, goes inside and returns. She extends an open palm towards me and reveals a gold band with tiny blue topazes.

'I also have photos of the wedding.' She shows me photos of herself in the gold-braided red dress.

I see Aziz standing in a group photo. 'So Aziz worked on the farm?'

'Yes. He always had his eyes on me, passing me, making vulgar remarks about how one day he, too, would have me. I never told Ahmed. It would have been too upsetting and dangerous. I would have hated for there to have been a fight and someone hurt.'

'What happened when you left the saffron farm? Were you forced to leave?'

'Yes. As I walked across the courtyard to the privy, Aziz grabbed me from behind and forced me to go to our room and get my passport. He then held a knife at my throat, and we went outside to a waiting taxi. I was terrified but too frightened to cry out in case he stabbed me. I was pregnant, you see.

'We travelled for hours into the dead of night, for how long I do not know as I slept, somehow. I heard Aziz instruct the driver to not stop and, if he did, to waken him while he went to the bathroom or bought petrol. They worked as a team.

'Aziz told me that he wasn't going to touch me and that he just needed me, needed a woman—especially a pregnant one—to make his journey easier. He said he knew I was pregnant as he could see it in my eyes and had heard Dilara telling one of the other girls.

'At some point during the pitch-black night, we stopped near a field. Aziz hauled me out and forced me inside a stone hut which had rough sleeping benches around its walls and stacked firewood. He lit the fire, boiled water on a kerosene stove, made tea and heated some tinned food. I only ate a mouthful and sipped the weak tea. I said I needed to go to the toilet, and he followed me out and stood beside me and watched me squat by a bush. I died of shame and embarrassment as he shone the torch of his phone on me. I wept silently at my hopeless situation, for I knew that if I tried to run, he might have a gun, and, anyway, I had no idea where we were.

'I lay on the bench in the dark with my eyes open but unable to see anything. I was determined not to sleep. I could not let these men touch me. Then I smelt the rancid stench of stale tobacco on a tepid breath near my cheeks. I panicked and screamed and shouted, "No! No!"

'The taxi driver had his bristly chin on my cheek and his hardness pressed against my thigh. I pushed him off me with all the force I could muster and sent him crashing to the floor. Aziz woke, turned on the light of his phone, jumped upon the taxi driver and punched and pummelled him to the floor.

'He shouted at the taxi driver that I was his and that he'd told him so and that he was paying him to drive a taxi, not have his pleasure with me. Aziz kicked him and told him to get up as we were to leave in half an hour.

'I was safe for now and we left in the taxi. In the dawn light I saw the outskirts of a big city, and Aziz told me it was Istanbul.

We drove through its narrow streets until we stopped in front of a luxury hotel. Aziz ordered me to get out and I did as I was told. I thought I might be able to escape, but he held a gun to my ribs and pushed me in front of him. At Reception, Aziz registered us as a married couple, and a porter guided us to a suite on the top floor. Once our suite door shut, Aziz pointed to the bathroom and told me to help myself, and he turned and phoned someone.

'I did as I was told and bathed as I felt so unclean after being in such close proximity with them. When I came out my clothes were gone, and Aziz handed me a box and told me to wear what was inside it as I was to be the wife of a Taliban. I opened the box and pulled out a full length black chador. I changed into it and have worn it every day until that day Ahmed appeared in my tent at the camp behind the stadium.

'Aziz kept me imprisoned in that hotel in Istanbul for many, many days, maybe even more than a month. I could no longer measure time, sitting on the sofa watching Turkish soap operas or listening to Aziz's rambling, incoherent talk. He told me how he'd joined the Taliban and fought for Afghan freedom from our Western enemies, how he'd killed people in the name of Allah, how he'd succumbed to temptation and been sucked in by the Americans to feed them intelligence about his comrades, and how the Americans rewarded him with gold, jewellery and women's bodies. He told me these stories over and over and ended up sobbing, for the Taliban, in reprisal, had blown up his house and killed his whole family who lived in it. I placated him, kept him quiet, nursed his ego, but then he would wake in the middle of the night in a blinding rage and scream and threaten to kill me with his knife. I was terror-stricken, and a guard who sat outside our suite would rush in and pin Aziz to the ground and save me.

'On the last night we were there, what I feared most happened. I was asleep on the divan and woke to the touch of his hand on my face. He curled up beside me and started taking his pleasure from my body. I could have screamed, but he would have killed me. He told me he'd done it before, and I wept as he lay on top of me. I thought only of Ahmed and prayed he would never know. I carried his baby in me and I had to protect it. In my head I recited verses from the Koran over and over and asked God to forgive me.

'In the morning Aziz told me to pack my things in a plastic bag he gave me and pull the veil over my face as we were to drive to Greece. He boasted that he had opium on him to smooth the palms of those whose help he needed to get there.

'We drove in the taxi to the Greek border, and the driver got out and spoke to the border guards. We remained seated in the car, Aziz in his pristine white tunic and me with the veil over my face. We were like royalty. The guards came over to the taxi, and Aziz wound down the window and handed them a small package after which they waved us through. On we travelled through Greece, and whenever a police officer stopped our taxi, Aziz wound down the window and handed the officer a small package, and we were waved on our way.

'Two days later, we arrived in Patras, and Aziz told me he planned for us to travel to Italy, either by ferry or smuggled on a private yacht. But I ended up living in a dirty tent behind the stadium, kept prisoner inside by Aziz with his knife and a gun and unable to escape. By now I was heavily pregnant and knew my time was near. Then the pains started and went on all night, and all I can remember of that night was great fear, and I cried out so loudly that Aziz got up and left the tent.

'I called out after him and begged him to call a woman to help me. But he was gone. I was alone with only a chink of early morning light filtering into the tent. Between the searing pain of the contractions, I cried and cried until a woman I'd never seen before appeared at the opening of the tent. She said something I couldn't understand and knelt beside me. She held my hand for the next few hours and helped the baby out, an angel from heaven. She washed him as he cried and wrapped him in a towel and placed him to my breast. More blood came, and she cleaned that up. I thanked God that I was all right and so was the baby. She left me and later Aziz returned and boiled tea for me and gave me some bread.

And that's how it was until Aziz stabbed Ahmed. Me, the baby and Aziz who fed me.'

I stand and hug Hanna. 'You've had a terrible time, but you're happy up here, aren't you?'

'Of course.'

'I'm going back home to get Ahmed and bring him here to you. I now know his story is true. Abed needs his father.'

When Ahmed and I arrive at the olive farm, he jumps out of my car and hurries over towards Hanna as she stoops over the vegetable patch. I remain beside the car and watch them from a distance, their black silhouettes against the sun's dying rays. She stands, pauses and holds out her arms, and the two embrace and kiss. He bends and picks up the baby, his son, and lifts him high into the air against the sky, and father and son chuckle with delight.

# - 14 -

Dimitri's leg heals, and we travel in my car to Kalamata from where I have to go south to explore the Mani Peninsula and write an article for Chloe. The day is hot and dusty, and we juggle the air-conditioning and the car windows to get the right temperature.

'Too windy,' I say when the windows are down. 'I'm getting dust all over my hair.'

'Too cold,' Dimitri says when the windows are wound up and the air-conditioning turned on.

As we enter Kalamata, Dimitri says, 'It's in the centre somewhere, near the main square. I've been there before. I'll recognise the street when I get there.' In his head he seems to have his own personal navigation system: he looks up at the sun, takes a reading and reaches our destination.

Kalamata, like most Greek towns, has its dilapidation: roads with holes and patched bitumen, footpaths of broken cement, piles of windswept rubbish and rows of wire fences covered in clinging plastic bags. Once-grand homes stand abandoned with rusty chains securing their gates, and factories and warehouses, empty shells of broken windows, stand desolate. Outside street cafés, men sit and wait and watch, spinning out time with a coffee or a glass of beer.

The road ends at the main square which, at 7 p.m., is filled with people sitting under umbrellas. We park and walk across the square, dragging our bags as we head for the Hotel Gold, which Dimitri's uncle owns. 'It's up here somewhere,' Dimitri says. We leave the square and walk along a narrow street until, ahead, I see a sign *Hotel Gold* adorning a slightly skewed bronze board above a café.

Dimitri sticks his head through the plastic curtain at the door of the café and calls, 'Yiannis.' From the dimness within I see a man sitting sideways on a raffia chair. He stands and ambles towards us. He's large, overweight, with cheeks of a ruddy hue and a head topped with a thick mane of silver hair.

'Oh, oh, Dimitri, welcome,' he says. 'Come in.'

The two hug and kiss and shake hands and effuse greetings. 'And who's this?' he asks of me. Dimitri introduces us, and after another embrace and more kisses and hand shakes, uncle and nephew, arm in arm, drift towards a wooden table. I follow them and we sit.

I look about the café. Its décor seems stuck in a decades-old time warp. The wooden tables wobble on the floor, old sporting posters and photos of Yiannis with friends and clients pepper the pale-green walls and dusty shells and fishnets adorn the walls above the crowded bottles behind the bar.

Yiannis proves a jovial host, smiling and eager. I soon learn from him that the edge went from his life when his wife deserted him a decade before and fell into the arms of a German she met on the beach at Kardamyli. She decided she didn't want to clean toilets anymore, nor serve rude tourists in the Hotel Gold and café, and so she abandoned Yiannis and their two children, Fotis and Dina, and left Kalamata for Munich, where, having taken her half-share in the Hotel Gold, she set up a shoe shop with her new husband in the most elegant street in Munich.

Dimitri and Yiannis chatter like squawking birds in a torrent of words that leaves me far behind with its dialect and talk of family. Above us a fan circles and dispenses wisps of air that dry our foreheads. Without any bidding a waiter appears and places glasses and water on the table.

'This is Fotis,' Yiannis says, putting his arm around the young man. 'Fotis, you remember your cousin Dimitri?' Dimitri frowns. 'Fotis. Fotis. You know, my boy Fotis.'

More smiles, embraces and gushing greetings follow, and Dimitri sits back and looks at his youthful cousin. He is handsome, with deep eyes, a smooth, delicate face, gentle movements and a timid smile. Dimitri tells him that he's certainly grown and asks what he's doing.

'University and helping here. When I can,' Fotis says.

'Good boy,' Dimitri says, slapping Fotis on the shoulder.

Fotis disappears and returns with bottles of beer and plates filled with fat Kalamata olives, pecorino and bread.

Dimitri picks up an olive. 'Yours?'

Yiannis nods. 'At least we've got our olives. Not many tourists come round here. They all go and stay at the beaches.'

After we satiate our hunger, Yiannis guides us up the stairs at the back of the café to show us our room on the first floor. The cream walls are dull from decades of neglect, and the marble stairs clatter under our feet. Yiannis fiddles with the lock until he eventually succeeds in opening the door. We enter, and an odour of tobacco and cheap deodorant greets us.

'Thanks, Yiannis,' Dimitri says. 'We'll be down in a little while for dinner.'

I open the door of the bathroom and see a basin, a shower and a toilet with a bin beside it for soiled toilet paper. Greek plumbing has never, it seems, coped with the invention of toilet paper. I always ignore the bin and hope there'll be no blockage. Even now I know I will ignore it though I would hate Yiannis to have a plumbing crisis.

I flop on the bed and lie next to Dimitri and bathe in the cool air emitted from the air-conditioning unit above us. Its fan roars as loud as a jet engine.

'Cool but noisy,' he says, looking up. 'I think tonight we'll need to decide between heat and silence or cool and noise.'

We roll over and embrace, but I'm too sticky. I need a shower. I tumble off the bed, enter the bathroom, turn on the shower and pull the plastic curtain. Three points of the shower nozzle spray water sideways, hitting the curtain and flooding the floor, but I shower and foam up with gel and shampoo. Dimitri opens the bathroom door, and the water flows out onto the bedroom floor.

'Hey, you going to be all day in there?' he says. 'Any room?'

He steps into the cubicle and soaps my back and then all over my body until laughing, we kiss, massage each other's bodies and make love, flooding the bathroom and half the bedroom. We walk about wrapped in towels and mop the floors with towels pushed around under our feet.

Feeling gay and light in our clean t-shirts and open sandals, we go downstairs. On the way down, Dimitri explains to me that Yiannis is his only uncle, and as he, Dimitri, is an only child, Yiannis is one of his closest relatives.

'I wish I could see him more often,' he says, 'but I never have time.'

It's always the way with the family, I think, until suddenly it's too late.

We find Yiannis in the same position as we left him.

'Coming out for something to eat?' Dimitri says to his uncle. 'Sure.'

I hadn't noticed before, but Yiannis's breathing rasps as he speaks, and he gasps as he gets up. We go outside and he lights a cigarette.

'We can go over to Yorgos on the other side of the square,' Yiannis says. 'He's my friend. Sends me tourists to stay in the hotel. He'll give us a good meal. He grills octopus.'

It's dark now, and the square is full of music, kids playing and waiters shouting. As we walk across the square, I feel I ought to take Yiannis's arm as he looks unsteady on his feet. We salute Yorgos. Fotis sits at a nearby table, so we join him.

'Ah, Fotis,' Dimitri says, 'you off duty at the café tonight?'

'My friend Andreas is there now,' Fotis says. 'Papa gives him a meal in exchange for doing a couple of hours a day.' His English is perfect. He cocks his head to one side and gives the suggestion of a smile.

'Is Andreas at University with you?'

'No, he dropped out. He couldn't afford to live in Patras. Not enough money for the rent. I couldn't either. There's no work anymore in Patras.'

'So, he's come home like you?'

'No, he's from a village down in the Mani. There's nothing there. Only sheep and goats. He stays here with us and with other friends. There's casual work like tourism here, also picking fruit and vegetables, and the olive harvest in November.'

It's all so tenuous, I think.

Yorgos brings over the grilled octopus, Greek salad and chips, and we jab our forks into the food. The grilled octopus, succulent and fresh, has the tangy flavour of burnt wood and the sea. I watch Yiannis, who neither smokes nor talks much, and I realise he's breathless and struggling as if it's all too much of an effort. His face reddens when he has a coughing attack.

'Why did you drop out of university, Fotis?' Dimitri says, a note of concern in his voice.

'Too difficult.'

'What were you studying?'

'Civil engineering, specialising in anti-seismic buildings.'

'What do you mean, too difficult? Did you fail your exams?'

'No. Too difficult accessing the professors and teachers. You know how it is here. To get anywhere in this country you have to know someone or have money. You have to be the friend of a friend to get ahead. I don't know anyone. At university, knowing the right people counts, otherwise you are on your own. You have to know someone to get the right work experience. Like an architect or the owner of a construction firm. Also, I need to work to pay my rent and eat, but there's no casual work in Patras. All the migrants do it. Ruined the job market for us students. They'll take any pay they can and don't mind living in tents. They rob food from the markets or the tavernas where they wash dishes.' Fotis, nursing a beer and more voluble now, has lost his shyness, and a sense of injustice rises from within him.

'The wars of the workers,' Dimitri murmurs.

'Half the people who start university drop out. It's too difficult. Not the subjects. I passed all my exams, no problem. It's all the rest. Look, I'm sorry for holding the floor.'

'No, don't apologise. I'm glad you told me. It's like that in this country. It's true.'

Fotis grabs the last of the octopus and chops it up. Dimitri turns to me and says quietly, 'He's right, you know. My father was a doctor, and he helped me get my foot in the right doors to do my hospital internships. Lots of my friends went to

London or Italy to do medicine. They had money. I could have gone abroad too, but I didn't need to, back then.'

Dimitri wipes the oil off his plate, and Yorgos places melon and figs on the table as well as cinnamon cakes and custard.

'Yes, the world is made up of little kingdoms,' Dimitri says, 'and you have to be in the right one to get ahead.' He stuffs the oily bread in his mouth. 'Anyway, there's no money now to pay anyone with qualifications. Just think of it. People like Ahmed are stopping people like Fotis from completing their studies. Doesn't seem right, does it?'

A trio of musicians gathers by the bar. A moustached man plays a bouzouki, accompanying a woman in a slim, black dress who intones a Greek love song—its Eastern sound flows out of the Ottoman Empire.

Yiannis stands and says he's on his way and he'll see us in the morning. As he walks out, I say to Fotis, 'Will he be OK getting back to the Hotel?'

'Of course,' Fotis says. 'Why?'

'Is he well? I mean, he seems to be having trouble … breathing. That cough doesn't sound too good.'

'No, he's fine. Probably should stop smoking, though.'

The boy seems oblivious, I think, as Dimitri sings along with the woman in black.

'So, Marina,' Fotis says. 'What brings you to Kalamata?'

'We're heading to the Mani to do some walking and hopefully end up in Kardamyli. I'm writing a travel article for a website.'

'Oh, I see. I have to go down that way myself tomorrow morning. I could show you where the trails are.'

'Sure. We plan to depart about eight.'

The singer finishes her song, and shouts and claps follow. It's our cue to go, so we stand. Dimitri goes over to pay Yorgos, but he says Yiannis has already done it. 'No problem,' Yorgos says, waving us away.

I wish they'd let us pay. They are too generous.

Back at the hotel we confirm the next day's outing with Fotis and wish him good night.

We climb the stairs, and Dimitri jiggles the key in the lock of our room's door. Inside, the floor seems to have dried. I sit on the edge of the bed with my phone and look up Hotel Gold on Trip Advisor. The comments are so negative that I snap the phone off, and a wave of sympathy for poor Yiannis rushes over me. Not even Fotis seems interested in trying to make the hotel more modern.

We strip and lie on the bed, embraced in a spoon, but cannot sleep due to the incessant roar of the air-conditioning's jet engine above our heads.

'We'll have to turn that thing off,' Dimitri says.

With a click, the roar dies down, but our peace is short-lived as the room's temperature soon climbs.

'Open the window,' I say.

Dimitri opens the window, and a wisp of cool air breathes across the bed. But festive noise comes from outside below. I look out the window and see it's just people shouting and bouzouki music emanating from an open window across the street. We try to sleep to the sound of the music. But to no avail. The noises of the night serenade us: the clatter of engines, music, voices and finally the rubbish trucks at 5 a.m.

I wake exhausted. Have I slept? I don't know.

# - 15 -

Dimitri is still sleeping when I wake. 'It's twenty to eight,' I whisper. 'We should get downstairs. Fotis will be waiting for us.' He murmurs and opens his eyes.

Ten minutes later, we arrive downstairs. Fotis is not there, but Yiannis is, sitting on the side of his chair. Has he been there all night? I wonder.

'Ah, hello, my young things,' he says. 'Sleep well?'

'Sure.' Dimitri doesn't mention the roaring air-conditioning unit above our bed.

In the corner of the café four young men sit round a table, drinking frappés and eating croissants filled with ham and cheese.

'Andreas!' Yiannis calls over to the corner. A young man gets up and comes over to us. 'Dimitri. Marina. This is Andreas, Fotis's friend from University.'

Andreas has the sloping nose and curly locks of a javelin thrower pictured on a Hellenic vase. He's of a good height, with a taut chin and athletic arms. As we shake hands, he smiles charmingly and his eyes twinkle.

'Welcome to Kalamata,' he says.

Perhaps he should be running the Hotel Gold, I think.

'Bring over some breakfast for these two,' Yiannis says to Andreas. He turns to us and says, 'Coffee?'

I request a frappé and Dimitri orders his usual Turkish. I look over at the three men in the corner. Their chatter distracts me because they speak in some Middle Eastern language.

'Yiannis, are those guys immigrants?' I say.

'Yes, I give them breakfast and something hot in the evening. They're good guys. They help me with the olive harvest, and I find jobs for them round the town. You know, through friends.'

'And where do they sleep?'

'Here, or in my old village, Alykas, up in the hills. Fotis'll take you there today.'

'And you don't charge them rent?'

'Course not. Someone's got to help them. Young men get hungry. They need to be satisfied at both ends. I can only satisfy them at this end.' He laughs and pokes his hand into his mouth. He then chuckles and gasps. 'Can't do the other!'

Andreas places our coffees and a plate of cheese pies on the table. I get out my note book and jot down: *Greek generosity, hospitality = philoxenia. Mediterranean largesse, compare with Sicily.* I want to pay for our breakfast and dinner last night, but Dimitri tells me not to or else I'll offend his uncle.

Fotis appears and greets us with a slightly slurred "Hi". It seems he's just got out of bed. He beats up a frappé at the counter and wraps a feta pie in a paper napkin and soon, wakened by sustenance, asks if we're ready to go.

We get into our car and follow him and Andreas ahead as we leave the town. We soon climb up into the Taygetos Mountains. The road switches back and forth and squeezes under overhanging rock carved into tunnels that allow passage for a single car only, and as we skirt a deep gorge which drops below us, I feel a tremor of nervousness.

'Do you know where we're going?' I say.

'Yep, sort of,' Dimitri says. 'I climbed these mountains with my father when I was a boy. We are going to the family village.'

Fotis's indicator flashes, and we turn left off the main road and take a minor dirt road that ascends gently into the mountains. Ahead, a village appears, clinging to the side of a hill, and we halt as the road ends.

Fotis jumps out of his car and says, 'Here we are.'

We set off on foot towards the village. The terrain is flat, shaped into a terrace by a stone wall, and we pass abandoned houses with rubbled walls eroded by the elements and covered in the clinging tendrils of giant creepers.

Fotis walks ahead of us, his little finger linked into Andreas's hand. I look at Dimitri, and he murmurs, 'Oh, I see.' They disappear around the side of the ruins of a larger building, an old church, and when we get there we cannot see them anywhere. We head back the way we've come and look below at the terraces partially covered in a wild undergrowth let to have its own rampant way in this forgotten world. We pause and stand in silence.

'It's eerie here, so quiet, isn't it?' I say, turning to Dimitri and taking his hand. 'I can't hear any birds.'

'There's no silence like the silence of abandoned human dwellings,' he says.

Dimitri guides me over to a roofless house.

'This is my grandfather's house,' he says. 'What's left of it.' We enter a space surrounded by crumbled walls and the remains of a fireplace. 'This was the centre of the house. They cooked over the fire, a table here, one big bed for the whole family in the next room, and the animals penned and sheltered beyond that wall. They were poor, very poor, and life was hard, eking out an existence in these mountains. Some vegetables on these terraces in summer, a few fruit trees over there, walnuts and chestnuts up the hill, and of course sheep and goats providing milk, yoghurt and cheese.'

We move "outside" the house and walk down the slope, passing ruins on either side of us.

'There were great feuds going on between the people of these villages,' Dimitri says. 'The people were either bound by great kindness or feuding with their neighbours over the hill. I can see why my grandfather's parents left for the valley, where they prospered and could grow pumpkins and potatoes in the sun.'

'What are those plastic tents down there?' I say.

'Where?'

'There, half hidden in the bushes.'

'They don't look ruined by the elements, do they? Let's go and have a look.'

We scramble down the rocky hill, stones slithering under our feet, till we come upon two small plastic tunnels, like those used to grow tomatoes. Dimitri opens the flap of one and says, 'Oh … I see. Marijuana plants.'

'Oh, no,' I say.

I hear movement among the low bushes beside another crumbling edifice covered in sheets of plastic. Fotis emerges with Andreas, and several immigrant men appear from the undergrowth.

As they walk towards us, I hear Dimitri seething under his breath. 'What the fuck do they think they are doing?' he says.

I'd never heard him angry before, but now he is.

'Fotis!' Dimitri says. 'What the fuck do you think you are doing growing dope here?' Before Fotis can reply, Dimitri adds, 'I bet your father doesn't know about this.'

'It's only for personal use. For us,' Fotis says.

'Personal use? I've heard that before. What's this? Your father feeds your friends, lets them use his house and this village, finds work for them, and you turn round and cultivate cannabis on his land.'

Dimitri opens the flap of the other plastic tunnel and looks inside. I see a healthy crop of plants in there. Dimitri turns to his cousin and says, 'And you say you've dropped out of university because you can't afford it?'

I'm surprised at how hard Dimitri is on the boy as he hardly knows him. But he's his cousin and is older. He has a right to.

Fotis bows his head. Yes, there is shame there, but he gives a wry little laugh and says, 'Those guys are from Afghanistan and know how to do it. They taught me how.'

'Geez, I hope you're not growing poppies.'

'Course not.'

'Do you want me to tell your father or shall I call the police?'

'Oh God, no, please don't!'

'Well, I'm coming back here in a couple of days, and if this stuff, and the Afghans, are not gone, I'm calling the police and telling your father. Do you think he needs this disappointment? He's not well, you know. He can hardly breathe. His lungs are stuffed. And remember, you're going to receive a piece of this property one day, and you might be able to do something constructive with it like set up an ecotourism destination here for hikers.' Dimitri turns the screws. 'Your boyfriend, Andreas, looks as if he might have what it takes, to do some such thing, but I'm not sure about you. It'd be better than wallowing in a prison cell, wouldn't it?'

Fotis blushes, and his olive skin takes on an orange hue.

Dimitri turns abruptly and starts walking uphill towards our car. He turns round and calls back to Fotis, 'No need to show me where the trails are. I know my way round these hills. I thought we cousins could have had a nice day out together, but I've changed my mind now. Do you care? ... Probably not ... But think about what I've said.'

We stride up the hill, but Dimitri stops and turns again. Fotis remains standing, fixed on the "street" below and looking up at us.

'By the way, Fotis,' Dimitri shouts, 'don't smoke dope. It blows your brains out. If you do that, you'll never be able to do anything with your life. Stop doing it now. I'm a doctor, and believe me I know what I'm talking about. Think about that too. You're my cousin, my flesh and blood, and I care about you.'

We head off towards our car in silence, panting as we climb the hill.

I've just seen Dimitri reprimand his cousin, but he's kept his cool, kept the lid on his anger. I myself would have exploded in an emotional outburst in such a moment, but Dimitri has roundly told Fotis a few simple home truths about the consequences of his actions.

One day, I see Dimitri might have to tell his own son—our son—about life's choices. His purpose and calm delivery draw me to him, the doctor and healer. But there is no son yet, I know, but there will be, one day, in the new room with its stone walls, next to ours at back at the house. It's nearly ready for him.

# - 16 -

We drive back down to the main road and turn left, away from the ruined village.

'We'll drive along here for a couple of kilometres,' Dimitri says, 'then turn off up the mountain and walk to this hamlet I know. It's about two kilometres up the hill. It's not too steep.'

Dimitri parks the car under a clump of unkempt olive trees and we commence our ascent by foot. The sun beats down upon us relentlessly, as does the incessant heat radiating from the stone walls lining the track. In our knapsacks we carry water bottles and rolls filled with cucumber, oregano and tomatoes, and soon sweat trickles down my back. We scramble up, the gravelly stones giving way under our feet, and after a kilometre, I tire although the coolness of a miraculous spring flowing between mossy stones somewhat mitigates the heat. We stop and drink energising draughts of cold water. The spring thins to a thread of a stream which we follow, climbing under the shade of oleanders with their cool green sheaves of spiked leaves and small flowers of pink and white. Overhead, poplars, aspens and olive groves speckle the mild slopes in silver and green. Dimitri finds a willow beside the stream, now with only a suggestion of water, and slumps to the ground under the tree, and I collapse beside him.

'Let's eat those rolls,' I say. 'I need something for the next bit.' I place two slices of cucumber on my forehead to cool off.

'It's not far,' Dimitri says. 'Just round the corner.'

I've heard those words before on hill climbs, I think wryly.

But he's right, for as we round the corner, the terrain flattens out into a green plateau and ahead a cluster of houses cling to the hillside. We slow to an amble and take in the view, a vista of verdant-cushioned hills and a tapestry of fields filling the valley far below. A wisp of cool air tiptoes across my brow, a well-timed mid-afternoon gift providing succour from the enduring intolerable heat suffusing from the baking rocks.

We reach a grassy square covered in the comforting shade of surrounding plane trees. Donkeys stand tethered to the tree trunks, and under the shade men and women sit or lie on coloured rugs. They greet Dimitri with enthusiastic hugs, slaps on the back and smiles. Dimitri draws me in and introduces me. They remember his father and uncle from their crumbling village in the gorge below, where these men now wander with their munching goats, and also remember Dimitri, too, as a young boy walking in the hills with his father.

They invite us to sit and offer us a plate of almonds and bowls of warm milk. Children appear and smile shyly, and the women bid the young girls to hand out food. The sunlight dapples upon the women with their scarved heads and the men with their brimmed straw hats, producing a picture painting. Rings of cheese hang in hessian bags from the boughs and drip whey. A half circle of houses, with stone walls at the bottom and wooden walls on top, surround the grassy square. Each house has a wide veranda boxed in for extra living or sleeping space. A stone pen lies beyond the houses, corralling the sheep and goats at night. There are no ruins here.

We have disturbed the afternoon siesta, and the women rise and round up their animals for milking. Some prop on stools beside the herd while others steer the goats into the stone-walled pens under the veranda. The houses on the hillside face south, nurtured by the sweet breezes from Africa and the arc of the sun as it sweeps from east to west. The mountains behind provide shelter from the freezing Siberian winds. We are in a pastoral scene, a moment fixed in a past century.

I jot notes in my journal in anticipation of writing a serious article for Chloe. This hamlet lives in precious isolation, and often I am loath to reveal such places in a tourist guide for fear of inundation and contamination by the outside world.

Dimitri talks to the men about Greek politics, and an old man laughs and says, 'Be careful of the Jews if you are going to the villages over there.' He points to towards the other side of the valley.

'What do you mean?' Dimitri says.

A conversation ensues about the people over the hills. The old man says, 'Ah, they think they can rip us off, them over there, but we can beat them at any game, especially when it comes to doing a deal.'

'What are they talking about?' I whisper to Dimitri.

'Oh, they're always going on about Jews round here.'

A huge copper pot bubbles above an open fire outside one of the houses, and a delicious aroma effuses from it. Every now and then a woman appears, stirs the pot contents, adds some spices and returns indoors.

The women finish milking, and night arrives. The moon sheds light almost as bright as daylight. A man brings out a kerosene lamp which illuminates our faces with an amber hue.

'They've offered us a bed on one of the verandas,' Dimitri says to me. 'Are you happy to sleep up here tonight?'

'It's a bit too dark to walk down that hill now!'

We sit on the patterned rugs, and the women in their baggy trousers dish out the casserole into terracotta bowls. The food has bubbled away all day, and the meat is as tender as butter. It's rabbit and vegetables laced with cinnamon, cumin, nutmeg and other unknown spices. Leaves of mint sprinkle over the tzatziki into which we dip our flat bread.

Dimitri talks with the men about hunting rabbits, shooting birds, the Jews who live over the hills and the Bulgarian gypsies who steal their goats. As the men speak, they slip strings of tortoise-shell beads through their fingers and twirl and flip, followed by a mesmerising click, click, click. Most of their talk I can neither translate nor understand, but their voices rise when they pat the long rifles and carved crooks by their sides and say, 'We have to watch out for them. We have to watch out for them.' They seem as threatened by strangers, stealthy Jews and gypsies as their animals are by rapacious birds and slinking foxes.

The women serve almond cake. I know this is a special treat for us, and we partake of it respectfully. Though full of the spicy casserole, I accept this hospitality with grace. I smile and wash it down with the rather rough retsina. A man offers Dimitri ouzo, and he drinks a small glass to complete the ceremony of hosting guests. The women start to move into the house, and we take this as a cue to follow them and climb the outside staircase to our boxed veranda. They lay a large horse-hair mattress on the floor for us, and we slip between sheets of thick linen which they keep in a walnut chest in the corner.

The room has no light, but we don't need it as the half-open wooden shutters allow the moon to shine across our room in silver shafts. Dimitri lies by the window with his foot propped on the sill. Every now and then he uses his toes to swing the shutters.

I release a stifled giggle and whisper, 'Our own personal air-conditioning. Ah, just a bit more air, that's right. A little trickle of air from those hills up there is creeping across my face. Perfect.'

He twiddles the shutter with his big toe.

We try to sleep, but resonant snores come from the next room, and the dogs beneath us under the house bark at calls from a faraway hill. A woman's voice releases a stream of invective to quieten the dogs but to no avail. None of this disturbance quietens an incessant cicada in the dark above my head.

'Do you think we are going to get any sleep?' I say.

'Probably not,' Dimitri says. 'It's midnight.'

But somehow we slumber for a few hours until we hear gunshots echoing about the valley.

'Are you awake?' I say.

'Course,' Dimitri says.

'What's that?'

'Hunting for wild boar or rabbits. It's a sport, you know.'

The dogs bark again. I doze for an hour until the jangling of bronze bells sounds below, and the women order the goats to assemble for milking. Roosters crow in a ruthless chorus.

'Is the night over?' I say.

'Probably,' Dimitri says.

We rise, open the shutters and see the women bustling about with pails and stools. The dawn sky in the east is streaked with silver and pink, and the day's first rays peek over the mountains.

By the time we dress and exit our room, it's daylight and most of the company already sit on the carpets below. The women bring out Turkish coffee in little brass pots, along with plates of sweet preserved fruit, freshly baked bread and pecorino. One woman, with her patterned scarf and gold earrings, has eyes that smile kindness and a warm heart, and the perfume of fresh bread exudes from her hands.

Dimitri tells me her name is Artemis.

'You slept well? More coffee?' she says to me.

'Sure, thank you,' I say.

The men wave their hands towards the plates of food and gesture for us to partake of more, and feeling obliged to accept their solicitousness, we stretch for more.

An elderly gentleman sits on a low chair beside Dimitri, and the family divert their attention from us, bow to him and attend him. He is the guiding presence, the leader of an indeterminate age.

'He is our grandfather, Papa Ephraim, the head of the family,' Artemis says to us. 'He owns all our sheep and goats, one thousand of them, that roam these hills. He has much money, hidden under the ground in terracotta urns.'

Ephraim has a white beard, which he strokes gently, gold teeth and, like Artemis, smiling eyes. He clicks his amber beads and nurses on his lap a crook with a dolphin's head.

'Have you seen his crook?' I whisper to Dimitri. 'Do you think he's ever seen a dolphin?'

'That's a beautiful crook,' Dimitri says to Ephraim, patting the dolphin.

'Here, take it, young man,' Ephraim says, passing it to Dimitri. 'It's yours.'

'Oh, no, I can't,' Dimitri says in protest, but the deed is done, and he cannot refuse the gift now. 'You're too kind, too kind,' Dimitri says, and as Ephraim beams, Dimitri puts his hand in his pocket and pulls out his Swiss pen knife.

'Please, take this, Mr Ephraim. You can use it, I'm sure.' Ephraim's gold teeth flash, and there are smiles all around the group. '*Kalá Kalá*,' they all cry, and our friendship is sealed.

We stand to leave and bow to Ephraim and shake his hand. Artemis comes from inside the house with gifts of food tucked in her apron: walnuts, cheese, bread and sugared fruit wrapped in a cloth. They farewell us as if we have stayed a month, and a great spirit of generosity emanates from these shepherds, full of the goodness of human nature. We exchange many embraces and slaps on the back, and as we commence our downhill walk to the car, they cry out, 'You'll come back, won't you?'

Soon we stand by the car and wave our phones about, but there is no reception.

'Where's the map?' I say. 'Ah, here it is under the seat.' I spread the map on the bonnet of the car and run my finger along a road which will take us to the sea. 'We need to go down to Kardamyli, here, then onto Kalamitsi to find Patrick Leigh Fermor's house. After that we should be able to find Bruce Chatwin's grave somewhere outside the village.'

# - 17 -

'There's the sign for Kardamyli,' I say to Dimitri. 'Turn right up there. That's it. Leigh Fermor's house must be along here somewhere. Closer to the sea. Keep going along here.' We slow and look for signs, and I see an arrow to Kalamitsi Beach. 'It must be along here. The house is built of stone. I've seen it in photos, a mosaic of terracotta and sand stone. It'll probably be difficult to find, you know, hidden amongst the trees.'

'So, you were talking before about Bruce Chatwin, that English travel writer,' Dimitri says. 'I read his book *The Songlines* when I travelled around Australia, discovering the Outback. Interesting book. I remember he wrote that the indigenous people are guided across the desert by their songs. There must be something in that.' He pauses. 'A real nomadic people.'

I tell Dimitri how Chatwin thought himself a nomad, wandering all over the world, only returning home when he felt like it. 'He laced that book with his theories of nomadism. He was married, but his wife never knew where he was because he was always away, travelling. Very indulgent of him. Very tolerant of her. Too easy, isn't it?' I release a wry laugh. 'He was the darling of travel writers in the eighties, yet critics like Salman Rushdie slated him for inventing things he did on his travels. It's all come out now because someone wrote his biography and got to the bottom of it. Even his wife says he attributed things to himself which in fact happened to her. I think people invent so-called "truths" all the time. Even historians.'

I tear off a chunk of bread and pass it to Dimitri. He munches on the bread until he says, 'I can't really see how someone who worked in Sotheby's and went to a posh public school could ever be a nomad.'

'I suppose you can never fact check a travel writer.'

I jot notes in the notepad resting on my lap, and my knees wobble as the car travels along the gravel road.

'Everything I write and send to Chloe could be an invention. How is she ever going to know whether or not what I am describing is true?' I chuckle.

As the car judders, Dimitri says, 'What's Chatwin got to do with Leigh Fermor and this house we're looking for?'

'You do realise Leigh Fermor's dead. The house is empty except for the old housekeeper.' I look at my watch. 'Oops, it's gone eleven, and I said we'd be there at half past ten. Anyway, Chatwin visited Leigh Fermor here when writing *The Songlines*. Chatwin loved Leigh Fermor's books that recounted his wanderings about Europe and Turkey in the 1930s. Chatwin wanted to get to know the great travel writer.'

'Oh, so that's it.'

'We're nearly at Kalamitsi beach. Perhaps we've missed the house. Best turn round.'

Dimitri reverses and we head back.

'What happened is that Chatwin and Leigh Fermor hit it off, and Chatwin stayed in a hotel in the village of Kalimitsi for several months and finished writing *The Songlines* in between long walks with Leigh Fermor in these hills, where they tossed around ideas about history, language, anthropology and the mind. You can see how Leigh Fermor influenced his writing.'

Dimitri stops, studies his phone and says, 'The house must be somewhere along here, according to Google Maps. Ah, I've got reception now. We best walk from here.' He opens the car door, then pauses. 'What did you say about Chatwin's grave?'

'Chatwin wanted his ashes placed near a church up the hill here. We'll have to look for it. Then I'll write it all up for those finely tuned Guardian readers who prefer to travel to a "pilgrimage" destination where they can walk on their knees and bleed, rather than carry round the burdensome label of "tourist" and have to stand in a queue for three hours to enter a museum.'

Dimitri pats my bottom. 'Oh, good for you.'

We follow a rough track until I see a building and pencil cypresses standing nearby as sentinels, then a blue wooden door set in a stone wall. A rope hangs by the door, perhaps having once held a bell but now only a frayed fragment.

Dimitri knocks, but no one responds, so he knocks louder and pushes the door. It opens.

'Hello? Hello?' he calls, and a woman appears from around the side of the house, wiping her hands on her apron.

'Kalimera,' I say. 'Sorry we're late.'

The woman, the housekeeper Angelina I imagine, looks at me quizzically as if to say, why are you apologising? I realise that excusing yourself for tardiness does not much enter into the ritual of apologies in these parts like it might in the Presbyterian woods where I come from. You just come when you can, are welcomed at any time and will be served accordingly.

'Sit down, sit down,' she says, gesturing to the stone seats placed around a mosaic table in the middle of the courtyard.

She disappears into the house. We look around and see piles of leaves windswept into a corner, chips in the tiles and mosaics, and unkempt trees that, though they provide shade, haven't been tamed since who knows when. Terraces of vines, olives and cypresses cradle the house, and the sea, a hundred metres beyond and below, spreads out from a small, shingled beach. Angelina returns with two frappés topped with chunks of ice and frothing milk.

'Sugar? Sugar?' she says.

'May we look about the house,' I say.

'Yes, you can walk around. But not inside. Just see through the windows. Nothing done much since Mr Leigh Fermor died five years ago. I just do a little cleaning and sweeping. He gave the house to a Foundation, you know. They start a little to fix it up, but no money now. No money in all of Greece. Those politicians, they steal it all. They take carloads of it to Bulgaria.' She gives a wry laugh and rolls her eyes heavenwards.

We slurp our frappés until our glasses are empty, then walk around the house, peering through the windows. I see dusty couches, rows of bookcases and an inlaid dining table in the living room upon which stand intricately worked bronze candlesticks. I'd heard about the gatherings of writers like the Durrells, George Johnston, Charmian Clift and Leonard Cohen around this table, where they partook of chicken and olives in red wine and engaged in what Leigh Fermor loved to do: talk of letters, art and human history. Leigh Fermor, with his volumes of books close at hand, would rise from his chair in moments of controversy and reference a volume and validate or invalidate a fact or date or geographical conundrum.

We finish our viewing and look for Angelina and find her watching television in the kitchen.

'Can we walk down to the sea?' Dimitri says to her.

118

'Sure, sure,' she says. 'You going swimming? I'll give you a towel.' Before we can say no, she hands us two large, white towels as soft as ducks' down.

We set off down the gravel path to the beach. The noon sun blazes above, and we strip and don our swimming costumes in haste, eager to enter and defile the water with its silver and turquoise sheen. I break the surface with care, paddle swan-like and let the surface ripple on my chin, but Dimitri runs and dives in and splashes everywhere, then leaps and jumps about, making tidal waves of foam. He strikes out with pure, sleek strokes towards a small island about 500 metres offshore, driving through the water like a fine-tuned hull. I look on with admiration.

He stops and looks back and shouts to me, 'I'm swimming to the island. Coming?'

'No,' I shout.

Half an hour later, I sit on the shingles but cannot see Dimitri. Has he swum around the island? Or exited the water and walked around it?

Three-quarters of an hour pass, and still I sit, awaiting Dimitri's reappearance. The heat beats down, oppressive, the silence is eerie and not even a dot of life appears on the horizon. Should I strike out for the island? I'm not a strong swimmer. I know I cannot do it. A tight knot of panic rises in my chest.

## - 18 -

My hands shake as I scroll my phone, looking for an emergency number. My well of panic unsprings and I leap into action. I need help now, not wait for emergency services like the police or ambulance, and can only think of Angelina up in the house. I scramble up the path towards the house, hoping she has gone neither shopping nor scavenging for early mushrooms. I run round the back to the kitchen and find her asleep before the TV, deep in the torpor of a siesta. I look about at the clusters of metal pots hanging on the wall, the patterned curtain below the sink and a gold ikon of the Virgin Mary in a corner.

'Angelina. Angelina,' I say with anxious urgency, but she continues to snore lightly, so I repeat her name with a raised voice, and she stirs with a little shudder.

'What do you want?' she says. 'Oh, oh. Sorry, sorry. It's you, yes. You need something? A shower? You have a good bathe in sea?'

She stands and places a carafe of water and two glasses on the table before I manage to explain my concern. She sees the worried look on my face and says, 'Where's your man?'

'We entered the water at the beach, and he swam out to the island. I returned to the shore, but by then he had disappeared. Round the other side of the island, I think. I just don't know. I haven't seen him for about three-quarters of an hour.' My voice crescendos as I rush my account. 'I need a boat to look for him.'

'Yes, yes, I see. You need a boat. A boat. Just one moment.'

'It's urgent. I mean, can you ring someone round here with a boat? Here's my phone. Or can we look for someone? We can go in my car.'

She goes over to the kitchen dresser, opens a drawer and pulls out a brown phone book.

'Mmm, now, let me see. Just one moment, please.' She flicks through the pages and searches in slow motion. 'Yes. I phone my brother.' She slowly dials a number and waits for what seems an eternity until, finally, a voice answers. A long conversation in dialect ensues, and when the phone call finishes, Angelina says to me, 'You go down to the beach now. My brother, Pano, he come in ten minutes with boat.'

I rush out the door, round the back of the house and through the courtyard. The stones slip under my feet on the path as I run down to the beach. Perhaps Dimitri is already back? But the beach is as empty as a dried-up shell. I scan the horizon, but it remains desolate. I cannot wait there any longer, so I wade out until I am out of my depth. My inner voice says, *Don't do this!*

I hear the thud-thud of a motor, and a small fishing boat draws up to me from around the rocky headland. A man's bronzed, creased face smiles below his straw hat, and he says, 'Hi, I'm Pano.' I explain in haste what has happened, but he interrupts me. 'Get in, get in. Yeah, I know everything.' He speaks perfect English and tells me he once lived in Oakleigh.

We head towards the island, and while the relief at having found help washes over me, anger rises within me. A speech forms in my mind, a stern lecture I'm going to deliver to Dimitri, bubbling with phrases like 'Why did you just abandon me there?', 'What did you think you were doing?', 'Don't you realise I've been waiting for nearly an hour for you?' and 'I had to go and get help.' Yet my anger and admonishment fade as panic and anxiety take over.

We round the island, and on the other side I cannot see Dimitri, on the island or in the sea. Terror rises within me, and I fear, indeed know, the worst has happened.

We motor slowly along the rocky shore, scanning the expanse of water and land. Suddenly, I see a distant speck in the sea.

'There, what's that over there?' I say, pointing. 'Head for that. Looks like someone swimming.'

As we approach, I see it's Dimitri, his smooth strokes barely breaking the surface.

'Yes, it's him! It's him!'

I shout out to Dimitri, but he does not respond. When we near to within fifty metres of him, he lifts his head and shouts, 'What are you doing here?'

I shout back, 'Where have you been? Where have you been?'

He dives under the water and swims, unseen, to the boat. He surfaces and says, 'Are you here to give me a lift?'

'Get in, man, get in,' Pano says. 'Your missus has been all over the place, looking for you.'

'You just disappeared round the island,' I say, whining. 'You have been away for hours.'

'No, I haven't.'

'Yes, you have.' I cannot assuage the anger in my voice as it trembles. 'I thought you'd drowned.'

'Well, I haven't, have I?'

We are arguing. Us, for the first time. I am not used to it, especially in front of this kind man who took time out to rescue him.

As the boat heads shoreward, I remain silent and sullen and look out at the approaching beach. But my anger resurfaces, and I cannot resist delivering my speech. 'This kind man, Pano, came with his boat to help me rescue you, as soon as his sister called him. Dropped everything to come and look for you. You do understand that, don't you?' I am in full lecture mode.

Silence envelopes us, and when the boat slides up on the shingles, I jump out and help Pano pull it up on to the beach. Dimitri remains mute in the boat, then he, too, gets out and assists Pano.

'You two OK?' Pano says. He heads up the path to the house.

I run after him. 'Thanks so much, Pano. I wish I had something to give you to thank you. You've been so kind.'

'No worries.' He must be from Oakleigh, I think. 'Angelina's giving me lunch. Might be some for you, too, if you hurry.'

'OK, maybe we'll see you up at the house.'

I return to the beach where Dimitri sits stock still. I'm a little concerned now.

'Are you OK?' I say.

'Sure, just felt a bit tired out there. I had a bit of a rest on the island. Examined some rock pools full of red anemones.'

I pat him on the shoulder, but he is strangely listless and his face has lost its colour.

'You look pale. Let me get you some water. I've eaten all the bread and cheese. I got hungry waiting for you.'

'I think I'm a bit low on blood sugar. Probably need a meal. Did I have breakfast? I actually feel a bit cold.'

'Pano says Angelina's making lunch for him and we could join them. Perhaps we should get up there fast.'

123

Dimitri pulls his clothes on, and several times he pauses and inhales and exhales deeply. The sun blazes above. Only mad dogs and Englishmen would be out in it now, I think. Dimitri fiddles with his clothes and brushes the sand off his feet.

'You sure you're OK?' I say. 'You'd better put this towel over your head. Maybe you've got a bit of sunstroke.'

As we walk up to the house, Dimitri struggles, low on energy, and we head round the back to the kitchen. I think, we can't just invite ourselves to lunch, so I resolve to ask Angelina for some bread. We enter the kitchen, which is as cool as an underground cellar, and find Pano sitting at the table and Angelina bustling at the stove. A salad, bread, feta cheese and a bowl of chips sit on the table.

'Please, please, sit down,' Angelina says. '*Kalá*, *kalá*, all good?'

'Yes, *óla kalá*,' I say. 'Dimitri needs some water. He feels a bit tired after his swim.'

'*Parakaló*.' She gestures towards a carafe of water and a glass on the table.

'I hope you don't mind if we have a bit of lunch.'

'No, no. Eat, my children. You like some lemon chicken?'

'Angelina's lemon chicken is the best in the country,' Pano says. 'You'll see.'

We sit at the table, and Dimitri shovels food into his mouth and colour gradually returns to his cheeks.

'So, what brings you here?' Pano says.

'Have you ever heard of the writer Bruce Chatwin?' I say.

'Sure. Read that book *The Songlines* when I was back in Oakleigh. All about the indigenous folk following songlines to find their way across the outback. Interesting, interesting.'

'Well, his ashes are buried around here somewhere.'

'That so? Now, where would that be?'

'At a church near the village of Exochori. St Nicholas.'

124

'Ah, yes, Agios Nikolaos.'

Pano provides us with directions, and he tells me he emigrated to Melbourne in the 1970s and worked for thirty years in a factory in Dandenong which made light switches.

'I promised my wife we'd return here when we had enough money to build our house among the olives over there. My son and daughter are still in Melbourne. One's a doctor in South Yarra and the other's a lawyer in Kew. They'll never come back here to live, but, don't you worry, they visit here every summer.'

Dimitri, now somewhat improved, stands beside Angelina at the sink. They chat in dialect above the noise of the TV that looks down from a shelf high up on the wall. Its screen broadcasts scenes of a demonstration on the streets of Athens, now a daily occurrence since the closure of the banks. Masked youths confront the police in the streets and throw Molotov cocktails. Police drag other demonstrators into police vans.

'Looks like those kids are trashing immigrant shops in some poor neighbourhood in Athens,' Dimitri says. 'They think those foreigners are personally responsible for shutting down the banks. People are desperate and have lost their sense of reason.' He pauses and watches the cacophony from the wall until Angelina reaches up and switches the TV off.

'Hell,' Dimitri whispers, before looking outside.

'We can't go out in this heat,' I say to Dimitri. 'Angelina, I'm sorry to trouble you, but would you have a spare bed so we can have a siesta?'

She guides us to the ground floor, and we enter a tiny bedroom as cool as a cave and with a bed as wide as an emplacement for two people in a camp site.

'We haven't slept for two nights, have we?' Dimitri says. 'Here, there's no air con, no dogs, no traffic, no gunshots, no roosters. I need to catch up.'

125

He lies down on the bed and closes his eyes, and within minutes I hear his rhythmic breathing.

\*    \*    \*

I wake, open my eyes and check my phone. It's twenty past four. Dimitri's arm is slung across my stomach. I run my fingers down it, and he stirs and looks at me.

'You needed some rest after that swim,' I say, smiling. 'It's nearly half past four. We'd better get going. I want to go up to Exochori. See if we can find Chatwin's grave.' Dimitri eyes look tired. 'You OK?'

He lies still for a minute, then squeezes my bottom and says, 'Sure I am.' He swings off the bed. 'We should pay for this room, don't you think?'

When we offer, Angelina won't hear of it, and she has a packet of food and a bottle of orange juice ready for us on the kitchen table.

'*Kalá, kalá,*' she shouts as we drive off. 'You come again.'

\*    \*    \*

A sign to Exochori directs us off the main road, and we pass between a school and the cemetery.

'The church must be round here,' I say.

'I'll park here, and we can walk,' Dimitri says.

We walk through the village to a grassy rill of land and see the church of Agios Nickolaos, a tiny Byzantine basilica, just beyond.

'Pano told us the ashes were scattered round the front, here on the left,' I say. 'Something anonymous. Chatwin didn't want a marked grave.' We search about amidst the wild flowers, oregano and thistles growing on a stony patch.

'Must be here,' I say. 'Thistles and herbs all mussed together. Very appropriate.' We turn around and look out over a tranquil panorama of the sea, which is as smooth as a sheet of silk.

126

'Oh, look over there,' Dimitri says, and he marches off into the high, dry grass which crackles under his boots. I can't see what he's seen. He bends his head low, and I hear the snapping of thin branches. He stands and returns to me, clutching a bunch of flowers. Roses. Deep-pink roses with tight clusters of petals.

'Here, smell these,' he says. He tickles my nose with the petals, and I breathe in a perfume intoxicatingly powerful yet soothing.

'Glorious,' I say. 'Let me smell … again … and again.'

'Do you know what these are?'

'Roses.'

'Yes, but special roses. Damascena roses, brought all the way to Europe from Damascus by the crusaders.'

'Ooh, that's so special. Let me crush some up and rub it on your neck. I might be able to squeeze out a bit of oil.'

'Not likely.' Dimitri laughs. 'You need five dozen roses to make one drop of rose oil. Or 5,000 kilos of rose petals to produce one litre of oil.'

'It's liquid gold!'

'Here's a couple blooms for your hat.' He breaks off a stem and pushes it into the band of my hat.

'Look OK?' I say.

'Beautiful.'

'Let's throw one on Chatwin's grave.'

'Good idea.' He tosses a flower onto Chatwin's stony patch amidst its wild flowers. 'Good spot to rest for eternity.' He releases a chuckle. 'Let's see if the church is open.'

We find a side door of the church, and Dimitri pushes it and it opens. We enter and pause as our eyes adjust to the gloom. Gold ikons rest on small altars in a side chapel, and the peeling frescoes on the walls badly need repair.

'Ah, you see that fresco,' Dimitri says, pointing to a dim image above my head, 'the one with St Nicholas by the sea, helping a man from the water. That's the story of St Nicholas saving Demetrios from drowning in the Black Sea. We all love St Nick on this side of the world. The Russians say if there's no God, at least there's St Nicholas.'

'Very apt,' I say a little facetiously, 'that we should be gazing upon the painting of a saint who saves people from the sea.'

'But I wasn't drowning.'

'I hoped not, but I thought that when you disappeared.'

As we walk towards the nave, I say, 'You know Chatwin was an atheist. But he sort of converted to Greek Orthodoxy after he became ill with AIDS. His funeral service was held in a Greek Orthodox Church in London, and his wife brought his ashes to Greece and scattered them outside this church. After a life of travelling he wanted to end up here. There must be a reason for it. Perhaps it's the sea touching the sky.'

We wander over to a small altar lit with candles, and Dimitri says, 'I'll light a candle for my mother. You going to light one for yours?' The new candles lie in numbered slots.

'Which number shall I pick?' I say. My hand hovers over slot seven. 'Yes, seven, I think. You and I met on the seventh. Remember? When you helped me over the gate?'

'Of course.'

Dimitri takes a candle from slot thirteen.

'Thirteen!' I say. 'That's unlucky.'

'No, it's not.'

'It is for us.'

'It's for my mother, not us. There were twelve disciples at the Last Supper, and Christ makes thirteen. A good number.'

We light our candles and push them into the sand. Dimitri crosses himself and says a little prayer. As we stand beside the baptismal font, I look up at the rough-hewn walls and see a peeling frieze framing the frescoed images. It's ages since I've thought of my mother, the accident and my family's bitterness over my having driven off the road and caused my mother's death. My eyes well with tears. Why is this place causing these unwanted thoughts to surface again?

Dimitri turns to me and says, 'What's the matter?'

Can he see my sudden sadness in this gloom?

'These candles are suddenly making me think of my family and my mother. You mentioning your mother has given rise to a knot of sorrow.'

'I didn't mean to. We Greeks always have our departed loved ones close by. You know, visits to the cemetery, flowers, ikons in a corner, candle lighting, masses recited in their honour. That's us. Melancholic, you know, like I told you before, but we also enjoy the good things. Food and wine, music, people and flesh.' He leans me against the font and presses my breast with his hand. 'See? Like this, playing in a church.'

'This isn't right, is it?'

'Probably not. No need to feel guilty, though. That guy up there,' he points heavenwards, 'is probably smiling down on us. I once read you people north of the Alps, with your Protestantism, live with guilt. It probably drives you along, but we down here by the Mediterranean live with fate and destiny.' He embraces me and kisses me. 'Yeah, relaxed, like us.' He laughs. 'Let's light a candle for us. Pick a number.'

'One.'

'A good number. We'll put it in together. To us.'

We each place a hand on the candle and press it into the sand.

'There we are,' he says, 'here together forever.' He pushes me up against the font again and kisses me lightly.

129

I look up and, unbidden, say, 'You're a mystery to me.'

'Why?'

'You just are.' I search for something to say, now I have uttered those words. 'So many new tales and images. A mosaic of your passions and knowledge plopped into my lap. Succour to my new life. A novel flavour.'

'Perhaps we are all mysteries to each other. Does it matter? Of course not. How boring would life be without mysteries.'

He takes my hand, and we go outside and walk about and take in the view before we climb the hill. The sky is lavender, a wide arc of velvet. I reach the top of the hill first as he lags behind. On previous such walks he has always led the way and I would play catch up. Now, when he reaches the top, he pants and catches his breath.

'Do you need something to drink?' I say, pulling Angelina's orange juice from my rucksack. 'Don't want you getting dehydrated.'

He takes a swig and, after a pause, says, 'I'm OK, I'm OK. Still getting over that swim.'

Am I reassured? I cannot decide. He looks pale.

'Come on,' he says. 'Better find the car. We need to get back to Kalamata and pick up our suitcases.'

# - 19 -

We amble along the main street in Exochori as it stirs from its afternoon siesta. Dimitri pokes his head into shops and disappears into one stocked with brooms, rakes, metal saucepans and watering cans hanging in bunches outside. I follow him in and squint to adjust to the gloom. He stands beside boxes of biscuits and flips through a rack of old ikons until he picks up one of Saint Nicholas.

'The guys in these shops collect all the stuff people discard when their old relatives die,' he whispers. 'I've found some great bargains over the years. People don't know what they're handling. See this? Exquisite, isn't it?' He turns the ikon over. '1858. It's a copy of the oldest ikon of Saint Nicholas, done in Constantinople in the tenth century. See the two crosses on the white stole? That's his emblem.' He runs his finger round the frame with its finely painted images of the Apostles.

'Yes, I see what you mean,' I say. 'They're so detailed.'

He draws me in. 'Let's see what the old guy wants for this.'

The owner sits on a plastic chair on the pavement outside the shop, and he and Dimitri negotiate.

'Fifty euro,' the old man says.

'No, no,' Dimitri says, raising his voice. 'Let's say forty.'

An argument ensues until they finally agree on 45 euro.

Dimitri removes and opens his wallet. 'Oh, hell,' he says to me, 'I've only got twenty euro. He'll want cash. Can't use credit cards round here. You got any cash?'

I pull out fifteen euro.

'We'd better find a bank,' Dimitri says. 'There's a Bank of Greece down there.'

But it's austerity, and with Greece being fiscally bled dry by its European family, we find the bank firmly closed.

'Try the cash machine,' I say. 'We're allowed 60 euro a day. You get 60 and I'll get 60. We need petrol too.'

Dimitri inserts his card, but the machine ejects it. 'Damn, the cash machine's empty. Give yours a go. You never know.' But the machine spits mine out too.

I recall having, in the distant past, hidden an emergency stash of cash in my car though I can't remember if it is still there or not. 'I might have some cash in the car,' I say. 'I hid some there, just in case.'

Back at the car, I open the boot and pull up the rubber matting covering the jack. I remove the jack and retrieve an envelope which I find contains bank notes that I quickly count.

'Thirty euro!' I say. 'You can get the ikon. And we'll have 20 euro left for petrol.'

Then the reality of our situation hits me, back in the real world, scraping to pay for the necessities of living.

But Dimitri takes my cash and hurries down the street, determined to purchase the ikon. It is still sitting by the loaves of bread on the counter in the shop when Dimitri hands over the 45 euro. The old man wraps the ikon in sheets of the local newspaper, and we rush back to the car.

'I want this for my collection of ikons,' Dimitri says. 'We'll place it next to the statues we bought at Olympia.'

'What about petrol?' I suddenly say, and we return to the shop and ask the owner if there's a petrol station in town.

He waves a finger at me. 'No petrol round here, madam. All finished.'

I gasp.

Back at the car, I tell Dimitri there's no petrol in town.

'We're going to have to look for some before we head back to Kalamata,' Dimitri says. 'We're nearly on empty.'

We head for Kardymali, hoping there'll be petrol there.

Dimitri spots the yellow sign of a petrol station as we enter Kardymali. We find ourselves in a queue, but at least that means there's petrol.

'Petrol's rationed, sir,' the young boy at the pump says. 'Only ten litres each.'

With that we'll get to Kalamata, but not all the way back to Kato Samiko.

Austerity is squeezing everyone, here in this world. There are no certainties, no cash, no petrol, but yes, there is still bread in that shop. I am too hopeful, perhaps.

\*     \*     \*

We drive to Kalamata over the mountains so Dimitri can return via his father's old village and check if Fotis has turfed out his immigrant friends and dismantled the marijuana tents.

'Feel like driving?' he suddenly says. He has always driven when we have travelled together in my car, and his request surprises me.

'Sure.'

He pulls over and stops, and we swap seats.

We wind up the hillside as the road switches back and forth, and I busy myself with the gears changing down and then roaring up. I become anxious about petrol and constantly check the gauge. Dimitri examines his ikon's paintwork and murmurs about its condition. 'This'll need cleaning,' he says.

He dozes for a while, then wakes and turns on the car radio. We listen to a woman singing a yearning love song, something wafting from the Middle East, but a voice suddenly interrupts by announcing "Breaking News". I remain focused on the road, rather than the announcement, until Dimitri says, 'Oh, Hell.'

'What's happened?' I say.

'That neo-fascist group, Golden Dawn, are attacking migrants and their shops.'

It takes me a few seconds to get the gist of what has occurred, that menacing Golden Dawn groups are roving the streets in Athens and Patras. It's always the way, I think. The extremists exploit the cracks opened by an incompetent government and direct their anger and hostility at the vulnerable underclass.

'They say they're attacking migrants in Patras,' Dimitri says.

'And the camp out at the stadium?'

'They're not saying. It started last night when a Golden Dawn mob stole from a Pakistani's shop in the back streets of Athens. A fight broke out with the owner, who was trying to ward them off, and they trashed the inside of the shop and smashed the windows. When the police arrived, the confrontation escalated and hordes of people crowded the streets. Not only the Golden Dawn anti-immigrant mobs but everyone from pensioners who have lost half their pension to government workers who haven't received a wage for months. Half the police are Golden Dawn too. You know—fascists. Doesn't take much.'

'I guess we won't know anything till we get back to Kalamata.'

'Turn left by that oak tree down there,' Dimitri suddenly says.

We turn off to the village in the gorge and bump about inside the car until we cannot drive further. As we walk down the hill, only the clear notes of birdsong break the silence. We pass through the ruins of the village and find the plastic tunnels smashed to the ground and all the marijuana plants ripped out as if done by force or in great haste. There is no sign of Fotis, Andreas or any of their friends.

'What does all this mean?' I say.

'I really didn't expect Fotis to take heed of what I said to him yesterday,' Dimitri says, 'unless someone else found this set-up and destroyed it. It's not looking good. We'll have a look around.'

But we find nothing among the ruins except a few torn pieces of clothing, two blankets and remnants of food not yet scavenged by nocturnal creatures.

We return to the car in silence.

'This looks concerning,' I say. 'Ominous, even. I hope Fotis is OK.'

Dimitri replies with a murmured 'Mmm'.

We get into the car, and I reverse with a roar up the track. Dimitri touches my arm, but I am ... what, angry? ... or panicked? I can't tell which. Something ... is it ... sinister? ... lies within these hills. We reach the valley, not far from Kalamata, and Dimitri suggests we stop for a meal. It's almost nine, and the charcoal grills will be fired up. I acquiesce to Dimitri's suggestion, though something quells my appetite, yet, later, when Suzanna, our patron, places fried melanzane and cold wine on our table, I fork them gratefully.

An hour later we arrive at the Hotel Gold in Kalamata. The main door is open, but we find neither Yiannis on his usual chair nor Fotis nor Andreas behind the counter. Dimitri stands at the stairs and shouts, 'Hello, hello.' No one replies.

'Let's go up to our room,' I say, 'and see if our stuff is still there.'

We go down the passage, and Dimitri knocks furtively on the door. No answer. Dimitri turns the handle, and we enter and find everything as we'd left it: our cases half packed on the floor and Dimitri's shorts slung over the chair. We pack everything and return downstairs. Still no one appears, and just as we decide to call someone, Andreas appears from behind a curtain at the end of the bar.

'Andreas!' I say. I'm suddenly relieved to see him. 'Are you OK?'

'Of course I am.'

'We've just passed by the old village up in the mountains and found everything smashed up and the marijuana plants ripped out. So, you decided to give it all up?'

'No, not at all. What do you mean? Were the other guys there? The Afghans?'

'No, not a soul about.'

'You mean, they've all gone?'

'Yes. Gone. Has there been trouble, here in Kalamata? With the migrants, I mean. We heard about trouble in Patras and Athens. Golden Dawn are demonstrating in the streets against immigrants. It's easy to get people on their side. Ordinary people have had enough.'

'Oh, God, no!' Andreas suddenly looks upset and angry. 'I told them to be careful. Now look what's happened. They're on the run again, I suppose.'

'Where's Fotis?' Dimitri says.

'At the hospital.'

'What do you mean? Why?'

'It's Yiannis. He collapsed last night. Couldn't breathe. They took him off in an ambulance.'

# - 20 -

Dimitri phones Fotis, who tells him that Yiannis is in the corridor of Accident and Emergency, struggling to breathe.

'We'll be there soon,' Dimitri says to Fotis. 'I've a friend, a doctor, who works there. We'll get Yiannis out of that corridor somehow.'

Andreas has put bread, grilled sardines and tomatoes on the table for our supper, but we've eaten already, so we keep him company while we watch the TV. A report from Athens shows footage of lines of riot police with plastic shields and batons waiting in Syntagma Square, then the Pakistani's shop window and the burnt-out premises owned by immigrants in the same precinct. The reporter grips the microphone while, behind her, weeping men wail and other demonstrators wave placards that read *Go Home Paki* and *Get Out Gays*.

'Are Golden Dawn homophobic?' I ask Dimitri.

'Very. They're like that because they're weak and afraid of their own inclinations. It's the same old story, punish others to mask your own fears about yourself.' Dimitri turns to Andreas. 'Andreas, are there Golden Dawn extremists around here?'

'Yeah.'

'Are you and Fotis being harassed? You know what I mean, don't you?'

Andreas bows his head and his face flushes. 'I guess so.'

'How? What do they do to you?'

Andreas stares out across the room, silent, thinking.

'They come into the bar and threaten us, calling us dirty faggots and pretty boys. One of them even grabbed Fotis by the shoulders, leered at him and called him a dirty bumboy and *poústis*. They told us that we and our dirty diseases best leave this town before they chucked us out, and that they had beaten up many friends of ours. Now, I stay out the back so I can see who comes in before I appear to serve at the counter. I'm scared they'll trash the bar. We have to be careful.'

'You could call the police, couldn't you?'

'Depends. Yiannis has only one friend in the police here, and he's not always on duty.'

There's that word again, I think. *Friend.* A friend who's a doctor, a friend who's a policeman. Here, you need friends on your side, or else.

'Andreas,' Dimitri says, 'we're going to the hospital now. Is it safe for you to be here alone?'

'Sure, sure. I'll be fine. Yiannis needs you. I'll watch from my hiding spot behind the curtain.'

'Can't you shut up the bar now?'

'No, we need the custom. There's not much custom because people have no money, so we've got to take whatever we can.'

'Call me if anything happens. Here's my number.'

* * *

Dimitri walks along the hospital corridors with a confident stride, in charge, in his comfort zone, knowing how things work. As I patter along behind him, a pungent odour of bleach, chlorine, antiseptics and rosemary wafting from a tray of meals assails my senses. It triggers all my fears, my grief and my shock at the time of the accident. My mother being rushed past me on a gurney, my head covered in gauze and my eyes too swollen to see her for the last time. I wish I hadn't come here, now with Dimitri, but duty bids me to be with him. An African orderly with her meals passes us and gives me a smile as bright as a halogen lamp. I smile back. I wonder if she gets paid. Probably not, I surmise, but no doubt she'll hang onto her job with all her might in the hope that one day she will.

'Doctor Andino here tonight?' Dimitri asks a passing nurse.

'Yes, he's behind that curtain with a patient. Should be out soon.'

'Good, we'll wait here.'

'Where's Yiannis?' I say. 'I can't see him anywhere.'

'Goran, you there?' Dimitri says towards the drawn curtain.

A young doctor emerges from behind the curtain and says, 'Dimitri, what brings you here?'

'My uncle, Yiannis Angelou, is in here somewhere. Had an attack of emphysema. Sounds like he needs something for his breathing. You don't happen to know where he is, do you? This is Marina.'

'Hi,' I say. He has shining blue eyes, and his jolly smile attenuates my repellence of the hospital odour. He emanates wellbeing, calm and warmth.

'Let me ask the nurse here,' he says.

He turns to a nearby nurse and says, 'Eleni, do you know where a patient named Yiannis Angelou is?'

'Over there, in that cubicle,' the nurse says, pointing. 'Emphysema. We're giving him oxygen.'

We enter the cubicle and find Fotis dozing on a plastic chair beside his father. A bottle half-full with urine stands under the bed, and a strip of band-aid holds closed the chipped door of the bedside cupboard.

'Fotis, how's it going?' Dimitri says. They hug, and I, too, kiss him and pat him on the shoulder. Our last meeting had ended in acrimony, and I want to assure him that we are on his side now.

'Ah, Dimitri, thanks for coming,' Fotis says. 'I'm fine, just fine.' Beside him, a masked Yiannis lies with his eyes closed and breathes oxygen tubed from a gas bottle.

'Do you want to get him into a ward?' Goran says.

'Sure, do that if it's possible,' Dimitri says.

'I'll fix it for you. We'd better keep him here under observation for a few days. See whether he can manage without the oxygen or if he needs to take a bottle home.'

We exit the cubicle, and Goran leans over a counter and asks a nurse to move a patient from the men's ward and give the bed to Yiannis.

What about the other patient? I think. But I say nothing.

We return to Yiannis's cubicle, and an orderly unplugs Yiannis's tubes and wheels him out.

'Thanks for that, Goran,' Dimitri says.

'Not a problem. I remember you got my mum sorted out at the hospital in Patras when she was on holiday there. It's a pleasure. I'll keep an eye on the old guy till he's discharged. Ring me if you want anything. Got that, Fotis?'

He steps out of the cubicle, and Dimitri turns to Fotis and says, 'Go up to the ward with your father and check he's OK. You should be able to come back to the hotel then. They'll look after him now. Goran's told them to.'

Dimitri and I leave the hospital and walk to his car. Even though it's now dark, the night remains warm and balmy. We drive back to the centre of town, park outside the square and walk across to the Hotel Gold. The front door is open and the place is in darkness. We enter and look about for Andreas, but he is nowhere to be seen.

'Andreas?' Dimitri calls out into the darkness.

A groan comes from the far corner, followed by a weak cry of 'Dimitri'.

We rush over and find Andreas propped in the corner, his face bloody and swollen and an arm lying skewed over his lap.

'Shit, bastards,' Dimitri says. 'What the hell have they done to you? Bloody hell. Andreas, are you OK?'

I fall to my knees beside him. 'Oh, Andreas, I'm so sorry. What happened?'

'We've got to call the police.'

'We've got to get him to hospital.'

'But the police need to see this.'

Dimitri and I argue, panic, about what, I don't know. He exams Andreas's face and arm. 'Andreas, any other injuries?'

But the boy can hardly speak.

We lie him on the floor and raise his legs. He cries out when we touch his arm, and Dimitri checks his pulse.

'Will he be all right?' I say.

'He's in shock.'

I find a blanket and cover him as he trembles.

We call for an ambulance, then the police and Fotis, and soon a myriad of people throng the bar. All talk at once and jostle for room to carry out their tasks. Fotis, crying, kneels beside Andreas and the police take measurements and ask the boy questions until medical orderlies roll him onto a stretcher.

The ambulance departs, as do the police with their iPads and notebooks, and Fotis follows an ambulance to hospital for the second time that day.

Dimitri rings the hospital and manages to reach Goran.

'Bastards,' I hear Goran say on the other end of the line, and I think, yes, the warmth of that man can turn to anger too. I hear him tell Dimitri that he'll look out for Andreas and not to worry as he was on duty all night.

I sit in a frayed raffia chair which scratches my legs. I feel tired. Very tired. It must be after midnight, and so much has happened in one day.

Dimitri walks about the bar and picks up broken glass and pushes chairs back into place. 'I guess we can see to this in the morning. Not too much damage.' He comes over to me. 'Where were we this morning?'

'Up in the hills with those shepherds.' I give a wry laugh.

'And here we are back again with the rubbish trucks in the street and the rattling air-conditioning.'

Back in our room we lie down with relief, the sheets pleasantly cool. The air-conditioning roars, but sleep envelopes us instantly.

# - 21 -

A phone rings from somewhere on a beach, then from a table on which there are stuffed peppers. My mind swims until I open my eyes and see Dimitri reach across me and pick up his phone. We are in bed somewhere, and a sudden crash of dustbins from a street outside hauls me into complete consciousness.

'Goran?' Dimitri says. 'Hello, yeah, hello. Everything OK? … The kid? … Ah, yes, sure … The arm's broken in two places? … The x-ray? … Needs to be operated on? … Yes, I get it … Yeah, sure, I'll get over there now … Short staffed? … What? No one's there at all? OK, I'm on my way.'

Dimitri puts the phone down, lies back and says to me, 'I have to go to the hospital. There's no one there to operate on Andreas's arm. They'll have to send him to Patras or wait till a surgeon comes tomorrow. Maybe. Guess it was lucky I was here.' He shuts his eyes. 'Should be pretty straight forward.' He stretches out. 'Let me lie for a minute.'

We lie side by side for a long moment. I stare at the ceiling with its peeling whitewash, and the light wobbles to the tune of a whirling fan. Dimitri turns to me, runs his hand over my body and says, 'Good girl, I'll be back soon.' He swings out of the bed.

'Let me try to make some coffee before you leave,' I say.

Downstairs, I find a tin of Nescafé, some milk in the fridge and a jar of stale biscuits on the counter. Pleased with the frothy frappé I make, I twirl my tray in true waitress style and lay out two glasses with straws and the stale biscuits on a table.

'Here, give yourself some energy,' I say to Dimitri. He stirs the beverage with a straw and, after finishing it, kisses me and goes out the door.

A TV sits on a shelf above the counter. I search for the remote and find it on the floor. I flick on the TV to the news channel—the only working one as all the others are closed down due to the exhaustion of government funds—which broadcasts the same clips as yesterday. Suddenly, I recognise the entrance to the hospital in Patras. The newsreader reports that demonstrators have been harassing immigrant patients when they are being wheeled on trolleys from the ambulance bay into Emergency. My gut tightens. What about our friends in the makeshift camp out behind the stadium? I wish Dimitri would return.

Upended chairs lie about the bar and broken glass litters the floor. I straighten the chairs and sweep the floor, and everything looks almost back to normal except for a smashed hole in a wall and a picture dangling beside it. As I walk over to investigate, I hear movement behind me. Fotis, dishevelled and looking as if he's just woken, appears from behind the curtain at the end of the counter.

'Fotis,' I say. 'You're back.' Relieved to see him, I hug him as I know he's had a bad night. 'Come, sit down. I've worked out how to make a frappé.'

I busy myself behind the bar while Fotis sits in silence as he leans on the table and holds his head in his hands.

'Here, try this,' I say as I place a frappé before him on the table. 'Hope I haven't made a mess of it. I could only find these biscuits to eat.'

'There are some apple pies in the freezer,' Fotis says. 'You need to put them in the microwave for five minutes.'

I heat the apple pies, and we sit, sip coffee and eat the pies.

Fotis revives somewhat and says, 'I thought Andreas was dead when I saw him on the floor last night.'

'Yes, you must've got a fright,' I say. 'And then you had your father collapsing earlier. A terrible day for you. I'm so sorry. They'll be all right.' My solicitude feels pathetic. I squeeze his arm. 'Dimitri's gone over to the hospital. He's going to operate on Andreas's arm. He's a pretty clever surgeon, you know. He'll check on your father too.'

'That's good.'

'Do you know what happened when those guys came here last night?'

'More or less. My dad's policeman friend turned up at the hospital. He's a good man. Sympathetic. He got Andreas to talk.'

'So you heard what happened?'

'Yes. They came in here and demanded drinks and food. They each drank about five cans of beer, ate all the food they could find and took the money from the till. Because there's no money in the banks, people like them steal what money they can from all over the place. Then they asked Andreas where the safe was. They reckoned Papa would have his savings stashed away somewhere. Most people do round here as they don't trust putting it in a bank. Andreas said he had no idea where the safe was, so they punched and kicked him and grabbed

145

him and forced his arm behind his back and kept bending it till Andreas said he thought it might be behind that picture, which it was, so they ripped the safe out and forced it open with a crowbar. They took everything. My dad's life savings. A life of working in this hotel.' Fotis's head bows and he weeps. I move and sit next to him and hold his hand.

'Bastards!' he suddenly says. 'The police said they think they know who did it, but they were all masked, so how can Andreas identify them?' He places his hands over his face and continues to weep.

No words of comfort form in my head, just anger at all the rottenness oozing up from the pits outside. Finally, all I can say is, 'Dimitri will be back soon. We'll know then how Andreas and your father are. Why not go upstairs and have a shower and change? Go on, you'll feel better.'

Later, Dimitri comes through the door, and I rush over to him. I hug him with an intensity which I suspect surprises him.

'You OK?' he says.

'I've been talking to Fotis,' I say. 'He's in a bad way. How's Andreas?'

'Let me sit. Yes, he's good. He'll be out of hospital soon.'

'Something's going on in Patras. More demonstrations. You should ring Zina at the hospital. And we need to find out what happened with the marijuana plants up in the village.'

'Wait, wait. I need food.' He slumps into a chair.

'Sorry. I'll prepare some food. Fotis is upstairs. He told me what happened to Andreas last night. He sat here, crying. I choked back tears, myself.' My eyes well. I can't help myself. 'Everything's going terribly wrong, isn't it?'

I soon lay cheese pies, bread, salami and olives on the table as well as cold water and a bottle of beer.

Dimitri turns on the TV. We watch in silence as we eat until he says, 'So, it's spilled over into Patras. There's something coordinated about all this. It's not just spontaneous demonstrations in downtown Athens. Yeah, Golden Dawn have got a lot of people behind them. They got seven per cent of the vote in the last elections and won eighteen seats. There's fifty percent unemployment amongst young people in Greece. They blame immigrants for taking their jobs. It's not true, of course. They won't do the jobs immigrants do. You know, cleaning toilets and picking tomatoes.'

He pours a glass of beer, drinks it and sighs. 'I needed that.'

He picks at the olives with a fork, and as he spits out a pip, I say, 'Do you mean that orders to get out on the streets and beat up immigrants have come from some central command?'

'Maybe. Look, they're in Thessaloniki too.' Dimitri points at the TV screen. He cuts up a cheese pie, devours it and gets out his phone and makes a call.

'Zina? It's Dimitri. What's happening at the hospital?' He listens, and I hear a long tirade on the other end. 'Shit. We're in Kalamata. There's trouble here too. I'll get back to you.'

Dimitri hangs up and says to me, 'There's mayhem at the hospital. I've got to get back there. Andreas will be all right by this afternoon, and Yiannis is breathing without a bottle. We should be able to get him out and home by the end of the day. They don't really have a bed for him at the hospital.'

Fotis appears from behind the curtain. His hair is wet, but he looks much better.

'Fotis, my boy,' Dimitri says. 'You OK?' Dimitri hugs him, and they remain fixed in an embrace as Dimitri pats his head. 'Bad luck. Bad luck for Andreas, but I've fixed his arm. A bad break. They'll call us when he is ready to be discharged.'

'Thanks, my cousin,' Fotis says. 'You're a saviour.'

He sits down and pours the rest of the beer into a glass.

'What happened up at the village?' Dimitri says.

'What do you mean?'

'We passed by on the way back to Kalamata. All your friends had left, and the plastic tunnels were smashed and the marijuana plants ripped out.'

'I don't know anything about it. You were with me the last time I was there. We left the Afghans up there to sleep and guard the plants. I haven't been back since. You're telling me they're gone and the plantation has been destroyed? So they were being hunted by those Nazis too. What the hell for? They've done nothing. Oh yeah, those Golden Dawn oafs wanted the plants. They'll be growing their own stuff now. Bastards!'

It pleases me that Fotis sees them as dull-witted. Violent followers but gawks.

'You knew them?' Dimitri says.

'Yes and no. Those Nazi thugs wanted the stuff. They bought a bit, but that was all. They must have followed us up there. They'll sell it now. They need the cash.'

'Can you contact your Afghan friends and find out where they are?'

Fotis gets out his phone. 'I've only got one number.'

He dials, and there is a voice. I can hear it myself. 'This number is not available.'

# - 22 -

We spend the afternoon closing up the Hotel Gold: hiding valuables, turning off services, shaking out bedding, jamming windows closed, looking for boxes and containers, pulling down roller doors, snapping shut bolts and guiding a weeping Yiannis into the car.

'You'll be back, you'll be back,' we say to him as we drive away, but no one can say when.

'You're safer out in the country with Maria,' Dimitri says. 'You know that, don't you?'

Amidst his tears Yiannis moans, 'I'm dying, dying.'

We travel in a convoy. Dimitri drives my car with Yiannis beside him, with his bottle of oxygen, and me in the back, surrounded by suitcases, boxes and all the accoutrements Yiannis might need for a long stay with his sister, Maria. Behind us, Fotis drives his car with Andreas, who nurses his face and grips his arm in a sling.

As we drive along the rough track to Maria's house, the setting sun turns the clouds of dust into billows of red and gold stars. The track turns, and when we arrive at the house, a flurry of chickens squawk and flutter away and dogs chained to a post bark as if the cavalry has come to attack.

'Hello, hello,' Maria says, stepping off the veranda. 'Yanni, Yanni, my brother.' The siblings embrace with exuberance.

Carrying boxes and suitcases, we follow her through the kitchen to a bedroom off to the side.

'Now, Yanni,' she says, 'this your room. I move out for you.'

A flowered water jug and a matching bowl for ablutions sit upon an iron washstand. The bed has polished walnut bed ends that match the carved chest of drawers and the wardrobe, and red terracotta tiles pave the floor.

'You'll be very comfortable here, Yanni. A nice armchair for you and a view of the hills.' She thrusts open the wooden shutters with a clatter and lets in an easy breeze coming from the undulating hills beyond.

We follow her out to the kitchen, where Fotis and Andreas stand with their bags.

'Ah, my boys, my two boys. Fotis, come here to your aunt.' She squeezes him in a hug and plants a firm kiss on each of his cheeks. 'You sleep out here, come now.' She leads us out onto a wired-in side veranda with two beds. 'You'll be very nice here, very cool. And you, my boy, what have you done to your arm and your face? Accident? In car?'

'Something like that,' Andreas says with a feeble voice.

'He's tired, aren't you, Andreas?' I say. 'Are you in pain?'

'A bit,' he says. I realise he means "a lot".

'You better lie down.' I steer him to the bed, and Dimitri empties his bag onto the bed and looks for painkillers. 'I'll get some water.'

Back in the kitchen Maria busies herself with food, drinks and a table cloth. She, with a faded scarf on her head and her short stature, reminds me of Beatrix Potter's Mrs Tiggy-

Winkle, and I suspect prickles might appear through her head-dress at any minute. Tin pots and pans cover the wall, and a saucepan bubbles on the stove, releasing a pungent aroma.

'Ah now,' she says, 'some Camomile tea for you, Yanni—ooh ah, no more cigarettes! And Fotis, for you? Orange juice? And a little wine for you, Marina? … with some ice?'

She disappears and then returns carrying a wooden board piled with rounds of flat bread sprinkled with oil and rosemary. 'I just get these out of the oven, now. Round the corner, there,' she says, pointing to the side of the house. I step onto the veranda and see a brick oven by the wall and smell baking bread emanating from within.

We devour the bread with gluttonous fury, for we haven't eaten all day. I take some wine and bread out to Dimitri, who sits beside Andreas and holds his hand. He talks to him softly, telling him he'll be all right, but the look in the boy's eyes suggests the trauma of the attack and the injuries he suffered still haunt him. I see Dimitri, the doctor, at work, but I don't say anything and leave the food and drink by the bed. At the door I turn and look at the two of them, patient and doctor, black silhouettes against the shafts of slanting rays whispering their golden motes into the room. Dimitri, half bent over Andreas and still holding his hand, silently strokes his elbow, infusing his limb with a light massage, till the boy drifts into a low-breathing sleep. I have seen this focus and intent of his when healing the sick migrants in their tents behind the stadium.

I find Yiannis asleep, gently snoring, in front of the television. The news rolls on, broadcasting the riots and demonstrations in the streets of Athens and Patras. Sirens wail as police brandish batons and drag contorted bodies into wagons. Fotis looks on, glum, his head in his hands.

Maria beckons me and says, 'I need tomatoes for salad.'

I follow her outside and walk behind her as she picks warm, red globes. 'Take this.' She hands me a cucumber. 'Now we go inside, under the house.'

She leads me to the cellar, and beneath the cheeses hanging in cloths, she slaps down a board on a table and slices some feta, which she puts in a basket.

'Now we go and feed the animals.'

We walk over to a rabbit hutch, and she opens the wire door and throws grass and vegetables into the enclosure. As she closes the door, she says, 'I boil up one of these for our dinner tonight. You know, bubbling on the stove. Ah yes, and something for the goats.' She turns and gathers a handful of hay. 'Come here, come on.' She throws it to the goats roped to the nearby fence.

'Come, you follow me inside and we go to the bedroom.'

In the bedroom she opens a drawer and says, 'You see here, inside this drawer, the board under my clothes.' She pulls up a board at the bottom of the drawer and removes a roll of cloth and reveals the contents below it. I gasp in incredulity, for she has envelopes of cash hidden away in the crevices of her furniture.

'Ah, you see?' she says. 'Now, if you need any money I have plenty here. They say on the TV there is no money left in the banks, but I have plenty here. Here, take this, you never know.' As she tries to hand me a wad of notes, her eyes sparkle bright blue and her face wrinkles in a smile.

'Oh, no no,' I say, hastily, 'we're fine, fine for now, thank you. Put it back.'

She rolls it up and replaces the board. 'You just let me know.' She moves over to the wardrobe and swings open the door. In amazement I see every shelf stacked with packets of sugar.

'You know, in times like this, you can never find sugar. I have plenty. In the war no one had sugar, but now I have plenty. People run to the shops and take all. You take what you need.'

'No, no, thank you. We are good for sugar. But thank you. Keep it for yourself.'

She shuts the wardrobe door, locks it and puts the key in her pocket. We return to the kitchen, where Dimitri looks solemn as he sits in front of the TV.

I find myself looking in at this moment from the outside. Beyond the hills riots rage and fighting rumbles in city streets, yet here, by this serene kitchen garden under the rays of the setting sun, beside tethered goats and caged rabbits, an old man dozes and, next door, a boy sleeps on a veranda.

I draw up a stool, sit beside Dimitri and say, 'It's not looking good, is it?'

He doesn't answer me and I don't want to press him. I place my hand on his leg and stroke it. I can tell he's desolate. We've been trying to hide our desolation, but now it's upon us. On the TV screen a car blazes on a street corner near the hospital in Patras where we used to drink coffee on the pavement.

'I should be there,' Dimitri says. 'It'll be chaotic at the hospital. I know what Zina's like. She'll just run about until she can't move. They have neither the equipment nor the staff to manage a situation like this.'

I do not know what to say to comfort him.

'No doubt the big chief is back at his holiday house on Corfu,' he murmurs bitterly. 'They all run off when things get tough. They always do.'

Still I sit, not knowing what to say.

'It'll be all over the news in a few days time,' he says with resigned sadness. He looks drawn. 'Understaffed emergency services, lack of medicines and even bandages and antibiotics.

That it should all come to this. Of course it has. Everything left to fester till it's too late. The house is collapsing.'

'Should we go?' I say.

'Course not. Aunt Maria has been cooking all day for us.'

Maria rattles at the dresser and brings out the plates used for special occasions. 'Marina, sit yourself down here,' she says. 'Dimitri, help me now with this stew. Wine, cinnamon and nutmeg, good for the winter. Yanni. Fotis. Yes, Fotis, you get the boy. He needs food too.'

As Fotis disappears out to the veranda, Dimitri helps his uncle to the table.

We sit cramped at the table, and before us are plates of Maria's rabbit stew with its herbs and spices deftly blended into the meat and vegetables. Yes, I am hungry, yet I hesitate as I go to pierce the rabbit with my fork. I'm not a vegetarian, not even slightly, but the thought of eating the once innocent rabbit now on my plate, however expertly dressed in herbs and spices, gets the better of me. I do not want to hurt Maria's feelings, so when she turns to serve at the stove, I quickly pass my rabbit over to Dimitri. The word vegetarian is unknown in her world.

Fotis reaches over and cuts Andreas's meat. 'Here, let me do that for you.' Andreas says nothing and scoops up his meat with his fork. I'm glad to see he has his appetite back after the anaesthetic.

Dimitri gets up and switches off the TV, and a sacred silence prevails, broken only by the tinkle of cutlery on crockery and a distant cock crowing at the wrong end of the day. The perfume of autumn grapes on the vine above us permeates the air more sweetly as the evening breeze stills.

When we finish eating the rabbit, I help Maria with the plates as she washes them and puts them back in the dresser.

She serves treacle-covered cakes and plates of the grapes from above. She chatters on, like a busy sparrow, about cousins and the priest and the church and the farmer next door who is mean to his children and the price of fish in the local shop.

Later, Dimitri stands and says, 'We'd better go now, Aunt.' He kisses her and I kiss-kiss her too. He hugs his uncle and Fotis, and with a slap on the boy's back, he reminds Fotis that he is in charge of the two patients and to look after his aunt as well. 'Call me if you need anything. We're not far away. And see if you can locate your immigrant friends. They must be hiding somewhere.'

# - 23 -

I tell Dimitri that Maria has shown me a wad of cash hidden beneath her clothes in the drawer in her bedroom and that she wanted to give me some. 'She thinks we might need it because she's heard there's no more money in the banks. Did you know she had all that money hidden in the house?'

'Well, not really,' he says, 'but I'm not surprised. Everyone has cash stashed away. No one trusts the Government, nor the banks, nor anybody in power for that matter, unless they're family or an old friend. They've experienced too much hardship and suffered too much hunger and cold through wars, riots and military crackdowns. There's little trust left in this country. Everyone's looking out for themselves and their families as best they can. The politicians certainly aren't going to make sure they're OK.' Dimitri gives the gear stick a fierce jerk. 'See, the peasants are right, again. Maria's not going to let this bit of rioting get to her. Good on her. She probably hasn't paid a penny of tax on those savings in the drawer. Why should she? Those guys in Athens have emptied the banks and carted all their booty off to Malta or the Channel Islands.'

Is it bitterness or just resignation I hear in his voice?

We turn up the drive to the house. The stars hover close in the moonless sky, and we get out of the car and stumble in the darkness up to the veranda.

It feels as if a hundred days have passed since we woke in the Hotel Gold. Time has taken on its nature of expanding and contracting at will, and that morning in the bar in Kalamata seems a distant memory.

Exhausted, we fall into bed. Dimitri, depleted of energy after a warm shower, rests in the comforting haven of cool sheets. I bend over, kiss him and say, 'Tired?'

'What are you doing tomorrow?'

'Let's talk about it in the morning.'

*　　*　　*

Next morning the road to Patras is frighteningly quiet with few cars and no trucks.

'Do you think the port's closed?' I say.

'Probably,' Dimitri says. 'Doesn't bode well, does it?'

We cross over a railway line, and as we drive along the road adjacent to the beach, a roadblock appears ahead and a police officer hails us to stop. Dimitri shows him his medical credentials and says he is on his way to the hospital. 'This lady is a nurse,' he says. The officer looks doubtful, and a moment of anxiety fills me as he walks away to confer with his captain.

The officer returns and says, 'It's dangerous along there. You'd better take the back roads.'

He waves us on, and we drive until we reach a crossroad where a car burns and hordes of youths eye each other off as the police stand and wait in riot gear.

'This doesn't look good,' Dimitri says. 'We'd better get out of here.' He turns right, away from the sea. 'We should be able to reach the migrant camp behind the stadium this way.'

We wind around the back streets of the town. It's early morning, yet the usually busy streets are empty. The roller doors of the bars, tavernas and supermarkets are drawn down, and closed gates bar entry to the schools. A dead city in daylight. I see a curtain in the window of a house move, and a woman glances out, then disappears. As we pass by, I hope they see the red crosses on the windows of our car and understand we come in peace, bringing medical aid.

Dimitri stops the car, and we walk down a narrow path until we come to the high, dry grass surrounding the stadium. The tents and cardboard shacks stand fifty metres away, yet there is no one about the camp. When we reach the makeshift habitations, I see why. Everything has been burnt or smashed to the ground. I push through the grass to the tent where Dimitri attends his patients. It stands askew, with debris strewn everywhere: mattresses, blankets, clothes, an occasional book, a photo, a wallet, empty tins and broken bottles. A camp abandoned in haste. Sudden gunfire breaks the silence, followed by what sounds like a bomb going off.

'That sounds close by,' I say, alarmed.

'They've gone,' Dimitri says. 'All escaped, to God knows where.' He sighs as he drops the flap of a collapsed tent. 'We'd better get back to the car and head for the hospital. Sounds like real fighting and mortars going off. Something organised. This is dangerous for you. Sure you're OK with this?'

'Let's get to the hospital. I'll feel safer there.'

\*    \*    \*

'Where's the PPE?' Dimitri says as he walks into Accident and Emergency at the hospital and takes charge.

'Over there,' Zina says, bending over a patient on a trolley.

Dimitri reaches into a near-empty box and pulls out two packs of sterilised gear.

'Here,' he says to me, 'put these on. There's a cap, gown and glasses. Go outside and help bring in the trolleys. The nurse will tell you where to take them. I'll be over there.'

I go outside where ambulance sirens wail, doors slap open and close and gurneys clunk when unloaded. I wheel in a young boy whose face twists in pain. Congealed blood covers his leg and a nasty wound oozes on his thigh. Inside, a nurse cuts his jeans and peels away the denim. I push him over to Dimitri, who inserts a drip and exams him.

'Burns, needs x-rays,' Dimitri says. 'I'll clean up this wound for now.' The flesh gapes, almost revealing the bone, but I have no time to linger, for the wounded arrive in an incessant stream, blinded by tear gas or impregnated with shards of glass from exploding Molotov cocktails or wounded by bullets or with limbs shredded by hand grenades. The police are now firing on the demonstrators, and the army has been called in. The media insist the fighting in the streets is just "riots", but the right-wing movement Golden Dawn proclaim "war".

Around midday I recognise a young man, Ali, from the camp, as he limps through the swing doors. He looks ghastly, with open wounds and burns. Blood streams down his face as he holds his arm.

I rush over to him and say, 'Ali, what's happened to you?' I pull over a trolley and help him onto it. He cries out in pain. 'Dimitri is through there. He'll see to you. Where's everyone else from the camp? We went up there but found no one.'

'They've all gone,' he says. 'Escaped two days ago. I stayed here because I have a girlfriend, from Pakistan, up at the shops. I want to stay with her.'

'Where have all the others gone?'

'To Zakynthos.'

'Where?'

'Zakynthos. Zakynthos. You know, the island off Katakolo. The people there are good people. They saved all the Jews who were living on the island during the war. They hid them from Nazis, in their houses. Not one Jew was taken from Zakynthos in the war. Now, they are looking after us. We take the boat from Kyllini, a good fisherman take us, and all are safe in Zakynthos. But I come back because I want to see my girlfriend, and I find our camp burnt and those people attacking my girlfriend's parents' shop, and we get caught in an explosion. We have to be careful. None of those people like immigrants.'

He lies back on the trolley, and slow tears roll down his cheeks. I take him to Dimitri, who inserts a drip and works on his wounds.

In the middle of the afternoon I wheel in another young man. He has so much blood on his head I can hardly see his eyes. So many young men. So many wounded.

'How am I doing, nurse?' he says. His limbs are in shreds.

'You're doing just fine, just fine,' I say, mopping up his blood with gauze pads.

'Thanks, nurse.'

I wheel him over to Dimitri, who squints at me through his perspex glasses and says, 'Leave him there. I'll give him a drip. He'll need something strong for the pain, with those injuries.'

'Are my legs OK?' the boy says.

He *is* only a boy, I think, with green eyes and loose brown ringlets. Some woman's son, a mother at home cooking rice patties at a stove.

'Yes, your legs are OK.' I lie.

A nurse cuts off his clothes and pats him down. Dimitri takes over and works on him.

I return two hours later and see a sheet over the boy's face.

'Has he died?' I say.

'Yes, I'm afraid so,' Dimitri says. 'I couldn't save him. He had lost too much blood, and we don't have much left in the bank. His lungs might have been damaged by the tear gas too.' He walks away and writes up his notes whilst conferring with the nurses.

I feel faint and sit on a bench in the corridor. I haven't eaten or drunk since breakfast. I have been so preoccupied with my job as gurney bearer that I've forgotten the time. And now this. A death. There have been others, but with this boy I made a connection. I feel wretched, but Dimitri seems to rise above it. So do all the staff. They have to. So much pain, so much injury and trauma, so many crying families looking or grieving for loved ones. I'm not used to it. The triage nurse works with ordered proficiency, directing patients here and there like a policewoman, but I have spent all my emotional energy on those I've wheeled inside. Zina and Dimitri work under the guidelines of learned procedures and busy themselves in their own world, two medics carrying out their interventions competently and instinctively.

I look about and see Ali sitting on the floor, for there are no more seats available. He has his arm in plaster and a bandage wrapped around the top of his head.

I squat in front of him and say, 'Are you OK? What are you waiting for?'

'My arm's broken,' he says. 'Dear Dimitri put it in plaster. A good doctor. Kind man. He also bandaged my head. All is OK. I just wait for papers to let me go.'

'Then where will you go?'

'To my girlfriend, Liyana, at her family's shop.'

'Is it safe?'

'I don't know.'

161

Dimitri walks over and says to Ali, 'Here are your discharge papers. You need to come back in fifteen days to have your plaster removed and your dressings changed. Don't try and remove anything yourself. Understand?'

'Yes, sir.'

'Good man. Look after yourself.' Dimitri gives him a smile. 'Where are you going now?'

'To my girlfriend's shop up here behind the hospital.'

'You be careful.'

'Do you think we can buy something to eat there, Ali?' I say.

'Sure. But the shop's closed. We must go round the back.'

'I need to get out of this place for a while. Dimitri, I'll go with Ali and get some food.'

'OK, but the streets aren't safe. You best turn round and come back if there are police or demonstrators hanging about.'

'I will. We'll be back soon.'

I strip off my medical gown and throw it on top of a full bin. No one has collected and disposed of the waste. Beside it, the bin containing new, sterilised gowns sits empty.

Despite the horror in the emergency room I cannot quell my journalist's curiosity, and I use the pretext of going for food as an opportunity to explore the neighbourhood to find out what's happening so I have something to write up for Chloe.

As I follow Ali up the hill behind the hospital, I recognise the neighbourhood, for we came here with Ahmed and Hanna for Abed's blessing in the makeshift mosque in a cellar underneath the Halal butcher shop. The streets narrow as the houses cram together in an ever tighter knot, and the shop fronts, mere holes in the walls, sandwich in between them.

We make our way through a maze of alleyways, and each turn of a corner disorients me further. We pass smashed "shop" windows, burnt tyres and upended cars and motorbikes. An eerie silence fills the alleyways, as if something has just occurred in this theatre of anger and hate, and the actors have exited, either gone forever or lingering just beyond the stage. The shop signs are written in an innocuous Arabic. Or is it Urdu? But the violent messages of the vandals read "Get out!".

We enter a laneway so narrow that we can touch the walls on either side at the same time.

'Here,' Ali says. He pushes and opens a door. We enter into darkness and the familiar odour of groceries. Ali turns on the light, and we find the whole shop trashed. Tins cover the floor, and the contents of broken bottles and jars, flour, spices, fruit and vegetables strew across the floor and on the counter.

Ali gasps, cups his hands to his face and shouts, 'Liyana! Liyana!' I follow him as he hurries to the back of the shop. He pulls back a curtain, revealing a tiny kitchen with a table, four chairs, a hearth and a sink. The only cupboard lies open and bare. Again, Ali shouts, 'Liyana! Liyana!' But no one replies.

'Where is the family?' I say.

'Her father, mother and sister all gone,' he says. 'I don't know where.' He gets out his phone and makes a call, but there is no reply, only that incessant beep that signals no one will answer, maybe ever.

He goes out into the alleyway and knocks on doors, but each door remains closed and responds with only a heavy silence. He pushes at a door and it gives, and we enter, only to see more trashing. Beyond the counter, a scream lets forth from behind a green curtain. I follow the boy as he rushes forward and draws open the curtain. An old man cowers on the floor in the corner and waves at us as if warning us to not approach. Ali speaks to him, and he calms down upon recognising Ali.

They talk in great haste, and Ali tells me the man watched his wife and daughter raped, and now he is a broken man and wants only to die. He had run along the alleyway, screaming, and warned the whole neighbourhood to leave then or else all the women and children would be raped. His wife and daughter left and ran up into the hills with Liyana and her parents and sister. The old man had remained at his shop.

'Never, I will leave this shop,' he says. 'I will die first.'

'We can't do anything, you know, Ali,' I say. 'We should go, now.' Ali, crying, hugs the old man and blesses him, and we leave him cowering in the corner.

I suggest we gather some food, quickly, and I find a plastic carry bag and fill it with what we can find on the shop floor. We then rush into the alleyway and hasten our way back through the maze of lanes.

I know there's fighting, injuries, looting and bombs out there, but I don't know where. It is almost more frightening waiting for an explosion than being in it. Only distant firing breaks the sinister silence. Our shoes tap loudly on the cobblestones, releasing a haunting echo.

As we enter the hospital through a milling crowd, I say to Ali, 'You stay with me for now.' Still he cries, desperate, his life shattered, and he slumps on the floor.

Dimitri approaches and says, 'You both OK?'

'Not really,' I say, and I tell him what I've seen. 'Ali needs some medication to calm him down. He's in a bad way.'

'I'll get it.'

*　　*　　*

Zina peels off her gloves, and she throws them in a bin and her stained gown in another bin. Who knows when this soiled laundry will be disposed of and when it will be replenished with new equipment?

'I've got to get home now,' she says to Dimitri. 'I've been here since six this morning. Can't focus. I'll make a bad mistake soon. I'll be back tomorrow, but my body and mind are in tatters. Jurgo is here for the night shift.'

'There's no one left at the camp,' Dimitri says. 'No need to go out there.'

'Yes, I know. Poor people.' She looks tiny and fragile. Behind her intense almond eyes and mass of short, brown curls, she exudes a passion for her work and an empathy for her patients, whatever their background. I see why Dimitri has teamed up with her. Their collaboration makes for an efficient machine.

'Did you know Aziz has died?' Zina says. 'Died in prison. Committed suicide. Hanged himself by his sheets.'

Dimitri gasps, then says, 'Oh, no. They should never have left him alone with those sheets. He had psychotic problems, schizophrenia. He was on medication and probably stopped taking his pills.'

'They say he kept crying out "Hanna!" every day. Who's Hanna?'

'Hanna was the young woman who had the baby in the camp. Aziz said Hanna was his wife and the baby was his. But we now know that's not true. There's a whole different story there. These immigrants make up a myriad of stories about themselves to get across borders from the Middle East and into Europe. Walking with a pregnant "wife" always gets sympathy. It's a long story. We've hidden Hanna. She's happy now and has removed her burka.'

Ali, beside us and somewhat calmer, wipes his hand through his hair and says, 'That man, my friend Aziz, is a poor man. God bless him.' He supplicates his palms heavenwards and gazes at the ceiling.

*     *     *

Ali, Dimitri and I stand outside the hospital. Twilight streaks the western sky, inexorably signifying the passage of time as another day nears its end. I pause and take a moment to watch the blending of colours on the horizon.

'Ali, where will you sleep tonight?' Dimitri says.

As Ali types a message on his phone, he says, 'I message my friend Hassan in Zakynthos. He tell the fisherman to come and get me at Kyllini and take me over to the island. I ask you good people if you can drive me to Kyllini. Then I am all right.'

Dimitri turns and disappears back into the hospital. We wait awhile, and I wonder what has happened to him.

He reappears and says, 'Just tried the cash machines. There's no cash anywhere in the hospital. We'll try all the banks on the way through the city. We need to buy petrol to get home.'

'Can we take Ali to Kyllini?' I say.

'Sure, if the gas lasts.'

We get into the car and travel along the seashore. The streets remain empty and quiet. A cat rustles in an overflowing bin then flees across the road. We stop at all the banks, but there is no cash. We drive on and find all the petrol stations closed with notices announcing "No petrol".

'So, there's been a run on petrol and the banks, and we weren't prepared,' Dimitri says. 'Only Aunt Maria has been prepared. Forever. We have no money, no petrol and a little food in a plastic bag which we haven't touched.'

Dimitri drives on towards Kyllini, applying a light touch on the accelerator. It seems to take forever to get there. We hope to find cash and petrol at this port town, but when we reach the town in the dark, everything is closed.

'Ali, have you got any cash?' Dimitri says.

Ali opens his wallet and reveals a 50-euro note. 'I need this for the fisherman.'

'I see. Well, there's a petrol bowser over there. Let's see if I can beg for some petrol.'

Dimitri disappears into the shadows. A light goes on in the house behind us, and I watch him talk animatedly for a minute, after which he returns to the car and says, 'Nothing doing. I'm sure he's hidden some petrol there, but he's not going to give it to me. There's your boat, Ali, and here's my phone number. Keep in touch.'

We watch Ali descend to the port and board a fishing boat which soon chugs out to sea.

*     *     *

We drive through Pyrgos, again hoping to find money or petrol. But the town, usually throbbing with people on an early evening in late summer, is hauntingly empty. I find this so unsettling that my heart pounds with anxiety. Dimitri is not speaking, nor am I, we don't have to. We just have our eyes peeled for banks and bowsers. He stops several times and begs for petrol, but to no avail. We exit the town, and with the petrol gauge on empty, we cruise onwards for ten, maybe twenty, minutes until the engine coughs and stops.

'Well, we're not going to make it home,' Dimitri says. 'I'll ring Fotis. Hopefully, he has petrol.'

Dimitri's call rings out into the black surrounds. Is Fotis there? Will he answer? Again, my heart pounds with anxiety. Finally, after the fifth try, he answers, groggily.

'Fotis,' Dimitri says, 'Have you got any petrol in your car? … Not much? How much? … I didn't get any yesterday. I forgot to fill up after we came back from Kalamata … I know … Ask Marina?' Dimitri turns to me. 'He'll need to siphon some petrol from your car into a can.' I nod. 'Fotis, do you understand? You need to siphon it … What? You can't? You don't know how? Ask Maria.'

There is silence until I hear Maria, shouting as if for some reason she thinks the distance between us requires shouting.

'You understand what you've got to do?' Dimitri says to her. 'Siphon the petrol into a can.'

'Of course, of course,' I hear her say. 'I siphon wine every day. Don't you worry.'

'We are at Epitalio … we'll wait for Fotis. Tell him.'

Our car sits stranded, off the road and next to a pine wood, on a night as densely dark as any night could get. The pines prevent even a glimmer of moonlight through the canopy. Dimitri guides us down a track, using the light of his phone. I'm glad to be out of the car, away from the city and hospital, and amongst these trees with their pungent perfume.

We come to a clearing where the pale moonlight breaches the pine trees, and I take some deep breaths and sit on the soft pine needles. We embrace and kiss, and the tension of the day recedes.

'Pine needles and pine smell,' I say, followed by a sigh.

'Mmm, I need this,' Dimitri says. 'We could just make love, right here and now.' But it doesn't come to that. We only embrace and affirm that normalcy and life exist beneath all the chaos.

Headlights approach, followed by a horn tooting, and with our clothes covered in pine needles, we scuttle back to the road and see Fotis standing next to his car.

'Fotis, my boy,' Dimitri says. 'Good work. Where's the can? Here? Maria did it all, didn't she?'

Fotis nods.

Dimitri empties the can into the tank of his car. He gives the engine a buzz, and it turns over. We're back on the road! I think, relieved.

'Thanks, Fotis,' Dimitri says. 'Now you can go back to bed.'

'Here, this is for you.' He hands him a hot casserole dish wrapped in a tea towel. 'Maria made dinner for you.'

'Thanks … and here's a hug for her.' Dimitri hugs his cousin and pinches his cheek.

*     *     *

We near Kato Samiko and stop at a petrol station on the corner of the main road. The shop is open, but "No Petrol" signs hang from the bowsers.

'Costas!' Dimitri shouts as he enters the shop. Costas, our local taverna owner, who is round and bald with bow lips, appears at the kitchen servery window. Dimitri has known him since they were in school together. Dimitri goes behind the counter and into the kitchen, and the two men hug and backslap each other.

'Give us two glasses of wine and some sardines on toast,' Dimitri says. 'We're starving. And you've got some petrol out there, haven't you?'

'Sure,' Costas says. 'Just for friends and family.'

'Fill it up, would you? I'll pay for all this when I get some cash.'

'You need money? You remember Angelino from military service. Well, he's now the manager at the National Bank of Greece in town. He'll give you whatever money you want.'

'Of course, of course. Thanks, Costas.' And Dimitri gives him another slap on his back.

# - 24 -

We sit on the veranda, and Dimitri unfurls Maria's tea towel and ladles her casserole onto the green plates. Despite Costas's sardines on toast, we are still hungry.

'She knows what I like,' Dimitri says.

The dolmadakia and peppers are stuffed with herbed mince-meat and rice, and the chargrilled fringes of the peppers crunch under our teeth, satiating our appetites. Later, we sit back, observe the moon and sip our wine. I stand and view the stars through the telescope. I'm an expert on the galaxies now.

'They're all still there,' I say. 'All those craters on the moon, despite what's happening down here.'

He comes up behind me and places his hands on my breasts. He smells of my lavender shampoo, for he showered before dinner, but the clamminess of chlorine, blood and wounds, which I've seen all day, still cover my body. He's practised at compartmentalising his work. I can't.

'I need a shower,' I say. 'I feel dirty.'

My time in the hospital takes me back to the year of my accident and the operations on my legs. I recall the doctor entering my room as if he was walking in slow motion, and him leaning over my bed and saying, '*We've put your legs back together. It'll be a long recovery, but if you stick at the rehab, you'll be able to walk normally again.*' He stood taller, looked at me and he said something I couldn't decipher.

'*What did you say?*' I said.

'*You're mother's passed away.*'

'*What?*'

'*You're mother's passed away,*' he said, kindly but too loudly. '*She had grave internal injuries. I'm so sorry.*'

He stepped over and sat on the bed, but I couldn't see him, rather, only the fan whirling above my head, round and round and round. Then he left, and I cried, and silent tears ran down my cheeks.

Now, here at Dimitri's house, I need to feel warm water flow over and cleanse my body, so I shower, and when I return to the veranda, Dimitri brings out pineapple cake and ice cream. We share the solace of his veranda—our veranda—and our spoons tinkle together as we dig into the ice cream and giggle.

Suddenly, I say, 'I'm so tired. That shower has turned my body to jelly.'

We go into the bedroom, and I lie down and soon sleep and dream of hospitals with disconnected actors passing through the theatre of my dream: Ali, Costas, Maria, my mother and an unknown man in a hospital gown.

Next morning, I find Dimitri at the table, talking on the phone. He mouths 'Tomas' to me, and they talk about the demonstrations, riots and hospital crises in Athens and Patras.

When Dimitri ends the call, I say, 'What are they doing in Athens?'

'Everything is happening around Syntagma Square,' he says. 'Students, unemployed workers, pensioners, immigrants, trade unionists, every type of group that has a grievance. They've all permanently occupied the square. They don't trust the government to make decisions in their favour during the negotiations in Brussels. There's riot police at the ready. And the government has declared a curfew. Everybody has to be off the streets by 8 p.m. They've already arrested hundreds of people.'

'I suppose they are all young people,' I say. 'Like those guys who came into the hospital today. Do you think they'll disappear like the *desaparecidos* in Argentina?'

'Well, we don't have a military dictatorship here. Yet. Only a fascist party inciting the populace.'

'Mmm, those immigrants did well to escape. They know all about it. They've experienced all this in their own countries.'

Dimitri pours Turkish coffee into a small cup and passes me a frappé. We eat crusty brioche with Maria's cherry jam.

'Tomas is coming to Patras in a couple of days,' he says. 'The Health Department has sent him to look over the hospital to check on infections, diseases, protective equipment, sanitation and so on. I can't believe they've let him come here. There must be someone in the department with some sense. Or a local politician who has seen the hospital being overrun and fears for his life if he ever ends up there. That's probably the real reason. I told Tomas we are short on everything. Antibiotics, sterilising equipment, masks. Even laundering facilities.'

'You'll be glad to see him. Unless someone sees the situation first hand, they won't understand.'

'Tomas reminded me about inviting you a while back to come and stay in Athens so you can report on the refugee camps there. You could go back to Athens with him. He gets through the roadblocks with his medical card. Think about it.'

'Yes, I will. I've read about the waves of Syrian refugees coming across to Lesbos from Turkey now. Chloe mentioned it the other day. I need to get on with my writing and send her a report on what I've experienced here and clear my mind of the stuff I've seen in the hospital. I'm just not up to it; seeing so many young people injured. Even girls with burnt faces.'

'Yes, it's hard at first, then you build a sort of bubble of detachment about yourself. You must to survive, or else you'll become a nervous wreck. Come here.'

Dimitri sits me on his knee. We embrace, and then he gets up and goes out to his car.

# - 25 -

The gravel screeches on the drive outside as a car comes to a halt, and a car door bangs. I go out onto the veranda and see Dimitri approach the steps.

'I've come home early,' he says. 'Thought I'd surprise you.'

'You did.'

He slumps in a chair and pours himself some water. He drains the glass and pours and drinks another. He's done more than a week of eighteen-hour shifts at the hospital while I've stayed home and worked on my articles. I've put off helping out at the hospital, even though I know I should be there to give them a hand. Fotis allays my guilt somewhat when he, having seen the turmoil at the hospital entrance when visiting Andreas and Yiannis, volunteers, with great enthusiasm, to push trolleys. Dimitri, touched by his cousin's gesture, tells me Fotis loves the job and feels a real rapport with the patients.

'He says he wants to be a nurse, to do the course at Patras University, whenever that starts up again. Any lunch left?'

'Mmm, just a minute.' I fuss about the kitchen bench and push across some cold meat, fresh bread and a spinach pie.

Dimitri sighs and says, 'I need some time out. It's chaotic at the hospital. I gave Zina the morning off, and now she's come back to let me go home. We do what we can there, but we're understaffed and running out of equipment and medication. There's nothing coming from Athens because the roads are blocked half the time, and nothing's coming in from Italy because it's too dangerous for ships to dock at the port.'

'I've been writing an article about it for Chloe all morning. Is there anything new happening?'

He gives a wry laugh. 'Better ask those guys in Brussels. Only they can get us out of this hellhole. The people want access to their money and the banks are closed.'

I don't often see Dimitri angry, but now there is a trace in his voice.

'Frustrating?'

'Yeah. Very.'

He lies back on the sofa and closes his eyes while I pack up my computer.

'Let's go to the springs for a bathe,' he says. 'I need to get out.'

*       *       *

At the springs Dimitri reaches out and pushes my bottom, and I climb over the gate and jump to the ground. He heaves himself over and lands with a little laugh. We hurry to the water's edge, only to find, to my slight disappointment, some young Germans there, slapping mud onto their faces and washing themselves. Dimitri removes his clothes and dives in, and I, more prudish, keep my bikini on and follow him.

We greet the Germans and swim to the entrance to the cave at the far end, where the steaming water enters from beneath the mountain. Dimitri surfaces from behind me and tries to embrace me, but I slip away and shimmy under the water. He tries again, but loses his grip and then paddles into the cave. It's too dark and claustrophobic for me, so I paddle over to the mud and the Germans. I float alone and watch the swallows swoop overhead. Suddenly, a black blur bursts from inside the cave and flies towards me. I realise it's a bat and duck under the water. When I resurface, the bat has disappeared. I, somewhat shaken, lie back and tread water while exercising my legs, then chat a little with the Germans and slap mud on my face and wash it away.

The sun sets and the air cools, and I think it's time to leave, yet Dimitri hasn't reappeared. A tremor of worry stirs within me. Suddenly, he's behind me, grabbing at my waist, but I slip away.

'Thetis,' he says.

I don't know what he means.

'You know what?' he says. 'There are hundreds of bats hanging upside down in that cave, and one brushed my face as it swooped past me. They're normally such shy little creatures and blind. And then it flew out of the cave.'

The thought of being touched by a bat repulses me.

\*     \*     \*

At home we shower, and I put on my pink dress, the low-cut one with the fine straps. We lie on a mat below the veranda as the incessant clicking of the cicadas bores deep into our bones.

Dimitri reaches behind him and removes a small package from the grape basket and hands it to me.

'This is for you,' he says.

The package is round and wrapped in layers of cream tissue with a mauve satin bow. It gives a ceramic clink. Something fragile, probably, I think.

I pull the ribbon and let it tumble to the mat. I look up and see him watching me, propped on one arm and smiling.

'Happy birthday,' he says.

It's my birthday. I hadn't realised he knew. 'How did you know?'

'Some time back, when I can't remember, I wanted to know your zodiac sign.'

I tear off the cream tissue and reveal a black and red cylindrical box made of terracotta, an exquisite copy of a pot from Attica with painted figures in a frieze on a black background, topped with a lid and a black nob.

I turn it slowly in my hands, and the ceramic feels smooth and sensual.

'My father gave this to my mother as a wedding present,' he says.

'It's lovely,' I whisper, touched by the beauty of his gift. The figures—with their bowed heads, finely draped clothes and laurel wreaths—are charming. 'Have you any idea what this was used for? It's too small to store olive oil.'

'No, not oil. It contained cosmetics. See that procession of people depicted on the pot. That's the wedding of one of the most famous marriages in Greek mythology. The wedding between Peleus, King of Phthia, and Thetis, the Queen of the sea nymphs. Thetis was always changing her shape from dolphin to horse to mermaid and back to human. Peleus had great trouble getting hold of her. Like me trying to catch you and slipping off today!'

Dimitri takes the pot and points to the figures. 'This is Peleus leading home his bride, Thetis, the one with the laurel wreath. Every god in the Olympian Pantheon, plus their entourages, attended their wedding. It was a mafia-style wedding.' He releases a laugh and hands me the pot. 'You know how it is with weddings. If you ask one member of the family, you've got to invite them all, every cousin, grandparent, aunt and uncle.

177

Art history books are full of depictions of that Big Fat Greek Wedding. Artists throughout the ages just loved painting this mythological marriage. It was a good excuse to spread plenty of nude bodies everywhere.' Dimitri laughs again and lies back on the mat and gesticulates to the heavens. 'Whenever you go to some big art museum and see one of those huge Rubens-style paintings with fleshy nudes all over the place, it's probably of Peleus and Thetis's wedding feast. They loved that stuff in Baroque times.'

Dimitri pops a purple grape into his mouth. He spits the pip towards the trunk of a nearby olive tree. 'Did you know Peleus and Thetis had seven sons, but only one survived. Achilles. You know about him, don't you? Him and his vulnerable spot. His Achilles heel. Where Paris, the Trojan leader, shot him with an arrow during the Trojan War and killed him. A great tragedy, but Achilles will always be our bravest warrior and hero.' He leans on his elbow again. 'Take the lid off the pot.'

I remove the lid and see a smaller package wrapped in the same cream tissue and tied with another mauve satin bow. I take it out and pull the ribbon, which falls through my fingers.

'This gift was also in the box when my father gave it to my mother,' Dimitri says. 'I want you to have it too.'

I unwrap the tissue and reveal a bracelet made of thick gold and with two rams' heads shaped at its opening. The gold is delicate, and the rams' heads with their finely incised horns and amber eyes are a wonder of artistry. I widen the opening and slip the bracelet over my hand. It fits perfectly.

'It's an armband,' he says. 'You're supposed to wear it up here.' He pushes it up my arm until it sits snugly above my elbow. 'Do you like the rams' heads? They have been used by ancient civilisations for thousands of years. Rams have always been symbols of power and virility. They protect the wearer.

The ram is the head of the flock. This is to protect you. Do you like it?' He seems anxious for my approval.

'It's gorgeous,' I say. 'I love it.'

My words sound trite compared to the emotion of the moment. He has given me a gift of such sentimental meaning that I'm overwhelmed and choke for words. I roll over and kiss him. It's what he wants, what we want, and we embrace fiercely on the ground, and he pulls up my dress and finds and squeezes my breasts below the straps. His hardness presses on my thigh, and I caress every shape and hidden nook on his body. 'You're too good to me,' is all I can whisper. We are soft sponge cakes, layer upon layer, feeding on its filling of cream. Turning it over. Tasting it. Devouring it.

Later, we lie back spent and look up at a sky of shot silk.

'Do you think we'll ever have an Achilles?' he says.

'With a vulnerable spot?'

'Yes.'

'Perhaps we've all got a vulnerable spot. It's what makes us human.'

'The gods should know.'

We wander back to the house and sit on the veranda.

'I've got something else for you,' he says. 'There.' He points at an envelope on the low table.

I hesitate, then laugh. 'Is this a trick? Or a surprise?'

'Mmm, a surprise, I hope! Go on. Open it.'

I pick up the envelope, open its flap and take out a bundle of folded documents. I flick through the pages and see photocopies of his and my passports, my birth certificate, translated into Greek—how he got hold of it, I don't know—his own birth certificate, a copy of the local paper and a document written in Greek that I don't understand. I'm not sure if I should be anxious or excited about these documents. Is this something to do with a planned holiday together? I think. But there are no tickets. Perhaps they are in my email inbox.

'Are we going on a holiday together?' I say.

'No,' he says. He smiles and holds up the document in Greek. 'This is a request for a marriage licence.'

'Oh! Oh!' is all that comes out of my mouth. I laugh and smile and cry as waves of delight—and relief that it is not something terrible—roll over me.

Dimitri laughs and smiles too, and we hug and kiss. He whispers in my ear, 'And I haven't even asked you if this is what you want.'

'Of course it is! Of course it is! I thought for a moment this was bad news. Oh, I'm so lucky. Yes, so lucky.'

'There's something else in the bottom of the envelope. I didn't put it in the Attica pot.'

I feel down to the bottom of the envelope and pull out a slim gold ring with a pale blue stone. He slips it on my finger.

We are to marry.

I'm too surprised and shocked to say the right words, and now, for a second time, all I can say is, 'I love it.'

My eyes well with the emotion of it all. 'I don't deserve this.'

'Yes, you do.'

'Oh, thank you. Thank you so much.' And we tangle up in a web of words and feeling and arms and pressing and flying.

'And when is this going to happen?' I say.

'The end of next month, when Tomas comes to be my best man. Katerina, too, will come to be another witness. Are you happy with that?'

'It's all arranged?'

'Guess so.'

I laugh again. 'In that little church in the square?'

'Suppose so, if you're happy with that.'

'Tomas is a wonderful singer.'

'I know. I love that church.'

'Why the local newspaper with the documents?'

'To prove I'm a resident of this town. Bit strange, but that's what they want. You don't mind my having rooted among your documents to find your passport and birth certificate, do you? I needed them to make the marriage application.'

'All for a good cause. Oh, I'm so happy.'

'It's getting dark. Time to go and celebrate. Alexi will be lighting up the grill.'

# PART TWO

# - 26 -

Dimitri hangs up his phone and says, 'We've been invited to a party.'

'Where?' I say.

'At the home of Giorgos Kanaris. In town. Well, above the town, actually.'

'Who is Giorgos Kanaris?'

'Our local Member of Parliament.'

'You know him?'

'A bit. Not well. His daughter's turning eighteen. I don't know why we've been invited to her birthday party. Guess we'd better go. People like him can get us desperately needed funds for the hospital. We need money urgently, and I don't think they understand.'

'Will we know anyone there?' I pause and think for a minute, then say, 'I haven't got anything to wear.'

'Just wear clothes.' He laughs.

My female DNA kicks in as I worry about clothes and hair.

Two days later, I select my pink dress to wear for the occasion and hope my sandals are high enough. I feel I should have curled my hair, but haven't. We drive on a gravel road up the hill behind the town until it peters out at the top where two large iron gates signal the entrance to a grand mansion. Dimitri pulls up at the gates and announces our arrival over the intercom. Video cameras installed on the gateposts record our presence. Justified paranoia? I'm not sure. The gates swing silently open, and we wind up a paved drive—lined with white roses, pink oleanders and fleshy geraniums in giant urns—until we reach a large parking space by the house, already full with silver and black saloons with German logos. I also see a Russian number-plated car with dark windows.

The main entrance is a curved portico embellished with marble pillars between which are statues of Greek gods holding bunches of grapes or in Olympian pose. The doors are wide open, and loud music and bursts of happy, vacuous laughter emanate from the rooms off the hall, causing the giant chandelier above my head to tremor and twinkle.

A man in white slacks and a yellow jacket tick-tocks across the marble floor and puts out a hand.

'Dimitri, my friend,' he says.

'Giorgos,' Dimitri says, shaking the hand.

Giorgos clasps my hand by the fingers only and raises it to his lips and bows forwards without kissing my bunched paw. He comes up smiling. 'Lovely to meet you. And you are?'

'Marina.'

'Ah, what a beautiful lady. My compliments, dear Dimitri. Come, my friends.'

He leads us through into an expansive salon with a glass wall overlooking an indoor pool. We wend our way through swirls and whirls of people, none of whom I know; people dressed in a palette of primary colours, and Amazonian women with heels inches higher than mine, bosoms bedecked in sculpted jewels, earrings of gold pendants and bracelets jangling on lean wrists. One such Amazon waylays Giorgos with a prolonged kiss, so Dimitri and I wander over to the gold-trimmed bar and busy ourselves ordering drinks and picking at the canapés.

'Imelda!' Giorgos shouts from behind us.

A moving mountain sashays through the crowd towards us. She wears a voluminous, turquoise full-length gown with chiffon wings that billow behind her. What appear to be feathers poke out from her hair.

'Imelda,' Giorgos says, 'come say hello to Dimitri. Dimitri, you know my wife?'

'Dimitri, darling,' she says, 'welcome to the party. And who is this charming little lady?'

As I tell her my name, she takes my hand in the tightest of grips and grinds the fingers her husband nearly kissed until she turns and shouts, 'Edris! Champagne! Champagne! Bring the champagne over!' She clicks her fingers, and a waiter dressed in black pants, white shirt and red bow tie emerges from the crowd. 'Edris, Edris, where have you been? Pour these people some champagne.' She adjusts his tray. 'Here, hold the tray like so and the bottle like that and pour slowly.'

Her feathered head bobs up and down above the tray and nearly dips into the champagne. The waiter demurely concentrates on pouring, and with great care his trembling hand succeeds in filling two flutes.

Imelda, who seems to find it difficult to concentrate on our conversation for more than a minute, looks over my shoulder and waves at an unknown individual behind me and says, 'Just a moment, please,' and swoops away.

I look at the waiter. I have seen his face somewhere before but can't remember where. Dimitri goes to say something to him, but Edris slips into the eddies of the crowd.

Giorgos corrals two passing girls with blond tresses and skirts barely covering their bottoms. Our voices rise an octave or two as the music from the terrace beyond the swimming pool throbs and lights flicker above the incessant chatter and laughter. The girls tell us they are having 'a whale of a time', and one bursts into uncontrollable laughter.

'Pleased to meet you,' one says with the slur of a Slavic accent.

'These are my little friends from Russia,' Giorgos says. 'Monica and Lada. Come to have a holiday in Greece, haven't you, girls? Some Greek sun away from the chill of Moscow. Who'd want to live there, eh?' With his hand fondling Lada's bottom, he bundles them off to the dancing terrace, and they gyrate under the shards of laser beams as he thrusts his swinging hips at them.

I turn back to Dimitri, but he is gone, having disappeared into the swell of the crowd. I manoeuvre to the bar again to give me something to do and see a face I recognise. Nina, a nurse at the hospital.

'Hello,' I say. 'I didn't expect to see anyone I knew here. You know these people?'

'Vaguely,' she says. 'My brother's a friend of the birthday girl.'

At the hospital I've wheeled patients into Emergency with her, but it's always been business there. Tonight, she wears mauve and with her hair curled. 'Are you drinking?'

'No, I'm on duty tomorrow.'

'Where do these people get all their money? I mean, do they steal it from the government coffers?'

'No, Kanaris has Russian connections. He owns a bank in Cyprus where the Russian oligarchy stash away their spare roubles. Putin and his cronies cream off what they need and hide it in Cyprus. It's all very easy there. The Cypriot Government just turns a blind eye, and away they go.'

'Oh, I see. Then Kanaris helps the Russians invest in Greece?'

'Something like that. You've been to that new resort down the coast, Al Baia, haven't you?'

'No, can't say I have.'

'Well, it's owned by Kanaris and built with Russian money. Kanaris took over some delicate coastal wetlands, carved out a huge port deep enough for mega yachts, built luxury hotels and palm-fringed promenades by the sea with strings of Italian designer shops, five-star restaurants, sunbathing beaches and bars serving fancy cocktails in crystal glasses. All the Moscow and St Petersburg middle classes flock there for their fix of summer heat. You should see them lying there with their Russian bulks, sipping champagne topped with sticks of cherries. And Kanaris makes a huge profit while exploiting the Bangladeshi immigrant workers who clean the rooms, wash the dishes and weed the gardens, all in exchange for a fistful of rice and a few euro which they send back to their families in Dacca.' She turns up her nose in the disgust. 'It's the way of the world.'

'So Kanaris uses the surplus cash he gets from these investments to throw mega parties?'

'That's about it.' She looks over my shoulder and waves at someone she knows. She wanders off, our conversation ended.

I am alone again, but Dimitri is nowhere to be seen. I pour myself a glass of fruit juice and nibble on a canapé. Suddenly, Nina reappears at my side.

'Ah, you're still here,' she says. 'Some Russian guy cornered me, thinking I was one of Kanaris's party girls. You know what I mean. He had a paunch big enough to make you bilious and had so much vanity feeding his ego that it emanated like a bad odour. What a jerk! Quick, give me a drink.'

She pours something brown from a bottle into a glass and takes a mouthful. She seems to have forgotten about abstinence and her hospital shift tomorrow.

'You know what I think about the guys here?' she says. 'They spend a lifetime trampling on everyone as they climb their way up the ladder, and when they get to the top, they spend the rest of the time trying to regain their virginity. Pathetic!' She downs the rest of the contents of her glass in a couple of gulps and trips off into the foam of people.

Imelda comes by, sweeps me up and says, 'We are dining now, come along.'

We enter a large dining room with a long table decorated with mauve agapanthuses and blue cornflowers. Candles in silver holders stream down the centre to the far end where Dimitri sits with Kanaris on one side and the two Russian girls, doe-eyed, on the other. Imelda guides me to a seat between two men I don't know and across from two matronly revellers with silver and gold adorning their chests and in their hair. Imelda sits opposite me, and I wonder what I can say to her for the next few hours. Dimitri sits far away, in another country, and I am somewhat annoyed he hasn't even come to find me, let alone save me from this horrid woman.

'Edris!' Imelda shouts.

The waiter appears, and I now recognise him as one of the migrants camped by the stadium. I had spoken with him often, in English, for he was a PhD student in Mathematics at Kabul University. He'd fled, fearing for his life, when the Taliban closed the university and many of its teachers disappeared. He always wore a cap when I spoke to him, and now, with his shock of black curls, I understand why I failed to recognise him earlier. Here, he is being told how to pour champagne. My heart sinks for this gentle young man.

190

'Edris, bring out the oysters. And tell the rest of the boys in the kitchen to help you. You remember how to open them with those special knives, don't you?'

'Yes, madam.'

'Good.'

Edris brings out trays of oysters on sculptured ice, and the hubbub at the table turns to confusion as the guests lean in or stand to get their fill of the shellfish.

Imelda plonks several shells on my plate. I am loath to tell her I can't abide raw fish or meat of any kind, so I make a gesture of splitting them open.

My worry about conversing with my hostess allays, for the three women talk incessantly about their children, school exam results, the universities they attend in England or Italy—because 'the standards are so poor in Athens now'—family holiday homes on Hydra and the prices of clothes in Harrods, for they all have flats in either Chelsea or Kensington or, daringly, Brixton. Their bejewelled heads nod and their painted nails scratch as they force open the oyster shells.

'Edris!' Imelda shouts again, clicking her fingers.

'Yes, madam?'

'More oysters, please, and serve the smoked prawns.' She turns and looks over at me and says, 'Nice boy, isn't he? I found him at that migrant camp, the one behind the stadium.'

'Oh?' is all I can say.

'Yes. I went there one day for a bit of adventure. I got friendly with him. He speaks a bit of English.' She juggles an oyster shell, forces in the knife with her chubby fingers and prises it open, then throws back her head, lets the meat slide onto her tongue and swallows. 'You know how it is, one thing leads to another, and we became, well, more than just friends, and I ended up going there every day. I'd give him a bit of cash every now and then for food and bought him a blanket. When they burnt down the camp, I told him he might as well come here and work for us. It'll be winter soon and cold out there.'

I wonder whether she'll throw him out when she tires of him.

Imelda gives a wry laugh. 'My husband has his Russian girls, I've got my Arab boy. You won't tell anyone, will you?'

'Of course not.' I lie. I know I'll tell Dimitri as soon as we get into the car.

# - 27 -

Platters of food continue to arrive at the table. Edris is busy, and I see he's got the hang of balancing multiple plates on his arm. He reaches over guests' shoulders, filling glasses and removing crockery.

The women continue to talk over each other, like high-speed trains, about trips and travel, Africa, Asia, yachts, islands, food and resorts. One woman murmurs, 'Michelangelo! Michelangelo!' Another woman, from a land on the other side of the table, and who errs towards an off-beat look in an Indian print, leans back and puffs on a hand-rolled cigarette.

'I have been in Uganda,' she says, 'giving my time to the natives. I'm building a school with the Kanaris Foundation.' I imagine her brick-laden hands in a bin of cement. 'You know his Foundation. We do good works all over Africa. I go down there in the cool season, you know, too hot at other times, and come back here to rest, in Hydra. I'm writing a book about it and giving the proceeds of the sales to my African charity.'

She seems to trump the other ladies' trips with mention of her charity work and blows out a smug billow of smoke.

An Adonis, with thick-lensed glasses and a little finger curled at the end of his fork, sits silently beside me and concentrates on peeling his prawns and splitting open his oyster shells. Suddenly, he looks at me and whispers, 'Pfft! Foundations! They're just tax dodges. That cow says she's writing a book. She can't even read. Don't know how she even managed to decipher the signs directing her to the airport.' His sardonic tone scares me. He sinks silently back to his task at the dinner plate and picks up a shelled prawn with his fingers and dips it into the sauce on his plate.

Several guests rise from the table, why I don't know, but I use this as an excuse to push back my chair and say, 'Pardon me, I'm just off to the bathroom for a minute.'

I see Edris hastening with a pile of plates towards a door in the far corner and follow him as that's where I really want to go, the kitchen. I push through the door and onto a sloping passage, presumably to aid the pushing of food trolleys to the dining salon, and stale cooking smells fill my nostrils. Edris pushes open a swing door at the end of the passage, and I follow him into the kitchen. The room is deserted. No cooks, assistants, waiters or dishwashers. Mountains of dirty dishes and platters of half-eaten food pile on the benches, and pots and pans sit stacked on the stoves, awaiting scrubbing. Edris stoops over a far bench, placing strawberries and cherries on a five-tiered birthday cake and arranging desserts on trolleys.

'Edris, where are all the kitchen staff?' I say.

'I don't know. They've all disappeared. Gone home.'

'So, you are doing all this by yourself?'

'I guess I'll have to. I'll manage.' He continues decorating the cake.

'Do you like it here?'

'I have to. I have no choice.'

'I imagine a few years ago you could hardly have believed yourself in this situation. Do they pay you?'

'Sometimes.' He bows his head and his lips curl.

I don't want to upset him. 'Are you trapped here?'

'Sort of. I'm a man of science, not a servant.'

'I know that.'

He stands behind the bench, and a noise comes from the floor beside him. I walk around the bench and see a small bear eating from a dish whilst tied with a gold chain to the leg of the gas stove.

I gasp in shocked surprise and step back. 'Edris, what's that?'

'It's madam's pet bear.' He drops some vegetables and fish into the bear's dish.

'They can't keep a bear in a house!'

'*They* can. It's my job to feed it.'

'But where did she get it?'

'They go on hunting trips to the Rhodope Mountains in Bulgaria. They have a hunting lodge there.'

'What do they hunt?'

'Oh, everything. They shoot whatever they find: boar, birds, rabbits and bears. They have their own guides.'

'Bears? They shoot bears?'

'With luck.'

'What? They missed this one?'

The bear looks up at me dolefully, and I feel a wave of pity for the poor beast.

'No, they found this one. Someone else shot its mother. Bit of the Wild West up there. Lawless. That's why they like it.'

'But … how did they get it back here?'

'Oh, the gamekeeper hauled it over the hills in a truck to the town where Kanaris has his private plane parked, then flew it to Patras.'

Suddenly, I want to get out of the kitchen as the bear makes me uncomfortable. 'I'll help you up the ramp with these desserts. Let me push this trolley, and you take the other.'

'You shouldn't really, you're a guest.'

'I don't mind. Come on.'

I follow Edris into the dining salon and find some guests still seated, while, through the glass panes, others throw themselves in the pool with joyous abandonment or gyrate on the dancing terrace. A blaze of fire shoots up from the horizon, only to explode and crackle as the night sky fills with falling stars of glittering hues. The revellers shout with delight and wonder as more rockets fire and explode in the sky.

'Fireworks! Fireworks!' they cry. 'What wonderful fireworks for the birthday girl!' And they break into exuberant applause and euphoric cheers.

The lights flicker and the dining salon plunges into darkness except for the feeble candlelight. The music cuts out, and the pool's underwater lights fade, turning the water black.

'Oh! Oh! Oh!' the revellers cry, and some scream in surprise.

'Giorgos!' Imelda shouts. 'There's a blackout. Somebody go see what they are doing in the kitchen. Something must have blown in the kitchen. Edris!'

'There's no one in the kitchen, madam,' Edris's voice says from the darkness to my right.

'What?'

'There's no one in the kitchen, madam, and no one's cooking. They've all gone home.'

'Gone?' The candles flicker. 'Then go get some more candles, Edris.'

'Where from, madam?'

'Somewhere in the kitchen. Giorgos, where's the switchboard?'

'In the cellar,' Kanaris's voice says from the darkness to my left.

'Edris, look for the switchboard in the cellar.'

Using the light of my phone, I return to the kitchen and look for candles in every drawer but find nothing.

Edris passes me in the semi-darkness. I follow him to the cellar, where we find the Adonis standing on a chair and looking at the switchboard with his phone light.

'Everything is on,' he says. 'Nothing has blown here.'

We go back upstairs and find the guests helping themselves to the desserts on the trolleys: ice cream cakes, meringue and cream pies, and chocolate mousse. They walk about in the semi-darkness or prop themselves on the edge of the table or in corners on the floor. Some drip melting chocolate ice cream on the brocade sofas, while others guzzle spoonfuls of all the sweet delicacies they can find. A priest, wearing a flowing black cassock and a bushy beard, sits on the floor and feeds a bare-shouldered, busty woman in a tiara. With the dimming of the light all niceties and manners are thrown out the window.

'There is nothing wrong at the switchboard, Mr Kanaris,' the Adonis says.

'We'll have to call the power people,' Kanaris says with a slur. 'Now, where's the number? Are there any lights on in the town?' He moves past me and stands at a large glass window and looks out at the town below. 'There are lights on everywhere, streets lights, next door, even the blocks of flats. It's just us. Everyone else has power and we don't. I'll try phoning the power people.'

'The power people! The power people! The power people!' the revellers cry.

His face glows as he flicks through his phone, but he can't seem to find the number. 'Does anyone have the number? And someone get more candles!'

# CHRISTINA A. DUDLEY

The guests ignore him, too intent on devouring their dessert, and some cut into the five-tier birthday cake.

'Light the candles! Light the candles! Light the candles!' the revellers cry.

But no one can find matches or a cigarette lighter.

'There must be a cigarette lighter somewhere,' a voice says.

'The lady in the Indian dress, the Indian lady, the lady that helps the Africans,' another voice says. 'She's got cigarettes.'

'The Indian lady! The Indian lady! The Indian lady!' the revellers cry.

But no one knows her name, and a flurry of hunting for her ensues. Imelda rushes to the bathroom door and knocks and tries the handle, but it is locked.

'Get out! Get out!' she shouts. 'We need your lighter.'

But all is silent within.

The wan tones of a guitar come from the pool. Heads turn, and a guitarist strums whilst he sits on a pool chair. The Indian lady lies on the ground at his feet and drifts off as she waves her hands and nods her head.

Someone beats pots and pans to make music, and the guests burst into a sugar-rush revelry. The duchesses and their men twist and gyrate and wave their arms about in the dim light, and some pluck at powerless guitars and produce tinny tunes. Even the Adonis sways before a fan-waving duchess in gold and yellow. The younger revellers near the pool leap and frolic about in the water, and the darker it gets, the louder their screams of delight sound. A voice shouts, 'The pump is off, the filter is off, and there's shit and vomit in the water. Beware!' But all ignore the warning. The confusion, chaos and bedlam throw the guests into a medieval frenzy. I suspect Kanaris and Imelda couldn't have hoped for a better party, each guest denuded, liberated and free.

I look for Dimitri and find him in a corner, talking to Edris.

'Ah, there you are,' I say. 'Couldn't see you anywhere.'

'Edris said you were down in the kitchen with him.'

'Yes, he has a bear down there.'

'A bear?'

'Yes, a bear—'

But our conversation is lost in the hubbub as the guests sing Greek folk songs, songs of the War, of their peasant fathers, of Communist marches and partisan camaraderie. All we can do is sit, watch and listen.

The music and singing lulls, and Dimitri says, 'Time to go.'

Imelda enters the room, leading the bear on its gold chain.

'Come, my darling,' she says. 'Come, my darling, dance with me.' She runs around in a circle, dragging the bear, until she collapses to the floor and hugs the poor beast, whining and crying. 'Ha, my dear, my darling, let us dance.' She stands, and guests form a circle round the bear, and it stands chained and bewildered while dancers shout and tease until the animal falls to the ground in an immovable heap.

'We've got to go! We've got to go! We've got to go!' the revellers cry.

A grand duchess sweeps into the room and shouts out in the flickering candlelight, 'Giorgos! Open the gates!'

'Giorgos!' Imelda shouts. 'Buzz the gates!'

'Where's the buzzer?' Kanaris says.

Dimitri and I follow the guests as they rush down the marble staircase, past the Olympians in the foyer and outside to the gates, but the great sheets of iron do not respond to Kanaris's pressing of the buzzer and remain shut.

I run back up into the Salon and shout, 'The gates won't open! There's no power! They're blocked! Is there a key to open them?'

'A key?' Imelda says, puzzled. 'A key? Yes, the key. The butler has the key. But where's the butler? Look for the butler. Edris! Look for the butler.'

'Where's the butler?' Edris says.

'In his rooms next to the kitchen.'

'But all the staff have left.'

'Left? Left? Go and look for the butler. My dear Marina, go and help the man. He can't understand me.'

'Yes, he can.'

'The butler. The butler,' she keeps repeating.

Dimitri and I go down the slope towards the kitchen, and I knock on the door next to it. No one responds. Dimitri tries the door and it gives. Under the light of my phone, we see a couple copulating on the butler's bed. The girl beneath looks up, startled. The birthday girl.

'What do you want?' she cries, trying to cover herself up. 'Get out!'

'Where's the butler?' Dimitri says. 'We need the key to the gate. We can't get out.'

'How the hell would I know? It's not in here!'

'Yes, how the hell *would* you know.'

We back out and close the door. We walk up the ramp, opening the doors and cupboards, looking for keys. We open a door and see a couple kneeling by the toilet, snorting lines of cocaine laid out on the seat.

Dimitri opens another door, and we find a salon lit with flickering phone lights.

'Ah Dimitri, come in,' Kanaris says, dazzling us with a shining torch. 'Just in time for a personal tour of my collection.'

Paintings and high reliefs cover the salon walls, and Kanaris, surrounded by an intimate group of his art-loving friends, stands before a white canvas with three pale-blue brush strokes.

'My latest acquisition,' Kanaris says. 'A José Armenis. A New York Latino. Lives on the street, does street art, but this one is a rare canvas.'

'Aaah, an Armenis,' a grande dame coos, leaning in with her phone. Her feathered headdress brushes the frame.

'Careful, now,' Kanaris says, pulling her back gently. 'This one cost me two million euro from Christie's in New York.'

As he moves the group around the room, they wave their phones at the art work. When he stops in front of a cow's skull hanging on the wall, the torchbeams cause the animal's hollow eyes to penetrate the gathering, and the group gush banalities.

'Now this is my absolute favourite.'

'Oh, Giorgi, it's wicked.'

'Never seen anything like it.'

'So unique.'

'So offbeat.'

'So outlandish.'

'Something Kleinish, back in the sixties.'

The group chant, 'Oh, yes, oh yes, oh yes,' and clap with excitement. A man says, 'You mean *Keinholz*,' but the ongoing applause drowns him out.

'Cost me another two million,' Kanaris says, puffing out his chest. 'From Sotheby's.'

Glass cases, over at the far wall and enshrining sculptures of the Minoans and Mycenaeans, distract Dimitri and me.

'Where did he get these from?' I whisper.

'God only knows. They should be in a museum.'

A group breaks away and hovers in a circle in a corner and point the pale light of their fading phones at someone on the floor. We ease our way to the front and see a person with a long plait and of undefined sex bent whilst painting a canvas on the floor. No, not painting, but randomly poking the canvas with a brush, filling it with a myriad of dots with what seems a random choice of hue. In this sacred chapel of art only hushed tones are heard, respecting the sanctity of the art work.

A woman by my side whispers, 'It's to be viewed from above. One needs to be suspended above the canvas to interpret its true meaning.'

The plaited artist looks up meaningfully and hands my neighbour the brush and says breathlessly, 'For you, madam. Guide me on my journey.'

'Oh, Arkadia,' she says, 'you are giving me the brush? Yes?' She falls to her knees, bends over the canvas and brushes the sacred cloth with the feather in her hair. Her tears fall with the emotion of it and drip on the artwork, blurring the wet paint.

A man behind me whispers, 'Arkadia's come all the way from New York to paint this for Kanaris. He has works on display in MoMA.'

'O great one,' the faithful circle cry.

Arkadia in all his humility passes the holy brush from person to person until the group is in ecstasy over the significance of this painting, and the guests lean over and try with all the effort they can muster to view the image from above with their dwindling phone light. Then Arkadia releases the sceptred brush from the last guest's hand and randomly joins the dots with a myriad of seemingly unconnected lines.

'Paths to the Temple,' Arkadia chants, 'as those who've read the Ancient Texts know. Where the lines cross, that is the meeting point of the Ancient People. The temple.'

'Oh, yes,' the faithful circle cry, 'the meeting of the Ancient People! The meeting of the Ancient People!'

Kanaris taps Dimitri on the shoulder. 'Dimitri, my friend, let me introduce you to my art advisor, Simona.'

'How do you do, Simona?' Dimitri says as they shake hands.

'Pleased to meet you,' she says with an Eastern European accent, giving me a cursory glance.

Simona wears the uniform worn by female gallery owners, art critics and auction house assistants—a de rigueur tubular black dress, conservatively hemlined below the knee. The jersey knit clings to her bottom and breasts, with a cut low enough to invite looks of sexual potential from male clients without overriding the seriousness and knowledge of her profession.

'Lucky, aren't I,' Kanaris says, 'to have found this gem of a woman who hunts out these art works for me from all over the world? What do you think? You know Arkadia would never have come to my home had Simona not persuaded him. He's never left his street in South Baltimore. And never will again.'

'Extraordinary,' Dimitri says. 'I've never seen anything like your collection. There is much to be admired. So surprising.' I admire him for the ambiguity of his reply. 'Especially this work of Arkadia. You are so fortunate to have him in your house. A real original. Don't you think, Marina?' He squeezes my hand.

'You have a wonderful job, Simona,' I say. 'I admire you.' I am suddenly full of admirable words myself.

'You know,' Kanaris says, 'I never have to think about what I am going to buy. Simona does it all for me. Isn't that wonderful? She has such perfect taste and knowledge of the market. She knows exactly what I like. You know what I mean?'

'Absolutely. Time saving as well,' Dimitri says. But he's run out of words. 'Well, we really must be going. I've got a shift tomorrow at the hospital. Thanks, Giorgos, for a wonderful evening.'

But Kanaris is already looking over Dimitri's shoulder, eyeing someone behind him.

Dimitri embraces Kanaris, then somehow I do too, and our host walks off arm in arm with Simona.

We slip away as the group continue their viewing and hurry up the slope from the kitchen and open the last door and enter a room filled with a cacophony of music and flickering amber candlelight.

'Darlings, come in,' a bosomy matron with a painted face and a balloon of teased hair says. 'Welcome to the party, my friends.' She places her bejewelled hands around my shoulders and draws me into a party of women in sequins, satin and silk, blond wigs, bosoms, bottoms and male voices. Another woman, with a brush of blond hair, sings a melancholy song from a dais at the far end of the room. 'You see, my darlings, we've found all the candles.' Drums rap, saxophones blurt tootle-toot and the trumpets and trombones pipe as the ladies sing and shout on the dance floor. A parallel party while the rest of the guests are trying to get away. 'Come, my darlings, eat, drink.' Her tinsel eyelashes flutter at us.

'We're looking for the key to open the gate,' I say.

'The key? The key? What key? Which key?'

'The key to open the gate.'

'The gate? What gate?'

'The main gate. The guests are wanting to go.'

'The guests? What guests? The guests are here, my sweet. Come on.'

She tries to pull me to the dance floor, but Dimitri holds me back and says, 'We're going.'

We return to the big salon and find guests lying on the floor while others amiably dance to the tinny guitar or sing folk songs with a Turkish whine.

The Adonis rouses himself from the floor and says, 'There must be a manual mechanism by the gate.'

We follow him outside and find the rest of the guests banging at the iron sheets of the gates.

'Let us out! Let us out! Let us out!' they cry. But of course no one can hear them, for they are at the top of the hill, far from the common people below.

The Adonis pulls at the vegetation at the bottom of a pillar. Dimitri joins him, and as I shine what's left of the light from my phone on them, they pull and rip at bushes of azalea, oleander and laurel.

'Nothing here, nothing here,' the Adonis says.

'No, nothing here either,' Dimitri says.

They try the other side and tug at rose bushes, smash an urn with a stone and pull up moss-covered bricks.

'There's nothing,' Dimitri says, emerging from the bushes with blood-stained hands. He is supposed to use them in the morning. 'Is there an emergency power system?'

'Yes,' Edris says near me. 'The gardener deals with it.'

'Where's the gardener?'

'He's gone.'

'Gone? Where?'

'Gone home. But look what I found!'

'A ladder! A ladder! A ladder!' the guests cry.

A wheezing Duke props the ladder against the gate, but it's pitifully too low, and the row of metal spikes across the top dissuade anyone from climbing over them.

'The fence! The fence! The fence!' the guests cry.

But the fence, an impenetrable stone structure with shards of glass on top to keep out intruders, dwarfs the ladder.

Edris appears beside us and whispers, 'Come with me. But turn off your phones first. I don't want that lot following us.'

We creep around the perimeter of the garden, following the stone wall. Edris slips behind the bushes and forces his way through the tall laurel hedge backing onto the fence. 'You can turn on your phones now. They're not following us.'

We push our way through the narrow space between the hedge and the stone wall until we reach where the stone wall stops, replaced by a fence of tall iron railings. We stop and shine our lights on the railings.

'See?' Edris says, pointing.

Two railings have been forced apart so a slim body can pass through to the world outside.

'I spent quite a bit of time doing this, forcing these railings apart with a crowbar. Now I can go out when I want.'

Lights approach, edging along the wall.

'Someone has seen us. Quick! Slip through the railings.'

Edris slips through with ease, I go next but with more difficulty, and Dimitri twists and turns and pushes until he makes it outside. We slither and slide down a steep incline and look back when we hear voices.

'They'll never manage to get through,' Edris says.

Back up at the fence a voice shouts, 'Look! An opening!'

'An opening! An opening! An opening!' the trapped guests cry. 'We can get out here.'

We look up and see a huge woman stick her leg through the gap in the railings, but like an ugly stepsister, she shouts, 'I'm stuck! I'm stuck!'

We watch as one after another push and pull and twist and turn, but all to no avail as the iron railings will not budge. Dukes with paunches puff and pant and swear and groan and then, like all the rest, fall back into the inside of the hedge, exhausted.

'You see,' Edris says. 'I told you so. They're stuck inside.'

Lights shine in the streets below, illuminating the whole neighbourhood, but up on the hill the Kanaris palace remains a blackened fortress.

'How are we going to get home?' I say.

'Hope there's a taxi at the station,' Dimitri says.

'Is it dangerous to walk there?'

'Probably not.'

As we take the long walk to the station, my sandals heels hurt me, but I dare not walk in bare feet as I'll slice up my feet. I feel blisters blowing up with every step and lean on Dimitri's arm.

We find a taxi at the station, and the driver agrees to drive us down the coast to our house. I sit on the soft and springy leather seats, grateful to be off my feet, and lean into Dimitri and close my eyes.

## - 28 -

I wake in the morning and find Dimitri already up as he has an early start at the hospital. I go into the kitchen to make coffee, but he's already made it and sits watching the TV.

'Hey, have you heard the news?' Dimitri says. 'The Army has come in and quelled the rioting and demonstrations. Things seem to have settled down in Athens and Patras, for now. There have been many arrests. Rightly or wrongly, I don't know. Nothing's changed, though, for the ordinary people. The banks remain closed, and workers are too scared to go to their offices and factories.'

'How are your hands?' I say. I grasp his hands and turn them over and see a myriad of cuts on the back of them from pulling out the Kanaris plants the night before. 'You'll need to do something about those.'

'I'll get Zina to fix them when I get to the hospital.'

'Do you think Kanaris will provide money for the hospital?'

'Probably not. I suspect he'll be trapped in his house forever.'

'You didn't get near enough to him last night to discuss the hospital?'

'I was near enough all right, but the Russian birdies were in between. Not the right moment. That'll come when he needs something. You'll see.'

We stand at the kitchen bench and sip coffee while watching the TV. A reporter from the BBC waylays a delegate from the Greek Finance Ministry as he enters the headquarters of the European Commission.

'How are the talks going?' the reporter says.

'Not very well,' the delegate says. 'There's no movement on any side. I am optimistic, however, that our European partners will not wish to see one of their members go bankrupt. That's the path Greece is on right now, and it would be catastrophic for my country and also for the European Union if it should come to that.'

The delegate waves off the reporter, but then turns and says, 'The Greek voters have voted for us to re-negotiate our debts, but for the moment our European friends prefer to punish the Greek people by forcing us to close our banks. It's not their fault, and the people know it.'

Dimitri turns off the TV. 'It's not looking good,' he says dismally. He raises his hand to his chest and says, 'Oh, oh.' He pants and gives himself a pat. 'Oh, got a cramp from all that messing about last night. Pulling up plants in the dark and squeezing through those railings. Probably bruised something or pulled a muscle.'

'Sure you're OK?' I say, concerned.

'Sure, sure.'

'What about eating something? I know you won't eat anything once you're in the hospital. And then I'll drive you to the station so you can catch the train into Patras.'

I place a feta pie in the microwave and heat it for him.

\*　　　\*　　　\*

I spend the morning writing up an article about Ali and the attacks on the Pakistani community and send it to Chloe at noon. Mid-afternoon, she replies: *Great article, very informative, need to tweak it here and there for space reasons but basically all good. Thousands of hits on your other articles about what's going on in Greece. Will get back to you re payment. Chloe.*

In a burst of housekeeping I sweep the floors, dust all the sculptures and Greek artefacts on the bookcase and run a cloth around the frames of the paintings. I pick up the ikon of St Nicholas and give it an extra wipe. I pause to examine the exquisite gold leafwork bordering the image of the saint and see it's been painted with sacred care. After lunch I pick some oranges and lemons to take over to Maria.

I sweep up a spray of dust as I swerve into the drive, and the dogs set up a racket of barking and strain at their ropes. I stop and call out, 'Hello, hello,' and finally Andreas appears, with his cast removed and looking taller and more relaxed than I'd seen him for a while.

'Hello,' I say, and we embrace. I follow him into the kitchen where Yiannis sits watching TV. 'Yiannis.' I bend low and kiss him. 'Where's Maria?'

'In the garden,' he says.

I go outside and find her pulling up weeds in a far corner.

'Ah, my dear, come, come,' she says, and she hugs me.

'Can I help you pull up these weeds?'

'No, no, they're potatoes.' She points at a nearby basket full of them. She hands me a fork, and I dig deep into the soil and the cold, earthy smell of potato rises. I give a little flip and reveal a soiled potato. I pick it up and go to toss it into the basket, but I hesitate, afraid to bruise the precious crop.

As I labour over every turn of the soil, Maria works with practiced speed. She leans down in front of me, her back curved like a reaper in a Millet painting, her scarf tied at her neck, her skirt dragging in the soil and her wooden sandals clacking on the hard earth beneath us. I push my hands down deep into the soil and feel about, my own private treasure hunt, until my fingers touch the cool, firm skin and I ease out the vegetable.

'Now the carrots,' she says, and I see she already has three in her basket. I pull at the green fronds, give a twist, and the vegetable releases from the ground like a wobbly tooth. We work our way down the line of vegetables until she says, 'That's enough for now.'

I follow her back to the house, but she pauses and cuts a handful of grass and walks over to her rabbits. She rubs the dirt off some carrots, opens the hutch door and throws the grass and carrots into the enclosure. 'There we are, my dears,' she says. 'Now your turn.' She slices hay off a small bale and throws it towards the goats. Two black and white kids dance around their mother, and Maria picks one up, kisses it and holds it tight till it jumps to the ground. 'Off you go, little one.'

She is not engaging with me in chatter. Why should she?

We sit in the kitchen and wait for Dimitri to arrive. The dogs bark as the crunch of gravel comes from the drive, followed by the click of a pulled handbrake. Dimitri enters the kitchen and greets everyone, and soon we sit crowded in the kitchen, a mini festa, as Maria plies us with cake and tea, which we devour with relish.

Later, Dimitri drives Fotis, Andreas and me to the pool for a bathe before sunset. Along the way, I ask Dimitri how he got his car out of the Kanaris compound, and he says Kanaris got a neighbour to call a welder with an oxyacetylene torch to burn a hole in the iron plates.

'They couldn't get a welder till the morning, till the thinnest person they could find finally got out through the iron railings, and then the woman who got out didn't know where to go to find a welder. It was bedlam up there, people throwing punches when trying to get their cars out first, women asleep in bathrooms and impossible to find. There's still no power. Kanaris blames Golden Dawn. He says it's a terrorist attack.'

Fotis sneezes twice in the back of the car.

'Are you sick, Fotis?' I say.

'No, just caught something from one of those patients on a trolley. The pool will fix it. You know what? I received a message from Hassan, one of our Afghan friends from Kalamata. They're safe, up in the mountains with some shepherds. Above our old family town. They're living in a hut the shepherds use in summer, and a shepherd's daughter, Artemis, leaves them food in a stone box by a stream. Every day, there's fresh bread, feta, fruit and whatever casserole they are eating that day. He says they're fine and warm and have a fireplace in the hut.'

'Well, good for them,' Dimitri says. 'They'll be looked after. We spent a couple of days with those kind people. They're a long way from what's happening down here.'

Dimitri turns into the dirt parking space before the pool and parks next to a German car. We climb over the gate, jump to the ground and hide behind the oleander bushes to change. Two young Germans we met there another time glide about in the steamy water with masks of dry mud on their faces.

'Hello, here again?' I say to the girl, paddling over. 'You've discovered the secret pool too.'

'My parents told me about it,' the girl says. 'They come here every year. My father is a zoologist, researching the bats that inhabit this cave. I'm Helga.' She extends a muddy hand.

I shake her hand. 'Ah, so your parents are Hermann and Gudrun. I met them here a few months ago. We shared a long meal together one evening, up at an olive farm above Arini, and your father told us all about bats and how they were losing their feeding grounds here because of the human encroachment into fields and woodlands. Are you having an end-of-summer break in Greece? You've been here before, I suppose.'

'To Greece, yes often.'

'You like Greece, then?'

'We love Greece, don't we, Lukas?'

Her boyfriend swims over to us, and as I plaster my face with mud, I say to him, 'Not a good time to be a German in Greece right now, is it?'

'Well, the people are nice and polite,' Lukas says. 'They need our tourist euro. It's not a good look for Germany and the EU, trying to pull down the weakest member state. We don't like it, nor do our friends. The European banks go and lend the Greeks billions to buy armaments from German companies and then charge exorbitant interest rates on the loan repayments. It's a crazy system.' He busies himself rinsing his face.

Dimitri swims underwater and grabs my legs and pulls me under. I come up for air. 'That's what's wrong with banks,' I say. 'They're just there to dupe the weakest.'

'Something like that,' Dimitri says. 'I think it's called screwing the vulnerable.'

'Yes, too easy. The playground bully. The big banks, too big to go under, so that's it.'

Andreas and Fotis emerge from the cave under the mountain. Both have mud-splattered faces, and Andreas has covered his broken arm in a muddy cast.

'Your arm will be better than ever soon with that mud on it,' Dimitri says to Andreas. 'This spring and its mud have been known forever for their healing properties. It acts as an anti-inflammatory. Even the gods knew about it, and all the great Olympians passed through here on their way to the Games.'

213

As we paddle towards the back of the cave in the mild twilight, Dimitri says to me, 'Tomas came to the hospital today from Athens. The health department sent him to look at the infection rates in the hospital. I've been telling him for months that we lack basic antibiotics, sterilising equipment, PPE and masks, laundering facilities, even sterilised dressings in emergency and cleaning materials. And there are outbreaks of infections in the prison which they can't put their finger on.'

He swims around and around, then floats on his back and looks up at the sky before turning over on his stomach. He comes over and rubs his legs against my thigh. 'Mmm, nice.'

'It's getting cold,' I say. The swallows have gone and the bats swoop low. The slightest breeze kisses my forehead, but it has lost its summer heat. 'Let's get out.'

We pass Helga and Lukas, already on the stone slabs and pulling on sweaters and jeans, and I say, 'See you tomorrow. Maybe.'

We climb over the gate, run to the car, and I wrap myself in a windcheater.

'We'll drop you boys off on the way,' Dimitri says to Fotis and Andreas. He turns to me. 'Then it's home for us. I need some hot food.'

# - 29 -

I slice zucchini and eggplant, toss them in a paper bag of flour and deep fry them in boiling oil. While we were at the pool, Maria has walked to our house and left a pan of oven-baked lemon potatoes and a loaf of bread on the table.

Dimitri tears the loaf apart and mops up olive oil and feta cheese on a crust. Hunger invades him, I can tell. He walks over to his collection of miniature Mycenaean sculptures on the bookcase, picks one up and turns it round in his hand.

'There's something sensual about the shape of these figures, isn't there?' he says, examining it. 'I see you've been dusting!' He laughs and places it down.

He goes out onto the veranda and turns the souvlaki on the charcoal grill. I lay out the green plates and glasses on the table and light a thick candle. I then come out with the fried vegetables and potatoes.

'Souvlaki?' he says, walking over to the table whilst chewing at a skewer coated in oregano, garlic and lemon. Cicadas thrum, boring holes in the darkness with their noise; summer is still here. The scent of the jasmine curling round the veranda posts mixes with the early evening pungency of musk floating across the hills.

'That smells good,' I say, yet I can't keep my hands from the crispy vegetables. The stars hang low and the moon casts its light, and I rise and point the telescope towards the galaxies. We talk of the Milky Way, the infinity of the Universe and the mystery of light years, then lie down on the veranda, as we often do, and pick out the celestial bodies in the ink sky. Dimitri has recently read *Astronomy Now* and points out bodies in the Milky Way unknown to me. I'm slowly getting the hang of it, and our nightly stargazing transports us to another dimension.

Unexpected lights appear at the end of the drive leading up the hill. A car approaches the house, and as it pulls to a halt, the gravel crunches. We stand by the back door and watch the driver get out of the car and open the back door to let out the passenger. It's Giorgos Kanaris. The driver leans on the car and looks around, a hand on a holster.

'Ah, my dear Dimitri,' Giorgos says as he comes up the stairs.

'Giorgos! This is a surprise.' They shake hands, and Giorgos slaps Dimitri on his back before bending as if to kiss my proffered hand. He steps through the door and enters the house as if it were his private possession. He strides through the kitchen and into the living room beyond.

'Ah, nice space,' he says, looking about. He picks up our new St Nicholas ikon from the bookcase. 'Mmm, good quality. You can never be sure about these things, their authenticity. You have to be very careful.' He replaces the ikon and takes up a pottery vase. 'Ah, some pottery hunted down from somewhere?'

'Only copies,' Dimitri says, 'but we like them.'

Giorgos handles the artefacts Dimitri has neatly arranged on the sideboard and runs his hand over the wood sculptures. 'Nice collection. My compliments.'

Dimitri grimaces, and I sense his tremor of irritation. Do we need this man's approval? I ask myself.

Giorgos walks through the double doors onto the veranda, sits himself on the sofa, splays his legs and lights up a thin cigarillo. 'Smoke?' He waves a gilt-edged box in our direction, but we shake our heads.

I give a smile and say, 'Something to drink?'

'Just water.'

As Giorgos takes the glass, a diamond-studded ring on his little finger sparkles in the candlelight. He is dressed as if on some business engagement: an indigo suit of silk and linen, a pale blue tie and matching handkerchief, and soft calf loafers exposing his brown ankles. He props, one bent leg on top of the other, and displays a youthful casualness which does not, however, mask his sixty-something years.

'So, electricity back on at your house today?' Dimitri says.

'No, I couldn't get anyone to come and look at it,' Giorgos says. 'No one wanted to enter the house. I don't know why. The power was on all over the rest of the city. In the end I paid this fellow a thousand euro just to cross the threshold of the house. He took half the day examining every plug and wire in the house but couldn't find anything. He said we might have to go underground, pull up the floors, and then left with five thousand euro in his pocket. I went down to the kitchen and found the rest of the ice cream cake melted all over the floor. It was a sticky puddle.' He gives a little laugh. 'Then I opened the freezers, and the stink of decaying food seeped out.'

He puffs on his cigarillo and smoke drifts gently upwards. He looks across at me, makes eye contact and lingers seconds too long. He smiles, screws up his eyes and gives an easy smile.

'You're looking lovely tonight,' he says to me. 'You're a lucky guy, Dimitri.'

I find his charisma charming and magnetic, and now, no longer the host from last night on stage, he plays the natural seducer with ease as he flicks the ash off his cigarillo. I feel drawn yet awkward. They are like that, these men. I shouldn't be surprised, for their fondness for women feeds their desire to hone their skills of seduction. I glance at Dimitri. He looks unperturbed, almost smiling, as if to say "of course".

'You know,' Giorgos says, 'I can't get any of the staff to come back. They refuse to enter the house. They say they can't.'

'What do you mean?'

'They say an invisible wall prevents them from entering. They stand, lined up about a hundred metres from the wall, and go no further. The police and the army tried to enter the place, but they couldn't breach the invisible wall either.'

'Can you get back in?'

'Not now. I got out after they cut the hole through the gate and haven't been able to get back in. As I said, there's an invisible wall around the house. If you put your hand up, you can feel it, like solid air, but you can't see it.'

We are stuck for words, and I wonder if he is losing his mind. Silence hovers between Giorgos and the two of us sitting on the cane chairs opposite him.

'I find that hard to believe,' Dimitri says. 'I mean, are you sure? Have you been around the perimeter of the house? Are you here because you need help to get back in?'

'No, I don't need help. We've examined everything. Nothing doing. The only person who's able to get in and out is that boyfriend of my wife. Calls himself Edris. Comes from Afghanistan or some place.'

'Is Edris in there now?'

'Yes. He leant out of a window and shouted down to me when I was outside the gate. He said he would stay there to look after the bear. That bear! That ridiculous animal my wife brought back from Bulgaria.'

We sit in bewilderment. So, I think, Edris has kept quiet about his private entry and exit point through the railings.

'Well,' I say, feebly, 'I suppose Edris will clean up for you while this sorts itself out. And what's happened to your wife? She's not stuck in there too, is she?'

'Good God, no! She left in someone's car. She's taken over the Penthouse Suite at the Palace Hotel while she waits for our boat to come and pick her up to take her back to Hydra.'

Giorgos stubs his cigarillo on a plate containing the remains of our meal. As I pour more water into our glasses, I hastily repress a sudden urge to laugh. The thought of this man being stuck outside his house by an invisible wall seems, if it weren't so bewildering, hysterically funny.

'Look, I haven't come all the way up this dirt track to talk about my house,' Giorgos says, before sipping some water as the cicadas quieten. 'My daughter collapsed last night and ended up in Emergency at *your* hospital.' He emphasises "your" as if to say the hospital is Dimitri's own property and he's personally responsible for all the mismanagement there.

'Oh, I'm sorry to hear that,' Dimitri says. 'Must've happened off my watch. No, I wasn't there last night. Your daughter got out, did she, before the invisible wall went up?' Dimitri gives a hint of a smirk.

'That boyfriend of hers dragged her out, and they called an ambulance. Turned up at Emergency and there was mayhem. Chaos! Not a doctor or nurse anywhere. She lay for eight hours on a gurney in the corridor, gasping for breath. The boyfriend had to threaten an orderly before she got any attention. Then they put her in a cubicle and there was no oxygen. She couldn't breathe. Nothing!' Giorgos's voice rises and his neck reddens.

'Somehow a doctor appeared and gave her a shot of something and she came to. She nearly died. Have you got that?' His voice rises higher. 'Nearly died!'

'Well, Giorgos, it's a bad state of affairs in there. So sorry this happened. As I wasn't there, I can't comment on your daughter's situation. A frightening time for the girl, no doubt. Look, it's bad for everyone there. I'm afraid to say that this sort of thing happens every day. Ordinary people are dying because of the lack of equipment and staff.'

Giorgos repositions himself in his chair. Dimitri places his hands between his knees with his fingers touching and looks at Giorgos and says slowly, 'The hospital has run out of funds. There's no money to buy even the most basic medicines. Fortunately, we have some volunteer doctors and nurses from *Médecins Sans Frontières* who help us out when we are short-staffed. Our doctors and nurses work sixteen-hour days. We need help like a third world country, and we're in Europe.' I can tell Dimitri is trying to keep his cool. He sits back. 'And where is your daughter now?'

'At the Palace Hotel. We've got a nurse in to look after her, and I got some of the necessary medicines from a pharmacist I know. Cost me a fortune.'

'I see.'

We sit in silence again, and I pour more water. The clicking of the cicadas has gone, and a whiff of cool air comes down from the hills.

'Yes, I see,' Giorgos says. He puts a hand in his inside pocket, pulls out his phone and taps the keyboard. He is not phoning but making calculations.

'What do you need?'

'Everything,' Dimitri says, simply. 'The only thing we have left is the willingness and dedication of all the people working there, who sacrifice themselves for the patients, night and day, without remuneration.'

'What? Without pay?'

'Or reduced pay.'

'So, you need equipment, beds, medicines, space? That right?'

'Mmm. And that's just the beginning of the list.'

'In other words, we don't have a twenty-first century hospital in this city? Where have all the doctors gone?'

'Emigrated to Italy, England, America, Australia. They get paid in those countries and work reasonable hours. Here, we kill people because after twelve hours on the job we doctors and the nurses can't think or reason clearly.'

I study Giorgos intently. I don't know this man, nor the one who played theatre, the party man, the night before. There's humanity down there, somewhere. There must be.

He stands. 'I'm going to fix this. You'll hear from me tomorrow.' He steps forward and embraces Dimitri. 'Yes, you'll hear from me tomorrow.' He turns to me and says, 'Madam, thank you for your kindness.' He smiles charmingly again and kisses my proffered hand. 'Have a good night.' He strides through the kitchen and disappears. An engine starts and headlights swing down the drive.

'Do you think we'll hear from him again?' I say.

'Probably not. You know what they're like, these party people. Lots of promises and no delivery. Just wanted to blame someone for his daughter blowing her brains on coke. He'll find a private hospital to look after her. Can't imagine why she ended up in our hospital. The boyfriend probably didn't know any better.'

I dump the cigarillo butts and ash in the sink.

Dimitri is in bed when I get there, and we lie skin to skin, two spoons.

# - 30 -

A phone rings, but from where I can't tell. I open my eyes and see a shaft of early morning sunlight thrown obliquely across the bed. Above, a cobweb clings to the corner of the ceiling. I splay my hand over the sheets. Dimitri has gone. The phone rings again, and I pick it up with a tremor of anxiety. Is he all right? But it's Andreas, so early in the morning.

'Andreas?' I say.

'Yes.'

'Everything OK?'

'Not really.'

My throat tightens. 'Why? What's happened?'

'Yiannis is in hospital. We had to get an ambulance last night. He couldn't breathe, even with his home oxygen supply.'

'In hospital? How is he now?'

'He's in Intensive Care on a ventilator. They think he's got pneumonia. He's on an antibiotic drip.'

'Where are you?'

'At the hospital.'

'Why? Where's Fotis?'

'At home in bed. He's ill too. A fever. Dimitri gave me antibiotics for him. He's probably got pneumonia as well.'

'Oh, no. Are you all right? And Aunt Maria?'

'I'm OK, and Maria's always busy. She's out harvesting grapes on the top terraces.'

'Are you staying at the hospital?'

'No. Dimitri told me to go back to the house. There's nothing I can do here. They won't let me into Intensive Care.'

'Of course. Look, I'll call you later, to see how Fotis is.'

I hang up, give myself a hasty breakfast and text Dimitri as I know he'll not answer his phone. Unable to concentrate on my work, I decide to visit Maria's house to check on Fotis. As the wheels of my car spray the gravel on Maria's drive, her dogs release a cacophony of barking. When I stop before the house, their din dies down, replaced by a blanket of silence. I enter the kitchen. Only a flickering candle before an ikon of the Virgin Mary tucked in the corner disturbs the stillness. A vase of roses and oregano sits before it, and I picture Maria, as I have often seen her, murmuring prayers, there in the suffuse light. I go through the house and see Andreas asleep on the back veranda and Fotis, also on his bed, with his eyes shut and his breathing rushed.

Behind the house the terraces wind up, and I find Maria working her way to the top. Gasping, I reach her, yet she seems surprised and annoyed to see me. I almost turn to go back, but we talk as we climb. She is never out of breath, so used is she to these hills. She tells me in simple terms that Fotis will be all right. 'He is young and strong, takes after me,' she says. She adds that she is a little worried about Yiannis. 'Destiny will take its course as it always does. We cannot change the ways of God.' I help her pick the grapes, but only after she gives me strict instructions to not place mouldy ones in the basket.

'Do you need any help with Fotis?' I say.

'No, of course not. That young man, Andreas, is very attentive. He'll make sure he's OK, with glasses of tea and cloths of vinegar on his forehead. He'll pull through. You'll see.'

We continue cutting grapes in silence as swallows dive from atop a crumbling goatherd's croft. Maria slings the basket on her back and walks down the hill. My phone buzzes. It's Dimitri: *No need to come in. Kanaris is here, asking after you.*

Back at the house Maria packs a few toiletries for Yiannis and hands me a cheese sandwich before I take my leave. I look out on the back veranda and see Andreas awake.

'How's Fotis?'

'Weak, can hardly stand up. Walks two paces and he's out of breath. I hope the antibiotics kick in soon. He hasn't eaten anything.'

'I'll ring you later to see how you are going.'

*  *  *

I hurry into the hospital with the bag for Yiannis. Emergency seems less harried than a few days ago, and I greet several doctors and nurses as I come in. I see Nina, the nurse I spoke to at the Kanaris party, and also Zina as she comes through the swing doors, working harder than anyone.

'Where's Dimitri?' I say to Nina.

'Up in ICU, checking on his uncle. You can't go up there, you know. He's in the Infectious Diseases ward.'

'Can you call Dimitri and tell him I'm here.'

'Sure.'

I wait around, wondering if I should go, until Dimitri appears, followed by Tomas and Kanaris.

'Yiannis? How is he?' I say.

'I couldn't get near him in ICU and Infectious Diseases,' Dimitri says. 'He's struggling, though. They're doing all they can, but he's struggling. They might have to take him off the ventilator because there's some sort of strange pneumonia going about and other younger people need the breathing apparatus. We'll just have to see.'

Dimitri pushes back his green cap and wipes his brow. He looks white.

'I've just been explaining to Mr Kanaris and Tomas here that it's in this sort of emergency that we need more equipment, and we just haven't got it.'

'Don't you worry, my boy,' Kanaris says. 'I've been talking to Tomas here and taking notes. See?' He holds up a pad with notes and figures. 'By tomorrow night you'll have more staff. I've got my list of things this hospital needs and my list of contacts in China.' He wipes his brow with a white silk handkerchief and points to his head, indicating that he, in his cleverness, knows the right people when needed. 'I do business all over the world, and everyone loves a holiday in Greece.'

He turns to me and says, 'Goodbye, my dear lady. So nice to see you again.' He takes my proffered hand, bows towards it and kisses the air. Through the glass main doors of Emergency, I see a black limousine and a chauffeur waiting outside. Accompanied by his bodyguard, Kanaris exits and slides into the back seat, and the limousine drives away.

'You still working?' I say to Dimitri. 'No time for a break?'

'Not now,' he says. 'It's time for me to give Zina a break.'

'Perhaps we could manage a coffee at that taverna round the corner, eh, Tomas?'

'Sure,' Tomas says, looking over his glasses. 'Catch you later, Dima.'

Tomas and I walk around the corner and settle ourselves at a wobbly table on the pavement.

# - 31 -

I re-enter the hospital but can't locate Dimitri anywhere. The only person I find is Nina, and she tells me he is operating or upstairs in ICU. I text him but receive no reply. All I can do is go home.

On my way I call in to check on Fotis. Andreas greets me from the veranda and tells me Fotis is still in bed, unable to get up, and Maria is busy in the kitchen.

'How is he?' I say.

'The same,' Andreas says.

'Have you spoken to Dimitri?'

'Yes. He told me to take Fotis off the antibiotics, give him medication for his fever and plenty of liquids, and to give him Yiannis's oxygen if he has trouble breathing. I haven't had to do that yet.'

'You realise he has something very infectious, don't you?'

'Yes, Dimitri said to keep him isolated and for me not to go near him or Maria.'

'You should use the outside bathroom. You mustn't catch this. Uncle Yiannis is very ill.'

'I know. Maria has made some food for you. It's on the kitchen table.'

'I'll have to refuse it because we have to be very careful. I'll say goodbye to her from the veranda and then go. You keep away from her too. Eat outside here.'

\*   \*   \*

I hear the wheels of Dimitri's car crunch the gravel outside. He's back early, and I hurry to the top of the stairs, concerned that he, too, is ill. But he jumps out of the car, full of smiles, bounds up the steps and we hug.

'Everything all right?' I say. 'You're home early.'

'It's been a good day,' he says.

'Tomas told me you'd had a heart check-up.'

'Naughty boy. I was going to tell you myself.'

'It's not serious, is it?'

'No.'

I follow him into the bedroom and watch him undress. He enters the bathroom and turns on the shower, and we talk, accompanied by rushing water and billowing steam.

'That's why you had those chest pains,' I say.

'They're not really pains. Just beating, like an adrenalin rush. I thought it was because of my work load. I'll be right now—just need to take a pill everyday, and it'll stay under control.'

'Are you sure?'

'Course, I'm sure. Don't worry. I saw the cardiologist. It's just what I thought.'

'Why didn't you tell me?'

'I didn't want to worry you. It's not serious. OK? Come here.' We kiss, and linger on it, his lips pressed to mine, and he embraces my buttocks. 'Hey, are we going to do this right now? Or have a drink?'

'A drink, first, I think.'

We pick up a bottle of spumante and some bread and anchovies and wander out onto the veranda, his hand still on my buttock.

'You know what the worst thing about every day was?' he says.

'No, what?'

'Getting into the car and finding I didn't have enough petrol to get home.'

'Yes, and then looking for it.'

# - 32 -

I spend the morning gathering my thoughts, trying to type my notes for Chloe at The Guardian. There have been a lot of hits on my Greek Notes column as the rest of Europe look on and wonder whether Greece's debt crisis will cause contagion in Europe's banks. Instead of trying to decipher the intricacies of the financial meltdown, I decide to describe what's happening at the hospital and how the lack of equipment and staff impacts real people. Hard to understand in Germany and Belgium, I think wryly to myself. But my concern for Dimitri suffuses my thoughts, for last night he told me he has a heart problem. He brushed it off by saying, 'Oh, it's nothing,' but the thought and worry of it wrangles in my mind.

I decide to paint our new room. I tie my hair in a turquoise scarf and wear shorts and one of Dimitri's old t-shirts. The afternoon light beams warmly through the windows, and the music on the radio competes with the cricket chirp outside. As I stand on a ladder and paint the window frames, I hear an approaching car that sounds too close to be passing on the road below the house. Who's that? I wonder. I dismount the ladder and stand at the kitchen door and watch a burgundy soft-topped Volkswagen with its roof down pull up outside. For a second I fail to recognise the driver until I realise it's Giorgos Kanaris, dressed not in an executive suit but a frayed pair of jeans and a washed-out t-shirt. He appears to be without his usual entourage of driver and bodyguard.

'Giorgos, this is a surprise,' I say. 'What brings you here? Bit out of your way, isn't it?'

'Just thought I'd drop by to see you.'

'Dimitri's not here, I'm afraid. He's at the hospital.'

'No, it's you I've come to see.' He bounds up the steps and takes my hand and kisses it, pressing his lips to my fingers for a moment longer than necessary.

'Oh.' I feel my face flush with embarrassment.

He looks ten years younger in his casual clothes and with his hair windblown and mussed up.

'Do come in, yes, come in.'

But Kanaris doesn't need inviting, for he has already strode through the kitchen and entered the living room. He stops and surveys Dimitri's collection of artworks. He smooths his hand over a wood-veined bust of a female nude.

'Is this you?' he says.

'Of course not.' I flush again.

'Mmm, nice piece. Where'd you get it?'

'Athens. A gallery there.'

'Better get the name of it. I'd like one of these.'

He picks up Dimitri's Mycenaean gods, fingers our ikon of St Nicholas and murmurs approval.

I wish he wouldn't.

'How about a drink on the veranda?' I say.

'Yes, sure, why not. The view of the sea's stunning. Here, I'll give you a hand.'

'No, I'll fix it.' I want to get him onto the veranda, but he follows me into the kitchen and crowds my space. I lead him outside, plump up the cushions on the divan and remove magazines and books.

'Back in a minute,' I say. 'Fruit juice?'

'Sure.'

I bring out the green glasses with the juice and a plate of yellow lemon pastries which he waves away.

'This is juice from our oranges, but there's tropical if you'd prefer.'

'Orange is just fine, thanks.'

I place the glass in front of him, and he crosses his legs. He props one leg on his bent knee, exposing his tanned ankles above his calf-skin loafers, and sips his juice. Silence lies between us as below the cicadas shrill. He glances at me and then away, out to the sea beyond, and I wonder whether I should talk about the weather or apologise for my appearance by saying, 'Sorry I'm looking a bit untidy, but I'm painting our new room.'

Suddenly, he says, 'You don't think I've forgotten about the promises I made to fix things at the hospital, do you? You remember I made a list when I was last here. Well, I've been working through it. I've recruited some doctors and nurses from Albania to work at the hospital. They're already here.'

'But how did you manage that?'

'Contacts. I do business in Albania.'

Business? I think. What sort of business? Wasn't Albania run by criminal gangs? I rein in my thoughts. The man is sending doctors and nurses, and Dimitri needs them at the hospital.

As if he can read my suspicions, he says, 'You are probably wondering whether Albanian medics can be trusted. Well, they sure can be, only they get a pitiful salary, if any. I'll employ them, pay them and supply them to the hospital. They're jumping at the chance to get out of their country and into Europe.'

'That's good to hear. Dimitri and the other doctors need help. They're overworked and exhausted.'

'I've got medicines and equipment on the way too. Coming from China. Should be here in a couple of weeks.'

'Thank you for doing all this.' I pause before adding rather regrettably, 'I didn't think you'd do anything.'

'I knew you thought that. Now you know I'm a man of my word. If I promise something, I keep it. Not many people can be trusted around here these days.'

I don't know what he means by that, but I'm extremely grateful to him. Dimitri needs to work a normal eight-hour shift.

'Does Dimitri know about all this?'

'Yes, he showed the new medics around this morning.'

He looks across at me and smiles. He then leans over and pats my knee. The jeans, the smile, his promises and actions break the formality of our previous encounters.

'We'll soon have that hospital oiled and up and running. You'll see. And I'm finalising plans to build a new wing.'

I raise my eyes in surprise. 'And how will that be funded?'

'I've got the funds. I'll call it the Kanaris Wing.' He gives a loud laugh, at himself. I find his enthusiasm infectious. We could almost be friends. Is this the end of his visit? I wonder.

'Shall I make you some lunch?' I say, a bit too impulsively, I fear.

'No, no. I don't eat lunch, but I'll have a lemon tart and a bit more juice.'

He leans over, and as I place the glass of juice on the table, he covers my hand with his, holds it and then, with the lightest of touches, brushes his fingers up my arm to my shoulder.

# - 33 -

I wish Dimitri would come home. He should be early today because he's got help at the hospital.

Kanaris has gone. Some time ago. How he went, I can't remember. Did I kick him out? Force him out? Edge him out? Persuade him ever so gently out? I can't remember.

Voices fill my head, repeating phrases.

*Nothing happened.*

*Nothing happened? … Or did it?*

*No, nothing happened … at all.*

*Treat him with kindness. You should be grateful to this man. He has money, he's a decision maker.*

*What? Me? Be grateful?*

*Yes, you. Everybody needs his help. At the hospital. He's brought in staff and now he's bringing equipment. And paying for it. Just be nice. That's all you have to be. Nice.*

All I can remember—it's etched in my mind—is having no underwear on under my t-shirt. It was a hot, sweaty day. That's the only reason. I wasn't expecting anyone to turn up just like that. And he kept fumbling, edging up my body with one hand, up under my t-shirt, and up my leg with his other hand. And he was breathing hard. So hard. Then what? I slapped him. Slapped him away, didn't I?

Oh God! What have I done?

Just be nice. Calm.

'I think you'd better go,' I'd said.

Oh God! Now what have I done? Told him to go. 'Get out!' I've ruined it for everybody. Everybody.

And then he left.

I wish Dimitri would come home.

I sit on the veranda for a long time and look at the horizon, at the line joining sky and sea, two elements, two shades of blue. The cicadas scream on.

I mount the ladder again and paint the window frames, yet I can't keep the brush steady. My hand shakes, and I smudge the glass as unbidden tears roll down my face, which I wipe with a rag.

I step down from the ladder and go out onto the veranda and see the two glasses, the half-eaten pastries, the crumpled cushion on the floor and the cigarillo butt squashed on the ceramic ash tray. I clean it all up and smooth out the cushions in a rush, not wanting even a trace of this afternoon to tarnish the veranda. I want to shower, but I hear Dimitri's car outside, so I go to the kitchen door to greet him.

'Hey, what have you been doing? Painting?' he says. 'You've got paint all over your face.'

'Yes, that's right.'

He enters the kitchen. 'Guess who I just saw when I was coming out of the hospital? Giorgos Kanaris. That guy never stops talking. He goes on and on about all he's doing for the hospital and how he'll be able to get anything we need for the place through him. He says it's his new pet project. Oh, and

234

by the way, he thinks you're lovely and that I'm a very lucky man.'

I slump into the cushions on the divan. I don't want to tell him about Kanaris's visit, so I don't. I try to think of something to say. Calmly.

'Are you happy with the medics from Albania?' I say.

'Very.'

'That's good.' I get up. 'I think I'll have a shower. I'm really dirty.' He doesn't know why, and he'll never know how much. 'Can you light up the grill? There's calamari in the fridge.'

'Sure.'

My senses dull to grey fog. Usually I'd be glad to see him home but not tonight.

Later, we sit and eat the fish, which he has bathed in oil and lemon juice, and I pick listlessly at the grilled cheese. Dimitri seems oblivious to my languidness and enthuses about the Albanian doctors and their efficiency and professionalism. He jumps up and tells me of a distant star he needs to observe through his telescope, and he calls me over and invites me to look at it. He then turns me and kisses me deeply. We go to the bedroom, slip between the cool sheets and make love. Deeply. Passionately. I give myself over to him more than I ever have done before.

Afterwards, he says, 'Nice, eh?'

'Very.'

'Do you like your new ring? Happy with the idea?'

'Very. Very.' I kiss him deeply again. Thank goodness for you, I think.

We warmly embrace and sleep until a ringing phone wakes us. Dimitri lifts it up and puts it on speaker.

'Dimitri?' a voice says.

'Yes.'

'It's Andreas. They've just rung from the hospital. Yiannis has passed away.'

\* \* \*

We gather in Maria's kitchen, where she has already set up an altar in the corner, lit a candle before a gold ikon and placed a photo of Yiannis next to a vase of mini chrysanthemums. She wears black with a heavy scarf on her head and clutches a handkerchief which she twists in her hands and uses to mop her eyes. Weeping and grief spread across the table, into gold-rimmed coffee cups and onto the mauve dishes filled with cakes. Maria bemoans not keeping him at home. 'It was the hospital that killed him,' she says between sobs. 'If only, if only …' But her voice wavers off into the distant land of sadness.

Two days later Dimitri and I stand outside the church on the square. We nod to people and kiss and shake hands with the town folk who have come to grieve with Maria. Dina and Vassilis, the butcher and his wife from whom I rented my flat, Costas and Anna from the Boutique Olive Farm and Alexi, who grasps my hand and kisses my cheeks twice.

Inside the church Dimitri weeps beside me, for, he says, it's his mother's funeral all over again. The priest's chanting brings a solemn calm. He waves a gold thurible, and puffs of incense waft over the congregation, who respond in unison to an ancient liturgy. The female mourners, their bowed heads covered in black scarves, lead the chorus with quivering voices from the depths of antiquity.

I follow the priest as Dimitri helps carry the coffin out of the church, and I find myself beside Alexi.

'Perhaps I should come with you up to the olive farm,' I say, 'and help you get everything ready for the reception after the burial. We'll have plenty of time while everyone is at the ceremony.'

'Sounds good to me,' Alexi says.

I tell Dimitri I'm going on ahead with Alexi, then go over and get into Alexi's car.

We wind up the hill to Arini. It's been awhile since I've been up there, and we stop at the spring, and Alexi gets out with his glass flasks and fills them with the cool water gushing from the mossy stones. We cup our hands and douse each other's faces, laughing, which somehow, and I don't know why, brings back memories of Kanaris and the divan on the veranda. Back in the car, we continue to climb the hill, and my throat tightens and tears roll down my cheeks.

'Hey, are you OK?' Alexi says, looking over at me. 'You're not crying, are you?'

'No.'

'Yes, you are. I didn't realise you were so close to Dimitri's uncle.'

'It's not that. He was a good man, but I didn't know him that well. My tears have nothing to do with him. It's just that I had a bad day yesterday.'

'Oh, sorry. I didn't mean to pry.'

'It's OK.'

We arrive at the farm and get out and walk under the vine and into the kitchen. I manage to compose myself, and Alexi hands me tablecloths to lay on the long table under the shade of the grapevines and shows me the cutlery and glasses to set out. Back in the kitchen we work together, decorating the fish dishes and pastries he has prepared and filling red and yellow plates with sweet biscuits decorated with sesame seeds.

'Drink?' he says, handing me a glass of water from a flask.

'Thank you. I love your pastries. Let me try one.' I give a little laugh as I take a bite. 'Mmm. What's in this?'

'Sardines and dill.'

I pause and examine it for a minute, then say, 'You must be wondering why I was crying before.'

'Well, yes. You're not ill, are you? Dimitri OK?'

I tell him about what happened with Kanaris on the veranda and how I couldn't bring myself to tell Dimitri. I cry again, and as I prop myself on a stool, I wish my tears would stay firm, but they won't.

'Nothing happened, you know,' I keep repeating. 'Nothing.'

Alexi leans over and hugs me. 'You'd better tell Dimitri.'

'But I can't. He can't fall out with Kanaris, what with the new staff and equipment he's bringing to the hospital. They need it. He's paying for it all out of his own pocket. You know the government has no money.'

'The man's a bastard.'

'On the one hand, yes, but on the other, he's doing good. We need him.'

'Let's pick some grapes to put on these platters for table decoration. Here, you take this one, and I'll do the other.'

We stand on wobbly stools under the vine and fill the basket hanging between us. The drinks and plates of biscuits are on the table by the time the first cars drive into the courtyard.

Alexi and I serve the guests, filling glasses for toasts to the lost loved one and heating the sardine-filled pastries. We spend more time in the kitchen than outside. I pass by Dimitri as he comforts Maria and swaps childhood stories with Sophie, the butcher's daughter. I pause, hand him an extra cake, brush him with a kiss and move on.

The sky is gold when the last cars leave. Alexi hugs me and whispers, 'Thanks for everything.' I feel his warmth as a cool autumnal breeze comes from the hills. I squash into the back of Dimitri's car, between Fotis and Andreas, and we wave goodbye to Alexi.

# - 34 -

Dimitri drives me to the Patras railway station, and we stand on a platform, waiting for the train to Athens which is due any minute. Nearby, youths in beanies and hoods jostle for position. Some stare at phones while others converse in raised voices, as Greeks do, afraid their interlocutor might miss a word. Young men with nothing to do, following the pack, waiting. I'm travelling to Athens to stay with Katerina and Tomas so she can take me to the refugee camps. Next month, after my return, they'll come to Arini to witness our wedding.

'I wish I wasn't going,' I say to Dimitri. 'I hate to leave you now. We have so much to do for the wedding.'

'Oh no, it's going to be simple,' Dimitri says. 'Crowns of flowers under the grapevine, plates of all the food we love and lots of happy people and music. You'll see!'

I hug him and kiss him as if I am bound for a journey to the moon.

The train approaches and cushions to a halt. I step forward and embark at the door before us, away from the pack of jostling youths.

'You'll text me when you get there, won't you?' he says.

'Of course. I'll call you.' I lean out and touch his fingers, and the train moves away. Waves of emotion engulf me. I don't know why. I'll only be away for a few days.

I find a window seat and gaze out at the vista as the train passes disused factories, unfinished apartment blocks, broken cement, cranes, bulldozers and other machinery abandoned goodness knows how long ago. I've seen this view before, along many other railway lines, all revealing the backside of human existence, the forgotten shambles of life. I can hear the youths shouting in the next carriage.

A young woman sits opposite me and smiles. She has a long, glossy plait with a bow slung over her shoulder and a shiny black mini skirt. She reaches under the seat for her bag, unzips it and produces two bread rolls, which she slices in half with deft fingers, as if she does this every morning. She peels back the lid of a tin of sardines and tips the contents into the rolls.

'You like some?' she says, offering. She has a slightly gravelly voice, from too many cigarettes, I deduce.

'Er, no, thanks,' I say. 'So kind of you.' I don't want to offend her, but fish early in the morning isn't my thing.'

'You going to Athens?'

'That's right.'

'First time for you in Athens?'

'No, not really. I've been there before.'

'Athens is not a good place right now. You be careful. There are migrants everywhere there, stealing from people. They're hungry, but there's no food for them and no money. You know our politicians and bankers did a deal with that bank Goldman Sachs and wrecked our economy.' It's a story I've heard before. 'And now the Germans won't help us, and we are being invaded by migrants.'

She munches hard on her sardine roll, and after a minute of silence she sticks out her hand, 'Hi, Philomena's the name.'

'Marina.' I shake her hand.

'You know, Marina, we're just pawns in their games. I lost my job. I used to be a teacher, but they ran out of money and closed the school and just moved all the kids to another school, ten kilometres away, and sent all us teachers back home.'

She slumps back into her seat and finishes her roll, then removes a plastic water bottle filled with cold coffee and tips her head back. With drooping lips and a mouth turned sullen, she looks at me and says with a bitter voice, 'Can't buy anything on these trains. They're all robbers. Want some coffee?'

'No, thanks. You keep it for yourself. I've got some water.'

We sit in silence until I say, 'So sorry to hear you've lost your job.' My words seem inordinately pathetic in comparison to her plight. 'I can't possibly understand what you are going through.'

'Don't you worry about me,' she says, 'I've moved in with my grandparents. There's six of us living on my grandfather's pension. I'm just telling you to look after yourself in the big city.' She inserts earplugs, leans back again and shuts her eyes.

The train stops at the occasional station, where a lone station master has decorated the platform with a pot of geraniums. I suck at my water bottle and jot notes in my journal. I draw a few sketches too, as I often do. I'm no great artist, but I can do a reasonable pencil drawing of things I wish to remember. The plait over her shoulder, the black skirt, the sullen lips, the coffee in the plastic bottle, her deft fingers filling the bread roll. I then doze until a voice over the intercom announces "Athens".

'We're here,' Philomena says.

I jolt into consciousness. 'Oh, thanks.'

241

'Don't forget, watch out for yourself.' Her skirt stretches over her bottom in front of me.

'Don't worry, I will.' I grab my bag from the rack above, follow her and disembark into a shoving crowd.

I see Katerina waiting for me on the platform, and she greets me with hugs and a warm smile.

'Hello,' she says. 'You made it. So good to see you. Come now, we'll go for a little drive through the city and then head to my place.'

As she trips along the platform in chunky sandals, her skirt sways in tune with her hips and full hair.

She drives me through the city and points out the damage from riots in the main shopping district and Syntagma Square. Broken windows, carcasses of burnt-out cars, street corners where milling youths still gather with nothing to do.

'It's not a good idea to drive round here,' she says. 'Any of these kids could attack the car if we stop. They're burning with pent-up anger, frustration and hopelessness. Most have lost their jobs—if they had one. Just thought you'd like to see what's happened here and what the atmosphere's like.'

We travel down a narrow street near the centre of town, and Katerina pulls up outside a portico. She jumps out, opens the double doors and squeezes the car into an internal courtyard, a haven of citrus trees in terracotta pots and purple bougainvillea draping the walls. Pano rushes out of the house, and she picks him up and swings him around. 'Oh, my beautiful boy!' she says. She tickles him as we go through a pair of French doors into a cool living room. She shows me to my room upstairs. I look out the window to the courtyard below and then across the roofs beyond to a small square with a church and a market.

Later, as I sit and watch Katerina bustle in the kitchen, preparing dinner, Tomas appears, home from work.

'Well,' he says, 'has Katerina given you an eyeful of the mess our city is in? It's not good for tourism. After dinner we'll go out for a beer at that bar in the little square you can see from your window. I know the owner. It's a bit risky to go any further.'

By the time we arrive at the square at dusk, only a few customers sit about the bar. We sip our beers and talk about the hospital and then the camps, when suddenly, over Tomas's shoulder, I see a woman, with a familiar plait with a bow and black skirt, walking towards the square, and I recognise her as Philomena from the train. How can this be? This coincidence. She lingers near the tables until a silver-haired man sitting alone beckons her over. She approaches the man's table and they talk for a minute. He pulls out his wallet and hands her some notes, and he stands and they walk off together. I watch her become a distant spot down the narrow street.

Tomas notices my eyes drifting across the square and says, 'Seen someone you know?'

'Yes,' I say.

He turns around and says, 'Ah, yes, Philomena. She comes here every evening to ply her trade. She's one of many. You see, the jobless have to live somehow.'

'You know her? But I met her on the train this morning.'

'Really? She lives around here somewhere.'

I'm too taken aback by this coincidence. 'I don't like strange coincidences,' I blurt. 'They bring bad luck.' I don't know why I say this. Now anxious, I tell myself it means nothing.

I phone Dimitri as soon as I return to my room upstairs. I'm missing him already.

'Are you OK ?' I say.

'Of course. I'm fine,' he says.

I tell him of my meeting on the train.

243

# - 35 -

The next morning we reach the refugee camp at 6 a.m. Katerina shows her pass and tells the guard, whom she knows, that I am a social worker from an NGO. He waves us through the gates, and we head up a dusty road towards queues of people already lined up outside a medical clinic, waiting for attention.

'Here, put this on,' Katerina says, handing me a mask. 'You'll need this as protection against a bit of everything here. Look over there, the clinic opens at six-thirty, but the people start queuing at 4 a.m. because they are desperate for treatment. We'll visit the women's section first and see how they're faring.'

We arrive at an area surrounded by a wire fence that separates and protects the vulnerable women and minors from the dangers lurking in the rest of the camp. We meet with Katerina's translator and visit the tents and those few fortunate enough to have found a hut.

'I'm just a sanitation inspector,' Katrina says to me. 'I check the toilet blocks, drinking water, personal hygiene, cleanliness of living conditions, access to food, overcrowding, kids and all the rest.'

When inside the tents, we look about and then sit. Katerina talks to the women, who detail long lists of needs and complaints. I take notes. A foetid stench runs through everything. Bedding lies piled in a corner, an odour of stale frying oil penetrates the walls, and the children have runny noses and need their hair washed.

'A lot of the children have scabies,' Katerina says. 'Neighbours steal each other's food and washing materials, and the women wear nappies at night because they're too afraid to go to the toilet block after dark.' She flips the pages of her notebook. 'There is a sense of hopelessness here. Depression makes people give up on personal hygiene and their will to do anything, especially after having their application for asylum rejected over and over again.' She releases a wry laugh. 'You wouldn't believe this, but the government employs people to run this camp—people responsible for keeping the rubbish off the roads, cleaning the toilet blocks, supplying food, organising washing facilities and looking after these refugees—but they don't do a damn thing.' I see she's angry now, frustrated with it all.

We enter an office building signed *Camp Management*, and Katerina barges through the outer reception area and into the office of the director. She slams her list on his desk and berates him for the lack of organisation, the filth and rubbish, and the paucity of care and amenities needed in the camp. Her voice rises to a higher pitch, and she talks so fast in an Athenian dialect that I fail to understand her.

The director, Aristide, with his sagging jowls and sweaty bald head, sits there mute, almost bored and removes a white handkerchief from his pocket and mops his brow.

'Are you accusing me of stealing stuff?' he suddenly shouts at her. 'Are you? Have you any idea what's going on in this camp?

Eh? Probably not. Well, let me tell you, there's a flourishing black market going on here. Everyone's selling anything they can lay their hands on.' His voice rises a pitch higher than hers. 'Yes, that's right, everything from drugs to toilet paper. All brought in by the government and the goodly charities. I've just got to make sure there is some sort of peace kept between these gangs and no one gets killed while trading.'

'I'll be back tomorrow to check on everything that's written here,' Katerina says as she stabs her index finger on the list.

She turns and storms from the room. I follow her, and outside the room she says, 'Look, what he said is probably true, but I threatened him anyway that he'd lose his job if he didn't get his act together. I bet he's been creaming off some of the food stores and other stuff for himself and his family. I told him I had friends in high places who could easily find someone else to step into his shoes. Guys like him get these jobs through political friends and then just sit on their bums and try to get as much out of it for themselves as they can.' She calms. 'We'll head down to the medical clinic. You hungry?'

'No, I'm fine thanks.' I've lost my appetite. 'I'll take a swig from my water bottle.'

At the medical clinic the queue has become a milling crowd. We enter and find the inside cramped and hot. Katerina checks the cupboards for supplies, the sinks and benches for cleanliness and turns over the paper sheet on each bed. I stand at the doorway as there's not enough room inside.

Two volunteer women doctors from the Netherlands tend the room and deal with everything from febrile children to stomach pains, pregnant women and seizures.

Dr Jasmine takes Katerina aside and lists what the clinic needs: sutures, drugs, sterilising equipment, gloves, masks, sheets, oxygen tanks. Everything, it seems.

As we go to leave, a commotion breaks out amidst the crowd outside, and shouting and crying ring through the door. A young man approaches us, dragging a companion who has a knife in his back and blood splaying down his t-shirt. They brush past me, and I feel the warmth of the blood on my arm and gasp. The doctors slip into action, and Dr Jasmine, with a steady calm, briskly and swiftly unfolds a stretcher, has the victim lie on it and staunches the blood. As I watch in horror, nausea swells inside me, and I break free from the room's chaos and rush outside into the crowd.

I stagger to the other side of the road and sit on the kerb under the welcomed shade of an olive tree. My hand trembles as I sip from my water bottle. With a damp tissue, I frantically attempt to wipe the blood off my arm. I feel contaminated: by the blood, by the stench, by the tension permeating the air. I see the sun high in the sky, and I feel light-headed. All I want to do is leave. I need Katerina to get me out of here, but she remains inside the clinic. All I can do is wait.

Half an hour later she comes across the road.

'Ah, you're here,' she says.

'What happened?' I say. 'Is that boy all right?'

'He will be. I think.' She pauses and ponders. 'It's a nasty wound. They've staunched the blood and put him on a drip, but he's conscious. I don't think the knife hit any vital organs. They need to get him to hospital. The ambulances take ages. You know how it is, the refugees are always last, but luckily those doctors in there know what to do. They're doing this stuff every day. Delivering babies and saving lives.'

'Was the boy in a fight?'

'Something like that. Just as the director said. The boy overstepped the mark. Started selling his black market stuff on someone else's territory, and all hell broke loose. An argument, a few punches thrown about and then out comes the knife. The police will be called, and the perpetrator will end up in prison and wallow away there forever. It's tough.'

She sits beside me on the kerb for a minute and then says, 'Well, that's it for today. We'll go now. I need food, and the boys will be home from school soon.'

We drive home in silence, enter her courtyard with its flowers and lemon trees and step on the cool tiles of the living room. Katerina's maid has prepared meat balls and salad for lunch and placed chunks of crispy bread in a basket on the table. I am suddenly ravenous and dig in as we talk in low tones.

'I don't know how you can go there every day,' I say.

'I don't go every day,' she says. 'But you get used to it, and I've made good friends with some of those Syrian families. They are well-educated and speak good English and are so appreciative of anything I can do for them. I've become their lifeline to the outside world. I help them with their documents and get them to the front of the queue or to the top of the pile. It's quite satisfying.'

After lunch I go upstairs to my room and shower. Cleansed, I lie on the bed and wake to find I've slept for two hours.

Later, we head to the square—it's obviously an evening habit—and order beers and wine. Again Philomena appears. She exchanges money with a client and walks off down the road, but suddenly she turns, looks at me, and, strangely, beckons me to follow her. Has she recognised me from the train the other day? Or is this theatre? I turn away, but her presence and gestures make me uneasy.

Katerina looks across at me and says, 'Take no notice of her. She's like that. Weird. Odd.'

Upstairs in my bedroom I hurry to facetime Dimitri. I'm so glad to see him and talk of other things. I want distraction, for the day has brought me down. I tell him about the refugee camp, but he seems unmoved, for he has seen these things a thousand times himself.

He talks about harvesting the olives—one of his many enthusiasms.

'I've been getting out the nets for the olive harvest for when you get back. We'll have to get started soon. I'm just preparing everything. Cleaning up the baskets, looking for the beaters. We always have a good time harvesting. It'll only take a few days. Everyone comes around, and we eat and drink and fire up the grill all day. When we've finished, we can focus on preparing for our big celebration.' He pauses, concern on his face. 'Are you feeling OK?'

'Yes, I'm fine, much better, now I'm speaking to you. I wish you were here.'

'Me too. I so wish I was there with you, but I've got a bit of a sore throat. Probably caught it from Fotis. Hope I'm not getting anything.'

# - 36 -

I spend the next day writing up my notes and then send my report to Chloe. She writes back about how pleased she is with my eyewitness account of what's occurring in the Greek camps, especially given the reports now appearing on TV news bulletins every day about migrants flooding across the Aegean Sea from Turkey to Greece. *It's good to get your perspective on how it is*, she writes. Her appreciation of my report makes the grimness of the previous day's events worth the effort.

In the evening we go down to the square for drinks. Again, Philomena appears and plies her trade. Her presence unsettles me and spoils my viewing of the sun setting over the terracotta roofs.

Suddenly, she approaches me and says, 'Still here? Remember what I told you on the train. Look after yourself in the big city. There are dangers here.' She strides off arm in arm with her silver-haired suitor.

'I don't like her,' I say to Katerina.

'Don't let her bother you. She's harmless.' She tries to reassure me with a pat on my knee.

Back at the house I facetime Dimitri who, at only nine o'clock, is already in bed.

'Are you all right?' I say, a little anxious.

'Sure. I told you yesterday I had a cold coming on, and now I've got a bit of a fever. Thought I'd better try and shake it off before I return to the hospital.'

'I wish I was there with you. I miss you terribly. I like to do things with you. You know, cook together and sit on the veranda and eat and drink and talk about what's happening and why everything is as it is. Nothing tastes the same without you. Katerina and Tomas are kind and generous, but they have their own lives with their boys.'

The coldness of the glass screen tempers our parting kisses.

I lie awake and stare at the ceiling and the flurry of dust motes in the moonbeam crossing my bed. I remember the evening Dimitri and I slept in the shepherds' house in the mountains: the stillness of the summer night, the horse-hair mattress, his leg stretched out beyond the covers and propped on the window sill as his toes twiddled the shutter latch.

Next morning, I rise early, and we head to the camp again. We visit the men's quarters and find them in more disarray and impoverishment than the women's. Katerina berates the men for the lack of order and cleanliness, but a pall of depression and hopelessness hangs about them as if nothing matters any more. Yesterday, we'd seen the women making the best they could out of tents and open-air spaces, but the men, without their women, are lost.

A man with a stethoscope round his neck sits on a stool outside a tent, seemingly though precariously in charge. He speaks perfect English when he tells us he is a nurse from Aleppo and can diagnose the ailments of the people and administer treatment if he has access to medication. As he speaks, he sews up a wound in a young boy's leg, and I wonder if he was involved in yesterday's stabbing in the camp.

'I'm not supposed to be doing this,' the nurse says, 'but somebody has to, so I do it even if my qualifications aren't recognised.'

I go to ask him a question, but he suddenly stands and enters the tent behind me. I follow him but stop outside when I see, through the open flap, lines of men kneeling in prayer on sacks and rags as an imam, with his palms raised heavenwards, recites prayers for his congregation. They are secure in their realm.

Katerina walks on ahead with her notepad and lists, and I catch up as she sits on a bench with a woman I'd seen the day before at the women's camp. I join them and Katerina introduces me to Samira. She, too, speaks perfect English and wears a fawn hijab enclosing large almond eyes above full, smooth cheeks. She gives no smile, just a steady gaze.

'Samira is leaving this camp tomorrow,' Katerina says to me.

'Are you?' I say to Samira. 'How long have you been here?'

'Too long,' she says. 'If we stay here much longer, my daughter will catch meningitis. There is meningitis everywhere in this camp. Children are getting it every day and disappearing to hospital. They are dying of it, and our spirits are dying away, too, with every day we sit stuck here.'

She seems more forthright and determined than her innocent face belies.

'Are you leaving alone? I mean, just your family?'

Samira pauses and tilts her head skywards. 'My husband is dead.' Her almond eyes fill with tears, but she steadies her lips.

'Oh, I'm so sorry.'

'Yes, he died in the Aegean Sea, halfway between Izmir and Lesbos. The sea was very rough, and someone stood up in the boat. It tipped to one side, and my son fell into the water. He couldn't swim, you know, so my husband jumped in to save him, but they both disappeared under the waves.'

She pauses and dabs her eyes with a corner of her hijab and remains silent. I don't want to dwell on her tragedy, yet I wish to learn more about what set her on her path to Europe.

'You speak excellent English,' I say.

'Thank you. I taught English in high school so I suppose I should. All our students studied English. It's essential to get on in life. My husband was a professor of Engineering.'

'And where was that?'

'Aleppo. My city has been destroyed, and my school lies in ruins. It was perilous for my husband to go to the university.'

'I see. Have you left family there?'

'Yes. My parents are still there. I wanted them to come with us, but my father is ill and my mother wouldn't leave without him.' Again, tears well in her eyes. 'My sisters and brother left, but I don't know where they are.' She screws the corner of her hijab in her fingers. 'Aleppo is a very dangerous place. Very dangerous. We were living in the cellar of our house at the end, and I was most afraid the army would come and force my son to join the government forces. We never took sides, you know, we just wanted peace, but it didn't come.'

Katerina takes her hand and says to me, 'I've tried to get everything I can for their trip tomorrow. Rucksacks, a tent, sleeping bags, warm clothes, boots and tinned food.'

'Where are you going?' I say to Samira.

'Germany. I have a cousin in Düsseldorf.'

We move inside Samira's tent behind us. She shares it with three other families. Each has a corner with their possessions piled in place. Samira's daughter, Adara, who looks about fourteen, sits cross-legged on the bedding, staring at an electronic device. She looks up and smiles shyly.

'I see you are packed up and ready to go,' Katerina says to Samira. 'Is there anything else you need?'

'Toiletries. You know, things for women's days. We are two women now.'

'I see, I see. We're leaving soon. I'll pass by a chemist to see what we can find. We'll be back in the morning.'

I follow Katerina around the camps while she checks the toilet blocks and the mini hospital housing the medical clinic. She asks Dr Jasmine about the welfare of the boy who was stabbed the day before.

'He is back in the camp,' Dr Jasmine says, 'and is leaving tomorrow with your friend Samira. They stitched him up in Emergency and let him go. There's no room for refugees without papers.'

Late afternoon, we return to Katerina's cool living room and sink into armchairs with icy drinks and cream pastries which the maid has set on the side tables. The boys come home from school and take up Katerina's attention, so I go upstairs and take a longed-for shower to rid myself of the contamination of the desperation in the camp.

I call Dimitri as he is probably still at home with his flu. He takes a while to answer, then finally he appears on screen.

'Hi,' I say.

'Oh, hi,' he says quietly. He looks worse than yesterday.

'How's your fever?'

'Getting worse. I got Fotis to bring over some antibiotics for me. They should start working soon.' He gives a couple of coughs. 'Had a good day?'

'I think I've seen and heard enough at the camp for a couple more articles. It's hard going. I think I'll come back the day after tomorrow. I hope you'll be better by then. We have the olives to harvest before our big day.'

# - 37 -

We arrive at the camp at six-thirty the next morning but find Samira, Adara and their possessions gone. Katerina asks a woman in the tent when Samira and Adara left, but the woman stares back blankly, then pulls up her face scarf, gathers her children in and shrinks into the corner.

At the clinic Dr Jasmine tells us that they left an hour ago. 'They'll be on their way to the station.'

As Katerina drives us across the city towards the station, I notice the streets are strangely quiet.

'Where is everybody?' I say.

'Special Secret Service forces carried out dawn raids in towns all over the country,' Katerina says. 'They arrested the leaders of Golden Dawn, the anti-government group that led the riots and demonstrations, and now they're all in prison and facing years of interminable investigations and trials. It was on the news this morning.'

She turns the car into a side street.

'The station's down there,' she says with a nod.

We travel along the street, but I can't see any sign of Samira.

'Oh,' Katerina says, 'and the other thing that happened overnight is the European Central Bank has refused to ease Greece's debt obligations. No concessions, no nothing. So we Greeks will just have to pull our belts even tighter while the Germans send in their accountants to watch over us and regulate how we run our country. They'll lend us more money to buy German goods and squeeze us dry until we repay our debts. Just lovely, isn't it? *Lovely*. We need to be taught a lesson, that's what they think. We are a lazy, incompetent people.' There is bitterness in her voice, bitterness because the country has been ticked off and sent home with fiscal minders to make sure the government tows the line.

We round a corner and approach a line of people walking towards the station, each carrying bags and laden down with rucksacks. Katerina parks the car, and we walk, weaving past the refugees, searching for Samira and Adara, but without success. When we reach the departure platform for the train to Thessaloniki, I see Samira and Adara sitting on their luggage, next to another family from her tent and the boy stabbed at the clinic two days earlier.

We hurry towards them, and I say, 'Ah, Samira, there you are. We've been looking for you everywhere. You got here early.'

'Yes, we left at five-thirty because I didn't want to miss the train. I wanted to be at the front of the platform and be one of the first to board. You see all these people?' I look about the platform crammed with people sitting or standing. Waiting. 'Everybody's leaving, fighting to get out.'

'I've brought you the things you asked for,' Katerina says, pulling out a plastic bag. 'Tampons, some antibiotics, paracetamol, antibacterial cream, handwash and other things. Oh, and here's some euro. You might need it to bribe the police to let you cross a border. Or even buy some bread.'

'Thank you, thank you, you are too kind. We lost all our money when my husband drowned in the sea. He had our cash sewn into the lining of his jacket. All I have is a credit card.'

'So you're taking the train to Thessaloniki?' I say. 'Then where will you go?'

'We will have to walk from Thessaloniki to the Macedonian border. Or get a bus. We're not sure if the bus will take us or not. We're refugees without papers. Illegal. People don't like us. They don't want us.'

'Maybe that money will help you get on the bus.'

'Maybe.'

'And who's this boy?' Katerina says, nodding at the youth who had been stabbed at the camp.

'This is Habib. He was stabbed because he got into a fight. It's too dangerous for him to stay alone in that camp.'

'Alone?'

'He became separated from his family on the trip from Aleppo, somewhere in Turkey, and he ended up attaching himself to us in Izmir. It's safer for unattached children and young people to travel with a family. I tell everyone he's my nephew. I don't mind. He'll be able to help me when his wound's healed.'

A voice over the intercom announces the arrival of the train to Thessaloniki. It hisses into the station and its wheels grind on metal. The door of the carriage in front of Samira slams open. I turn to hug her. My eyes well and my throat thickens as we embrace, and all I can do is wish her good luck and a safe journey. Katerina, too, bids her farewell as a tear rolls down her cheek. They will need all the luck in the world, I think. We don't wave but watch the train move slowly away as Samira stands at an open window and looks out with a steady gaze.

After lunch back at Katerina's house, I go upstairs and lie on my bed. I'm tired from the early start to the day and emotionally exhausted. I cannot remove the plight of this woman and her travelling companions from my mind. I eventually fall asleep and awake refreshed, determined to write up my article on the day's events and send it off to Chloe. I want to be free of work when I return to Dimitri so I have time with him and for the olive harvest. I scan the BBC website for any news about refugees trying to cross the border into Macedonia. I find an article with images of armed guards, barbed wire fences and roving German shepherd dogs. The article reports the police only permitting 500 refugees to cross the Macedonian border each day. My heart gives a thump. Another photo shows an encampment of tents and groups huddled in the rain around fires burning in tin drums. None of this seems right.

I try to facetime Dimitri but he doesn't reply. He's probably back at the hospital and too busy.

\* \* \*

In the evening we go down to the square again for beers, and when we finish we head off across the square to walk down a side street. As Katerina and Tomas walk ahead of me, I feel a tap on my shoulder.

'Hello,' a familiar voice says. 'I thought I might find you somewhere round here.'

I turn and before me stands Philomena. 'What are you doing here?' I say accusingly.

'Looking for you. I thought you might like to meet some interesting people. People that you could write about in your articles about Athens.'

'How do you know what I'm doing in Athens?'

'I saw you at that migrant camp the other day, so after you left I asked them what you were doing. They told me you were writing articles about migrants for an online website.'

'So?'

'Well, it's just that I know someone that might surprise you, that you might be interested to meet. You know, a little scoop for your website.'

'It's not my website.'

'Well, whatever. Just thought it might tweak your curiosity.' She smiles charmingly.

Yes, she has tweaked my curiosity. 'And who is this person?'

'Someone connected to Golden Dawn.'

'Oh. And where is this person?'

'Just down this road and round the corner. Two minutes away.'

'I see.' I'm not sure whether to trust her, but she seems to be acting normally now. Piquing my interest. Enticing me.

Katerina and Tomas return to my side.

'Thought we'd lost you,' Tomas says. 'Are you coming?'

'Katerina, Tomas. You know Philomena, don't you?'

'Well, not really,' Katerina says. 'Just seen you around here sometimes.' She smiles and nods to the young woman.

'Philomena is going to introduce me to someone connected to Golden Dawn. Could be interesting to add to an article of mine. Apparently they're just around the corner here.'

'Well … OK.' I sense a slight tone of doubt in her voice. 'Will you be all right?'

'Of course.'

'You'll find your own way back to the house, then, I suppose.' She pauses. 'Don't be long, lights out early!' She laughs. 'See you soon.'

As Tomas and Katerina head off, I turn and follow Philomena down the street. Twilight turns to darkness as we walk down a side lane with no shops and lit with only an intermittent weak globe. We turn left, then right again, and the street narrows to a laneway with walls on either side within touching distance. Claustrophobic and disorientated, I lose my sense of direction. It seems we are not going to a taverna in a lighted street for a quiet drink.

'Do you know where you are going?' I say.

'Sure I do.'

'You said it was two minutes away, but we've been walking for much longer than that.'

'No, we haven't.'

The only light comes from the occasional open door we pass and where the black silhouette of a person stands sentinel. We turn another corner, and then another. I've no idea where we are, and we arrive at a door in a wall where Philomena presses a button. A buzz comes from inside and footsteps approach, but the door remains closed.

'Who's there?' a voice says over the intercom.

'It's Philomena.'

A keypad beside the door lights up, and Philomena punches in a code. The door clicks open. In the dim light within, a hulk of a man in dark glasses and a cap stands at the bottom of the stairs.

'Who's this?' he says, looking at me.

'A friend,' Philomena says.

'You know you're not supposed to bring anyone here.'

'It's all right. She's a nurse. She won't do any harm.'

I wonder where Philomena got "nurse" from.

'Huh, one of your lesbian friends.'

'And so?' Philomena scowls at him. 'What's it to you? Oh, shut up and let us pass.'

'Not so fast.' He blocks the stairs, pulls out a gun and presses the barrel to her neck. 'Come here, you little bitch.' Grabbing her by her arm, he frisks her whole body and then puts his hand down her shirt and up her skirt. He pulls out her phone and turns it over in his hand, 'Hmph! Nice try, but you won't have much use for that in here as there's no reception.'

Fear and nausea wash over me as I anticipate that I, too, will be frisked by this brute.

'Philomena,' I say, 'let's leave. I'm not interested anymore.'

He turns to me and a sinister smirk appears on his face. 'Ah, come here, you little puppy.'

He presses the gun to my cheek and grabs my shoulder. The stench of his sweaty armpits makes me bilious.

'Let's see—'

'Victor! Enough!' a voice with a thick Russian accent shouts from above.

The brute removes his hand and the gun and steps back. He glowers at me and says, 'Next time, my little puppy.'

Philomena punches him in the stomach, pushes him aside and shouts, 'Get out of my way, you arsehole.'

We climb two flights of stairs in the dim light and come to a small landing with a door. We enter and follow a long, narrow passage until we find ourselves in a living room sparsely furnished with a couch and two armchairs, a table covered with books and papers and an untidy kitchen corner where the remnants of past meals fill the sink.

'Anton! Anton!' Philomena calls.

The door opposite opens, and a tall, slim man with a grey beard and balding head walks in. He embraces Philomena and they kiss deeply in front of me.

'Ah, my lovely girl,' he says, pressing his hand on her breast.

Philomena goes into a long rant about how the hulk at the bottom of the stairs treated her. 'He put his hand down my shirt and up my skirt and pressed his gun to my neck.'

'Huh, that Bulgarian thug hasn't got one gram of grey matter in his head. I tell him that his job is to guard outside there and not move till I call him, else I'll call the police to take him away, and he'll never be seen again.'

Anton turns and looks me up and down. 'And who is this young lady?'

'This is Marina, a friend of mine.'

'And what brings you to Athens?'

I pause before I answer him and try to digest his Russian accent with its long vowels and hissing consonants. I know Philomena would have told him that I've been writing about migrants, yet if he's got anything to do with Golden Dawn, I figure he'll not like migrants, foreigners or anybody of that ilk.

'I'm writing articles about migrants … about the situation in the camps.' I try to qualify.

'And you writing for who?'

I quickly invent a name. 'Webnet.'

'Ah, let me see.' He takes out his phone.

I quickly tell him he needs a password to get into the site. 'It's only for subscribers.'

He waves the phone about and curses, '*Chert voz'mi*! There's no reception. Ah, this country, no internet, no money, no work and full of migrants. It goes to dogs.' He returns his attention to me. 'And what you find in camps?'

'A lot of people who need help.' I think this is the wrong answer. He's probably not interested in migrants who need help. 'There's a lot of disorganisation.'

'Ah, yes. Greek people, good people. Greek government, bad government. Steal all people's money and nothing left for people. Now we come from Russia and help Golden Dawn when they come to power. We help them win elections and give them money for debts. The Europeans don't do it. You see, they kill Greece.' He strokes his moustache with his fine hands and gives Philomena a little smile.

'Now, Marina, you have tea?'

'Yes,' I say. 'Thank you.'

He makes tea, rattles cups in the kitchen corner and places floral cups and hard biscuits on the table in front of me.

'You know Hermes Chloros?' he says.

'Your important leader? Yes. Of him. I don't know him personally.'

'Now they arrest Hermes, but we get him out. He my good friend. We been friends for many, many years. He come to Russia many time to our meetings with many important leaders from Europe. You know, Madame La Pen, Mr Salvini from Italy, Mr Nick Griffin from British National Party and Mr Orban from Hungary. All people from these countries don't like Europe. And Mr Nigel Farage, you know him? He good man. They all want out of Europe. They want to free their country from moneylenders. All people in those countries are tired of liberalism, globalisation and euro. They cry, back to drachma! Back to lira!'

Yes, I think to myself, the Russians are galvanising support from the European right-wing parties. I read about it in *International Politics*, that these parties are sympathetic to the Russian cause and funded by the Russian government.

Anton gives a little laugh. I don't need to interrupt him with any questions as he is a river of words, seemingly used to churning out his ideas at great speed to listeners.

'We want a new way,' he continues. 'Away from the modern West, where Rothschild, Soros, Schwab, Gates and Zuckerberg hold and control everything. It is most disgusting thing in history of world. I good friend of Mr Putin, and he agree we go back to family, Orthodox Church and unite in one great Eurasian community against America. You see, we start with Ukraine, who come to join the Great Russian Family, our new

Empire, that is where Ukrainians want to be. Not join with the West and Euro and NATO.'

'This is all very interesting, Anton.' I humour him. 'I think you have some very good points. I understand that many people agree with you, especially here in Greece where they've lost their jobs and the government can't pay its employees.'

'Now, you must write notes so you can put all in your articles. I give you name of my book. *Another Way* by Anton Dautov. Here, I write down. I want sell my book in UK. You buy online at this address. Tomorrow, I go back to Moscow.'

I put the note he hands me in my pocket.

Suddenly, from outside in the passage, there comes movement and arguing voices, followed by rushing footsteps down the corridor and a banging on the door.

Philomena screams. 'They're outside the door! They're after us! They're after you, Anton!'

She and Anton leap from their chairs and rush to a door on the opposite side of the room. They disappear through the door and slam it closed, and a lock snaps shut. A gun fires outside in the passage, and a man screams in pain in the passage. Is it Victor? I can't tell. I rush to the door to follow Anton and Philomena, but it is locked. I am alone in the room and can't use my phone.

Outside the door to the passage, a voice shouts, 'Dautov! Dautov! We know you're in there. Come out now, with your hands on your head.' They shout again, but in Greek. I can't tell who they are. 'We'll break the door down if you don't come out. You're finished.'

They bang against the door with what sound like the butts of guns. They rattle the lock, but their attempts to open the door are useless as the door is made of a heavy wood and the lock solid. I saw Philomena turn the key when we came in.

Shouting and arguing continues outside, and someone yells, 'Unlock the door, Dautov!' Footsteps retreat outside until only silence remains. Are they giving up? I think.

A man whimpers in the passage. It must be Victor.

'Victor, are you out there?' I call. No reply. I try again but louder. 'Victor, I'm alone in this room. Philomena escaped with Anton. Can you get to the door and unlock it? Have you got a key?' But no response comes.

I try every which way to use my phone. I look for a landline phone socket but can't see one anywhere. I lean out a small window which opens onto the narrow lane, but there is no reception whichever way I point my phone. I consider jumping to escape, but it is too high, almost three floors. If I break a leg I can't run, but if they find me here I might be arrested. I go over to the other door off the living room through which Anton and Philomena escaped and fiddle with the lock.

'Philomena! Anton! Open the door!' I shout, but all is as silent as a tomb.

I search for a screw driver to unscrew the lock but find nothing in any of the drawers or cupboards. I only find a knife. I attempt to unscrew the lock with that, but the knife won't turn any of the screws.

I lean out of the small window again to see if there's life in any of the buildings across the lane. But darkness reigns, and a shaft of moonlight reveals the buildings as abandoned, with no glass in any of the windows and with collapsed ceilings and roof. I recall Dimitri telling me that parts of Athens had never been repaired after an earthquake and that the allocated funds had just disappeared into unknown hands.

Dimitri! Oh, how I wish I was with him now, on our veranda, stargazing. He'll be wondering why I haven't called him. I am suddenly weeping and missing him badly. He'd know what to do. I have to get out of here. I wish I hadn't come to Athens. Philomena kept telling me it was dangerous.

I go to the door and cry out again, 'Victor! Victor! Can you hear me? Are you there? Answer me. The door's locked.'

I hear a whimper. Or do I? I can't tell. The sudden screech and whine of a cat comes from the lane below, and the light above me flickers and goes out.

'Oh, oh no,' I cry into the darkness. I squint to adjust to the gloom and stumble with outstretched hands towards the door and feel for a light switch, but I can't find one. Has someone cut the power? My hand grazes a lamp on a nearby table. I find the switch, but it doesn't respond.

The darkness closes in on me as do my thoughts. Black thoughts envelope my mind. The accident, my mother, my hand on the wheel; now, in the dark, I am convinced I took it off the wheel. Dimitri. He's not well; he told me so. 'Oh, Dimitri, how am I going to get out of here and look after you?' I say aloud. I stumble forward until I reach the couch, and I lie down and close my eyes. I'll wait till morning, I tell myself. Someone will pass below in the daylight. But what if they come back? Those people. The ones looking for Dautov.

*  *  *

Thumping on the door to the narrow passage snaps me awake.

'Give it another go!' a commanding voice outside shouts.

As the door judders, I jump to my feet. A shot fires and the wood around the door bolt splinters. I rush to the window and hide behind a curtain and peek through a gap.

'Now go!' the voice shouts.

Following an enormous thud, the door crashes to the floor, revealing a man holding a battering ram. Two uniformed men file into the room, their guns at the ready and torch lights beaming. My heart thumps loudly; I'm sure they can hear it.

'Captain, there's no one here,' the lead man says in Greek. I don't recognise the uniforms as police. Are they army?

'Where's that bastard Dautov gone?' the owner of the commanding voice says as he steps inside the room. 'Victor sent the message saying he was here. We've got the other guys from GD, but this is the one we've really got to get.'

'Captain, there's a door on the other side of the room,' the lead man says. 'I'll try that.' He steps over and grasps the door handle and tries to turn it. 'Damn, it's locked.' He rams his shoulder against the door, but it remains steadfast.

'Here, let me give it go,' the captain says. He pulls out his gun and fires a shot at the lock. 'Argh, nothing doing! Get the battering ram.'

As I grip the curtain, barely able to breathe, the battering ram is thrust at the door, which crashes to the floor, accompanied by the cracking of ceramic and the shattering of glass.

Shards crunch beneath the steps of the lead man as he enters through the doorframe. He throws aside a chunk of ceramic. 'It's a bathroom. There's no one here, not even a window to escape from. That dumbhead out there, Victor, he's led us here for nothing. Need to teach him a lesson on the way out.'

'Search this room,' the captain says, 'and see if you can find anything.'

I move my face away from the gap in the curtain and shake uncontrollably, desperate to calm my heartbeat and breath. Torchlight illuminates the curtain, and the barrel of a gun sweeps the curtain aside, revealing a beam of light that shines into my face, blinding me.

'Hey, look here, my friends,' the lead man says, 'a bubba girl.' I shake all over. 'Get your hands on your head. Go on, go on.'

The captain comes over. 'Well, what have we got here? And what brings you to this room?'

I can't reply, for I am paralysed with fear.

He presses his gun to my stomach. 'Speak, or I'll shoot.'

'I … I … I was brought here by a friend,' I say. 'For tea.' I nod towards the cups and biscuits still on the table. 'She went into the bathroom, locked the door and didn't come out again.' My mind rushes as I try to think up a plausible story. 'I called her, but she didn't reappear, and I couldn't get out of this room because the door was locked.'

'You English?'

I pause for a second. 'Yes.'

'What's an English woman doing in this godforsaken place?'

'I was giving my friend an English lesson.'

'Ha! Sounds like a good reason for a lesbian meet-up! And what's your *friend's* name?'

'Verena.' It's the first name that comes into my head.

'Verena what?'

'I'm not sure.'

'Ah, course you're not sure.' He turns to the lead man. 'Got to tell Intelligence about this one. Probably working for the British.' He turns back to me. 'You ever heard of Dautov?'

'Who?'

'Anton Dautov. He's Russian. He should have been here. But he's not. Only you, a British spy.'

'I'm not a spy. I'm not working for anyone. I've told you I came here to my friend's house. That's all. There's no one else here.' I go to remove my hands off my head.

'Keep your hands up! Right, let's see what you've got on you.' He frisks me all over, and I shudder as his hands touch my intimate parts. He pulls out my phone. 'Ah, this should be interesting.' He puts it in his pocket.

'No. Please. Give it back. I've many family contacts on there. I don't want to lose them.' I try to appeal to his human side, but my words waft into nothing. His ice blue eyes stare at me. 'Look, there is nothing there that could interest you.'

'Silence! We're taking you down to the barracks. Let's get out of here. Move!'

He twists my arm up behind my back. I hear a crick and cry out in pain.

We file out into the passage and pass Victor lying in a pool of blood. He whimpers, but the captain gives him a hefty kick in the ribs. I reel in horror at his bestial aggression and go into a panic: where are they taking me? To what end? My mind races, jangling with fear at what they will do to me.

The captain spits on Victor and says, 'You were supposed to do a job for us, but you didn't. Anton Dautov isn't in there. So just lie there and bleed, you bloody Bulgarian.'

'The man needs help,' I say.

'Shut up, you! And keep walking.'

'Where are we going? Where are you taking me? I've done nothing. I don't know that man. Please, let me go. I won't say a thing to anyone about this. Please, you're hurting my arm.'

He tightens his grip. 'Shut up or I'll break it.'

I find myself crying, uncontrollably, as the memory of Dimitri and me on the bed in the shepherds' house high in the hills overwhelms me.

The captain shoves me forward and ushers me along the passage, down the stairs and out the door. We cross a dimly lit street, and he pushes me into the back seat of a grey car. The captain and the lead man sit either side of me, and the captain shouts in some dialect on his phone as the car speeds through the empty streets of Athens, through every red light.

I am in a state of despair, with no way of escaping. How did I get myself into this? My journalistic impulse to follow a lead? To learn and hear something new? And now it has cheated me. The wrong road taken. Thoughts of Dimitri flood my mind. We never had to decide which road to take. We just went as one. Down the right road. Always.

The car slows to a stop in the dark before an innocuous building. They hustle me into the edifice, down a hall and into a small room with a table, a chair and a blinding light.

'Sit here,' the captain says, pushing me down. 'We'll be back.' He goes out and locks the door.

As I rub my aching arms, I look around the room for video cameras and see one in each corner. So they are watching me. Without my phone, I have lost any sense of time. I stand and walk around, then lie on the floor, but the cold cement penetrates my bones. I shut my eyes but cannot sleep. I need a clear head, devoid of despair, I tell myself, as I cannot let them bully me with their methods and questions. I sit again and sing songs in my head and talk to Dimitri about our walk in the mountains and the smiling shepherds.

The door opens, and I stand as the captain enters.

'Come this way,' he says.

I follow him up a wide staircase, with granite steps and a mahogany bannister, and along an open balcony until we arrive at a carved door. He knocks, and voice within calls, 'Enter.'

'Go in,' the captain says.

I step through the open doorway alone, and the captain disappears as he closes the carved door.

Before me, a grey-haired man in a leather chair behind the desk gets up. He wears a uniform and smokes a cigarette.

'Do sit down,' he says in perfect English and with the accent of some well-to-do English public school.

I look about at the bookcases, the low tables with gold boxes and a side table with a cluster of decanters on a silver tray. It could be a library in an English manor house.

He extends an open hand and says, 'Colonel Panagos. And you are?'

I pause for half a second. Have I lied about my name? No. 'Marina,' I say.

'Marina what? Have you no surname?'

'Evans.'

'I see. And what were you doing out in the middle of the night inside a building where a Russian rebel we are looking for is holed up?'

'I don't know anything about a Russian. I was invited there by a friend to give her an English lesson. She's Greek.'

'I don't believe you. The Brits are after him too. You're working for British Intelligence, aren't you? You lot are all over the place, trying to find out what's happening with the debt crisis here.'

'Absolutely not! I don't work for anyone. I'm not even British.'

'What's that? Are you American? That's even worse.'

'No, I'm Australian.'

'Australian? Spying for the Australians? What do they want to know about Greece? Half of Greece have gone to live in Australia already. Are you Greek?'

'No, I told you, I'm Australian. I was born there. I'm just staying with friends for a few days in Athens before I head back to the Peloponnese where I am writing a tourist guide.'

'That doesn't explain why you were in that room all night.'

I tell him about Verena going into the bathroom and not coming back, about where Katerina and Tomas live and about Dimitri working at the Patras hospital.

He walks over to a dark window in the corner, lifts a phone receiver and talks rapidly in Greek, before turning to me and smiling. 'We're checking you out.'

He exits the room, and the captain enters and stands guard over me.

'I need to go to the bathroom,' I say.

He talks into a mouthpiece, and a woman enters, leads me into a side room and watches me intently as I sit on the toilet. I shake with embarrassment.

I return to the room and wait. When the clock strikes five, Colonel Panagos returns and stands before me.

'Do you have a middle name?'

'Yes.'

'What is it?'

'Anne.'

'And your date and place of birth?'

I provide them to him.

Again he leaves the room.

I sit and wait, guarded by the captain. Debilitated, my anxiety rises.

The door opens, and Panagos reappears. 'We've checked you out. All you say is true. We've spoken to our contacts at the Australian Embassy and, luckily for you, your identity details add up. You can go. The Captain here will take you out.'

The captain grabs my elbow, and as he steers me towards the door, I turn and say to Panagos, 'Thank you.' A spring of courage wells in me. 'Are you people police or army?'

'Neither. We're an independent security agency. Hired by the government, or the police, or the army, to carry out special operations when needed.'

'I see. And accountable to no one, no doubt.'

'That's right.' He gives me a sly smirk.

The captain pushes me out the door, roughhouses me along the open balcony and down the stairs. I am in danger in the hands of this man who is answerable to no one. We head down the hall towards the building exit, but, suddenly, he pushes me into a side room off the hall. He grabs my shirt, pulls me toward him, runs his hand up my leg and presses his groin against me. He gropes at my breast and attempts to push me to the floor, but anger rises within me like an exploding volcano.

'No. Don't, you bastard!' I shout.

I flay my arms about, claw at his face and draw blood on his cheeks. He yells and slackens his hold on me. Sensing his vulnerability, I reach out and dig my thumbs into his eyes. He screams and staggers. I knee him in the groin. He crumbles to the ground, groaning in agony and cupping his crutch.

'And give me back my phone!' I say.

I feel around in his pockets and find my phone. He strikes out at me, but I avoid his clenched fists and rush out the door and the building and run as fast as I can down narrow lanes and streets, away, away from the building and its sinister ugliness within. I reach a square and hail a taxi with a frantic wave, and it moves towards me and, like a cruising ship of good fortune, stops in front of me. Breathless, I get into the taxi and scroll my contacts for Katerina's address and show it to the driver. We travel in silence. Tears stream down my face as dawn greys the passing streets.

At the house, I unlock the courtyard door with the key Katerina has given me, and the door clicks, shutting out the night. I breathe in deeply as the feeling of a safe haven, of summer flowers and a lazy fountain unburdens my body. I creep around to the back, go upstairs, careful not to waken the household, and enter the bathroom. I shower and let the long rivulets of water wash over me and cleanse the night away. I vow not to tell Katerina anything, nor Dimitri. I lie down on my bed and close my eyes.

*     *     *

273

A knock comes on my bedroom door. 'Marina,' Katerina says from outside. 'Breakfast. You don't want to miss that train.'

I sit and try to call Dimitri, but he doesn't answer. Wretched with disappointment, I console myself that he is operating.

I go down to breakfast late. 'Sorry, I got back from Philomena's house after one. I shouldn't have stayed so long.'

'Interesting people?' Katerina says.

'Mmm, quite. But I don't think I'll bother with them anymore.'

'More coffee?'

'Sure. Thanks.' I seem to have quelled her interest. 'I've missed my train. I'll try and get the next one. I'll just have another apple pie before I go.'

After breakfast I say my goodbyes to Tomas and Katerina. She and I hug deeply, for more reason than she could ever know. We are friends now, sealed, she with her warmth, her sassy body, her smile and her passion. My earlier jealousy of her—and the seemingly intimacy between her and Dimitri—is gone, replaced by a bond that binds us close.

I find my seat on the train, shut my eyes and drowse, only to wake nauseous and exhausted from the terror of the previous night. All that happened haunts my thoughts. I rock from side to side as I walk down the corridor and enter the toilet and lock the door. I drop to my knees over the toilet and vomit. As I retch, beads of sweat bathe my brow. Grasping the sides of the swaying corridor for support, I stumble back to my seat. I close my eyes and will the waves of queasiness to pass.

When I open my eyes, I see the black bow. Philomena. Sitting opposite me. Her sudden presence stirs an avalanche of emotion within me. Shock. Anger. Fear. Intimidation. Has she been following me?

She stares at me and says, 'Are you ill?'

I decide not to answer her trite questions. 'Why did you abandon me? Have you been following me all this time?'

'No, just a coincidence. As I walked past this compartment, I saw you sitting here.'

'Don't lie to me,' I say, raising my voice. 'A coincidence? Are you joking? You set me up in a trap last night. God knows what you're up to. And where are you going now?'

'I'm not going anywhere in particular. I'm just escaping. I've got to get away. They arrested my boyfriend last night. He's on the executive of Golden Dawn.'

'And what about that creep Dautov? Looked as if he was your boyfriend last night.'

'God, no. He just pays me for sex. Wants quirky stuff. Makes me sick. Ugh, him? My boyfriend? Are you mad? He'll be in Moscow by now.'

Nausea again washes over me, and I rush to the toilet and retch into the bowl.

When I return to my seat, Philomena looks at me and says, 'You *are* ill.'

'Of course I am!' I shut my eyes and keep them closed for a long time and try to quell my nausea. When I open them, she is still looking at me. Her penetrating gaze unsettles me, and I urge my ill self to move away from her.

I shift to the next carriage and, to distract myself, look out the window and observe the rubble in backyards and the cranes standing idle on working sites, yet her near presence makes me feel sicker. As the train slows, she appears at the open door of my compartment and says, 'Look after yourself.'

I say nothing. She disappears and the carriage door slams, yet she reappears on the platform of the shabby station, escorted by the captain and his offsider. They grip her arms. What for? I ask myself. Has she been arrested? A pang of nausea rises within me again, and I close my eyes and try to calm the urge to vomit until I drowse.

I stir to the sound of wheels scraping on the iron rails, and the train slows as it pulls into Patras station. I hastily gather my baggage and hurry off and look down the platform, eager to see Dimitri. I had texted him the time of my arrival, but he is not there. I look about until I see Fotis approaching me.

'Oh, Fotis, you're here. Where's Dimitri?'

'In hospital.'

'You mean he's back working at the hospital?'

'No, he's in bed in hospital.'

'What do you mean?'

'I took him there last night. He collapsed at home, so he called me to come and take him to hospital.'

# - 38 -

I follow Fotis through a revolving door and into the hospital foyer. Before us stands a new reception desk surrounded by glass partitions and padded chairs in the waiting area. The smell of fresh paint fills the air, and not a single trolley can be seen in the corridors.

'What's happened here?' I say.

'Your friend Kanaris has thrown some money at this place, as he said he would, and now they've got a new Accident and Emergency department. They've also revitalised some unused wards and hired a band of new staff from Albania. Dimitri was training them till he fell sick. The place runs like a slick machine now.'

'Where is he?'

'Dimitri?'

'Yes.'

'Through here.'

We rush through the swinging doors beneath a sign marked *Infectious Diseases*, only for a nurse with a horsey chin to immediately confront us.

'Sorry, no visitors beyond this point,' she says with a slurred accent. She must be one of the new Albanians, I think.

Fotis tells her we've come to see Dimitri.

'No visitors beyond this point. It's written there.' She points at a sign. She has wasted little time in taking charge and defending her corridor like she's commanding an iron battleship.

'Can you tell him that his cousin Fotis is here with Marina. I've just brought her from the station.'

'I'll see.' She marches away, and we wait a considerable time before she returns.

'He's not well, you know,' she says. 'You'll have to put on these surgical gowns and masks. In there.'

Her tone is bossy and rude, suggestive of how things were done when under a communist regime. She points to a door, and we enter and put on our sterile uniforms under her stern guidance.

We follow her down the corridor to the end. She pushes open the door, and I see Dimitri lying on a bed, surrounded by machines and tubes.

'Don't go too close,' she says, putting up a preventative arm. 'You've got ten minutes.'

As soon as the door closes I ignore her directive and rush over to Dimitri and embrace him. A frisson of anxiety stirs within me as I touch his smooth arms and place my hand on his shoulder under his bed clothes.

'It seems ages,' I whisper. He looks pale. Drawn. Fragile. I place my hand on his forehead. 'What's happened to you?'

'I've got pneumonia,' he says. 'Couldn't breathe last night, felt like an asthma attack. Had to get Fotis over to drive me here. I'll be all right soon. They've given me some antibiotics. Must have caught it from Fotis. And look at him now. Right as rain. Eh, man?' Dimitri gives Fotis a pat on his arm.

'*You* look tired,' Dimitri says to me. 'Have a bad train trip?'

'Mmm, I felt sick on the train. I vomited. Must've been something I ate. I'm OK now.' I lie. The smell of the hospital makes me nauseous. 'I just need a rest. How long will they keep you in here? Remember, we've got the olives to harvest.'

'I'm sure it won't be long. They'll put me on an antibiotic drip, if needed. We'll see.' He flops back on the pillow, exhausted from talking. He grabs the oxygen mask and breathes heavily into it.

'Are you all right?'

'Sure, sure,' he says, panting. 'That's what happens with pneumonia. The lungs are so congested that they can't even get enough oxygen to talk.' He puts the mask over his nose and mouth again and inhales in short breaths until he removes the mask. 'Did Katerina look after you?'

'She certainly did. She took me out to the refugee camp. So grim. And so sad. So many people left languishing, and children too.'

But Dimitri has his eyes closed and pants into the mask. He's already tired from our visit.

'Dimmi,' I say. He opens his eyes. 'We'll go now. You need to rest. We want to get you out of here as soon as possible.' I bend over and kiss him on the forehead. 'I missed you. Get well soon.' He gives a slight smile. 'I'll be back tomorrow.'

We go out into the corridor, and I see Zina approach us. I'm relieved to see a familiar doctor, a face I know. 'Zina! I'm so glad to see you.'

'Ah, Marina, you're back from Athens, I see. Are you here to see Dimitri?'

'Yes. He doesn't look good. He's exhausted and can hardly breathe. Is he getting better?' I sound anxious, I know, and hope for reassurance.

'He's only been here overnight, so let's say he's stable. We've been checking out his heart.'

'What? What do you mean?'

'You remember a few weeks ago he had a bit of a problem.'

'But he told me it was nothing, just a minor heart condition that could be managed with a bit of medication. He said it was run-of-the-mill stuff.'

'Men do that, just dismiss it as if it's nothing. And doctors are the worst. Ever seen how many doctors smoke? They tell their patients not to do it, yet they've always got one lit under the desk.'

'But Dimitri doesn't smoke.'

'I know he doesn't. All I'm saying is that he probably didn't take his condition seriously enough.'

My face falls.

'Don't worry, Marina, don't worry … we're onto it now. And he has oxygen. He'll be over it soon enough. We're putting him on an antibiotic drip today. That should knock off the pneumonia.'

'I'll be in tomorrow, Zina. I really need to know exactly how he is. I might call you.'

'Do that, Marina.'

Fotis and I exit through the revolving doors. In the foyer I see Giorgos Kanaris by the reception desk. I don't want him to see me, so I hustle Fotis out of the building.

We drive along the sea front. Fotis stops to buy petrol and take cash out of a machine.

'Ah, so there's petrol now, is there?' I say. 'And I see you can get cash from the machines.'

'Yes, now that the government has agreed that we do what Europe tells us, we've got petrol and money. Easy, isn't it?' He gives a wry laugh.

We pass abandoned cranes on building sites and detour to the water's edge to eat at the beach taverna. My nausea passes, but I feel weak and light-headed. We order iced water and fried bread with salad. I nibble slowly at mine as my hunger has waned.

'Now I'm really worried about Dimitri,' I say to Fotis. 'Do you think he'll be all right?'

'I'm sure those doctors know what to do. Anyway, if he's got what I had, he'll get over it with just a bit of a cough.'

We sit in silence, eating the salad and looking out at the sea.

'Nice here, isn't it?' I say. 'The sea looks so inviting, a calm mirror. I feel like walking into it and breaking its sheen.' I tear off a piece of bread and throw it to a pesky seagull. 'Dimitri and I had one of our first breakfasts here. Seems so long ago now. He always knows the good places to eat at, like this café hidden behind a curtain of scarlet bougainvillea with the sea at your feet.'

We finish our meal, and I doze in the passenger seat while Fotis drives on for another hour until he wakes me when he stops to drop me off at the back door. I lean over and embrace him before getting out of the car.

'Thanks, Fotis.'

'Not a problem. Let me know what happens with Dimitri, won't you?'

'Of course.'

Near the steps the nets and blankets for the olive harvest lie in a dusty pile with the beating poles strewn beside them and the baskets heaped on top. Dimitri has pulled everything out from under the house, but nothing is ready for use. I drop my bag on the kitchen floor and go out onto the veranda. The air is still balmy, and I lean back into the cushioned sofa and watch the sun sink towards the horizon as the sea gathers its reflection in streaks of topaz. I could fall asleep here, now, but know that I won't wake till morning, so I go to the bathroom, shower and get into bed.

In the morning I am still ill, and I sit looking at my cup of chamomile tea on the kitchen table. As I sip slowly, I notice a stale pie and half a peach on the bench, but I can't eat anything. I want to phone Dimitri but can't just yet, so I drive into town. I park the car in front of the chemist and go inside. The pharmacist smiles as she knows me.

'*Kalimera*, Marina. How may I help you today?'

'I'd like a pregnancy test.'

# - 39 -

After a week in hospital, Dimitri returns home, and the strength that seeped away whilst he was in hospital forces its way back into his body. Zina reassures me that he will be OK. 'He'll make a quick recovery,' she says. 'You'll see.' And he does, for he is soon able to walk about the olive grove and check the ripening fruit. He wipes out the baskets, shakes the nets and polishes the beating poles.

Harvest day arrives. Fotis, Andreas and Maria come for breakfast, and after coffee and cakes on the veranda we set off between the trees and lay out nets and beat the branches with our poles to dislodge the fruit. Later, Alexi arrives with a beating machine, and the fruit rains down in curtains of green hail. He stands beside me and teaches me what to do. 'Beat the branch, not too hard and not too soft. You have to be careful not to bruise the fruit but beat it off the tree at the same time.' An old radio sits beneath a tree, and Maria sings along with the bouzouki. When she chants her prayers, her voice emanates from a distant past. In the slanting light I look along the lines of trees, at the upturned heads of my friends in their chequered straw hats and bandanas, and see a finely painted pastoral scene.

In the afternoon Dimitri goes up on the veranda and cooks. Cooking for company corrals him into the best of moods, and when we gather to eat, he bustles about as he hands out plates and the dishes of grilled meat and fish. His hair flops over his forehead as his deft hands arrange the food. 'Come on, boys, you need this,' he says. 'Some wine?' Yet he fills our glasses before we answer. Alexi has brought his pickled zucchini, tomatoes, feta and fresh bread, and Maria has unwrapped her loukoumades soaked in her own honey. Harvesting the fruits of the land has warmed us to our friends, announced the end of summer and the end of illnesses. I see Dimitri eating copiously at the other end of the table.

Next day, we transport the olives up to the olive press at Alexi's farm and watch the green fruit rain down into the bins and then onto the stone press. Dimitri toasts the bountiful crop with early wine and embraces our harvesting companions.

Later, at home on the veranda, we lie on the sofa, languid with the wine. Dimitri has his hand on my stomach and his arm around my shoulder.

I turn to him and say, 'Guess what?'

'What?' he says.

'I've got some good news for you.'

'What sort of good news?'

'Something you'll be happy about.'

'What? I can't imagine. Is Chloe paying you double?'

'Nope. Something there.' I press his hand on my stomach.

'What?'

'I'm pregnant.'

'Oh. Oh.' His voice wavers, and he pulls me towards him and kisses me deeply whilst running his hands through my hair and over my face. 'Oh, that's wonderful news. I'm so happy. For you. For us. Very. Yes, yes, you'll be a marvellous mother.' He kisses me again and crushes me to his body. 'Let me feel it.' He presses his hands to my stomach.

'You can't feel anything yet,' I say. 'It's just a dot.'

'Are you OK? I mean, are you feeling all right?'

'Of course I am.'

'But you've been vomiting every morning. Why didn't you tell me before?'

'I wanted to wait till you were out of hospital. I wanted to celebrate here at home, not in that sterile place. Let's celebrate now.' We embrace again and slowly, tenderly, make love as the stars bear down and cocoon us under the universal ceiling.

The next morning Dimitri springs into new life as if this newly blooming being within me has regenerated his sick self.

'We'll have to finish that room,' he says. 'We'll get Ahmed down to finish painting it, and then we'll get the doors and windows done.'

Dimitri is still on leave but is not sick enough to prevent him from going off to fetch Ahmed and to buy more paint and order windows and a door. He returns with Ahmed in the car and a load of purchases. 'I've bought pot plants and a tree for shade,' he says. 'The room will need shade.' He is as excited as a little boy with a new present.

He guides Ahmed to the unfinished room. 'Now, Ahmed, my friend, this room's nearly finished. It's for the baby. Just need to tidy it up. Here's the paint you were working with before. Just give it the final touches, round the window frames and door.' He turns and disappears out of the house.

While Ahmed gets on with painting the new room, I sit at the dining table and type.

Later, I offer Ahmed a cool drink and check his progress.

285

'Ahmed, where's Dimitri?' I say.

'Gone down to bring the rest of the nets up from under the trees at the end of the last row. You want me to go help him?'

'No, I'll go down and give him a hand when I've finished my article. You stay here and finish this room. He's already talking about doing the floors and the lighting.'

I complete my article and see the sun low in the west. Gold streaks fill the sky, and a slightly chilled breeze blows through the open window.

'Ahmed,' I call out. 'I'm going down to help Dimitri. I'll get him to drive you home when we return to the house.'

I step off the veranda and walk down between the olive trees. It's quite a walk to the last rows, and I can't see Dimitri anywhere. A little knot of worry surfaces. I reach the last rows of trees, but he's nowhere to be seen. I call out his name and look over the fence to the goats next door. I call out again, louder and more urgent. I walk up and down the rows of olive trees until I see a large pile of nets hidden behind the trunk of the most ancient tree in the grove. I hasten towards it, fearing he might have fallen and broken something. Then I see him, lying on top of the nets. I call out to him, but he neither replies nor moves. Panic swarms me, and I rush towards him. 'Dimitri.' I fall to my knees beside him. 'Dimitri? Are you all right?' He lies crumpled down on his stomach. His eyes are closed, and his head is thrown back at an awkward angle. 'What's happened to you? Get up.' I touch his face. 'Can you hear me? Say something. Can you feel me?' I place the back of my hand to his cheek, but it is as cold as a landed fish. I lift his hand, but it is as lifeless as a rubber tube. 'Oh … no,' I whisper. I shake his shoulders, then try to lift him. I bury my head in his chest and listen for a sound. Not a beat. I roll him over and breathe into his mouth between pumps to his chest. Someone once told me how to do this, but I can't think clearly now. 'Come on. Come on.' Tears stream down my face as I pump and breathe, for how long I don't know, but still he lies there inert. Lifeless. Cold. I hold his hand and sob until I release a scream as loud and raw as a wounded animal.

What feels like a glass jar falls over my head as I lie beside him under the tree. Through the glass all is blurred, distorted, muted. There's Ahmed and a stretcher and uniformed medics. Then Zina from Emergency at the open doors of an ambulance on a driveway. 'He's passed away, Marina,' a voice says. The sterile revolving doors at the hospital. The Albanian nurse with her arms around me, just holding me. Through the glass, I sense another cream room. Fotis, crying, stands a blur before me. So, too, Andreas. They speak to me, yet I can't hear them, can't understand them. All I see are mouths moving. Maria comes in, crying copiously, and embraces me, burying her head in my breast. Shifting groups of medics and nurses in crushed trousers and caps wipe their eyes, touch my cheek and kiss my hand. The glass jar around me is as translucent as a medieval window. Then Fotis leads me away. 'We're going home now,' he seems to say, and he and Andreas take me by my elbows and steer me through the revolving doors. Outside, a blurred Giorgos Kanaris appears before me. He takes my arm and kisses my hand and says something like '... a compassionate man ... a good man ...' He pauses. 'Too good.' Then I am in a car, travelling I know not where. All I can say is, '... but where is he?' A voice says, 'They'll bring him home tomorrow.'

In a bedroom I lie and stare at the ceiling. The veins of wood on the ceiling above me wave and form and reshape themselves. Katerina is there now, consoling me, comforting me, urging me. 'You must eat, must sleep,' she says. Tomas appears at her side and tells me to drink this, and I sink into a well of sleep.

It is day, and I find myself sitting on a veranda—Dimitri's and my veranda—with people around me and a coffin before me. Maria lights a candle beside our St Nicholas ikon in the corner and puts wild oregano and an olive twig in a glass vase. She prays in whispers and presses a cross to her breast. Dina and Vassilis arrive with others from the town. They bring flowers and candles and lay them on the coffin. People take my hand and kiss it and offer condolences. Costas and Anna come down from the Boutique Olive Farm, and Alexi too. He sits beside me all afternoon and doesn't say anything.

Still the glass jar covers me. I'm in a church, so glad for the chanting. A throng of black-scarved mourners respond to the chants, but I am numb, harrowed, mesmerised, understanding nothing, just staring blankly at the nape of a neck in front of me. Incense wafting over the coffin, golden candles, the priest's enamelled book—I'm lost in candlelight. Shadows. Grief. Katerina leads me to a corner and we light candles. 'I know you'll want to do this,' she whispers. 'For him.' But all I can think of saying to him is, 'You left me.'

Up on the hill, crosses, blindingly bright and white, surround us. People crowd the hill, from the town, the hospital, the camp, Athens, his school. So many people unknown to me. The priest chants and people murmur and cry. Someone hands me a sod of earth and a bunch of lilies, and I drop them on top of the coffin. Katerina holds my arm as Tomas chants, his voice wavering up to the sky. Ahmed, Hanna, Edris and Ali stand beyond the crowd, with upturned palms and mouthing prayers.

I am told there are seven stages. Or is it five? Or three? Or forever? Forever, I think. A bleeding wound that leaves a scar.

I lie in bed and look at the veins of wood in the ceiling. I can see the cobwebs too. I lie on the veranda and look at the constellations. One day soon, I hope, I might be able to pick something out from the Universe, like we used to. But now, here in my present, I place my hand on my stomach and hear a voice say, 'Marina, you've got a little someone you need to look after.'

# EPILOGUE

# - Epilogue -

Through the glass jar all about me remains blurred, distorted, muted. For how long? Days? Weeks? Months? I do not know. I lie on my bed and, between fitful sleep, examine the veined wood ceiling. Later, I sit on the veranda and look out at the sea and stare at the line on the horizon where sea meets sky. I observe the stars through his telescope. A Mercury sky. I sip from a green glass and blow dust off his sculptures and ikons. Funny that, wanting to clean them for him. Though numb in my glass jar, I sense the presence of others coming and going, never leaving me alone. Fotis and Andreas sit with me on the veranda. Maria brings food. Tomas and Katerina visit and stay. They cook, rake leaves and pick oranges.

One day, I can't say how long after the glass jar fell over my head, I seek warmth from a cool breeze as a low sun in the sky fails to feed my cold bones. I drive to the thermal springs. When I arrive, the gates are open in expectation of visitors, but no one is about. I walk to the pool, stand behind a bush and change into my swimming costume. I dive from the wobbly stone slab and plunge into the water. Alone in a warm cocoon,

I swim idly about, pushing myself along on one side, like a lazy dolphin. I stop and scrape mud from the walls and plaster my face with a mask, cancelling everything.

I hear a splash and look up and see a woman sitting on a rock at the cave entrance. As she spreads mud on her cheeks, she looks over to me and says, 'Hello, Marina,' in such a way that gives me a fright. I know her voice, but not the short blond hair. Is she a German visitor?

'Hello,' I say. 'Have we met before?'

'Yes.'

'I don't recall where.'

'Don't you remember? On the train. You declined my fish sandwiches and coffee.'

'Philomena?'

'That's right.'

'I didn't recognise you. You've changed your hair and you've got a mask on now. I thought you had gone to prison. After you were arrested at the train station.'

'Masks, masks, masks,' she said. 'No, they released me. I told them my boyfriend wasn't my boyfriend, rather, a client.'

I swim away, unable to bear being near her.

'No, don't go away. I wanted to tell you how sorry I am about Dimitri's passing.'

I spin around. 'How do you know about him?'

'I ask around.'

'Whatever for?'

'I knew him once.'

'You knew him? How?'

'Oh, long, long ago, when he was at school in Athens. We knew each other then.'

I stiffen with fear. I don't want to know about his past, only the memory of the time we shared. Again I swim away.

'Oh, Marina, please, no, don't go away.' The dry mud on her face cracks and turns a creamy grey as tears dribble down her cheeks in fine grey streaks. 'I loved him once, but he disappeared, went to America and deserted me, and look at me now?'

'But that was years and years ago.'

'Yes, I've been stalking him ever since he came back.'

'Stalking him? *Stalking*? What, following us around?'

'Yes, up into hills, down to the sea.'

Had she spied all this time on us? I couldn't bear the thought of it. 'Are you crazy? Spying on us? Crazy, crazy, that's what you are. Mad, deranged, mentally deranged.' I am shouting now. 'You don't know anything about anything. You don't know anything about us. You couldn't possibly. People like you are a pest, a plague, a parasite, a jealous fiend feeding on the joys of other people. Lonely with a dead heart.'

I lunge forward to push her off her rock, but as swift as one of the bats flying above us, she slithers off and worms her way back into the cave. I rush to the edge of the pool and haul myself up onto the wobbly stone. I gather my clothes and run to the car and roar its engine and spray out a fan of dust in my wake as I surge away.

At home I stand under the shower, hot and steaming, and wash every crevice of my body to rid myself of her infestation. And then I collapse to my knees and release a long scream as tears stream down my cheeks, and the bell jar breaks, and my grief, my loss, my emptiness, pierces my harrowed heart.

Later, how long I do not know, I dial Katerina's number and wait until she answers.

'Katerina?' I say, choking back a sob.

'Yes. Marina? Is that you? Oh, it's so good to hear from you. How are you getting along? We're coming to Kato Samiko in a couple of days. We want to see you. Hermann and Gudrun, from Germany, are coming to stay, and we are bringing them with us. Are you all right?'

'Not really.'

'Oh, I'm so sorry. It all takes a long time, you know.'

'I know. Katerina, I was at the pool today and … and …' I can hardly get it out. '… I saw Philomena. She was at the pool. We had a conversation in the water, and she told me she used to know Dimitri.'

'You mean Philomena from round here? That's impossible. She died months ago, in some mysterious way, so they say. You said she used to know Dimitri?'

'Yes, at school.'

'She's lying, Marina. I knew Dimitri all his life. She never went to our school. It probably wasn't her. You've mistaken someone else for her. Anyway, as I told you, she died months ago. They found her dead by the railway tracks on the line to Athens. You know she was working as a prostitute, don't you?'

'Of course I do.'

'I think you may have imagined it. The mind plays tricks on you when you are suffering the trauma you are going through.'

'Are you saying that one of her clients killed her?'

'No. Nobody knows. She was buried in a hurry.'

'I'm sure it was her today.'

'It can't have been. She's dead. You must have been hallucinating. That pool, with its emanating gases and warm waters, can effect the brain like mind-altering drugs. It's good for the body but not always for the mind. That's what lives are made of, a mix of the imagined and the real. As I told you, Philomena's dead. You must try to rid your mind of these imaginings. It's not easy … sorry, I sound a bit harsh. I can't wait to see you. We'll talk about it when we see each other.'

I didn't understand. Was she trying to tell me that nothing was ever as it appeared to be? Had the glass jar distorted my sense of reality? Had I been hallucinating? I would probably never know, but I knew I would never return to the pool again.

\*     \*     \*

Years pass until one evening—with winter approaching, the rains arriving and the Arcadian winds blowing as chilly as ice—Alexi's car pulls up outside, and he marches into the kitchen.

'Hi, you,' he says. 'I want you to come up to the olive farm and stay for a while. We need a hand. We've got guests for dinner, but no one in the kitchen and no one to serve at the table. Ahmed told me to come and get you. He said you've been holed up on your own for too long and need to work, hard.'

I struggle to comprehend what he has said, yet I acquiesce, and he stands beside me in the bedroom while I pack clothes and gather things from the bathroom shelf.

'You can stay for as long as you like,' he says. 'We need help in winter and you need company.'

'But I've got my baby.'

'Well, she's not a baby any more, is she?'

'No, I suppose not.'

Melissa comes into the bedroom. She is eight. Eyes almond pools. Thick dark hair, with Dimitri's cowlick flopping over her face.

'Where are we going?' she says, watching me pack.

'We're going up to Alexi's house. He needs some help. We'll stay a while. Are you happy about that?'

'Of course. Will I be able to help with the goats?'

'Sure,' he says. 'We've got a new kid.'

\*     \*     \*

That night at the Olive Farm, it is Katerina and Tomas who arrive for dinner, accompanied by Fotis, Andreas, Hermann and Gudrun. I hug Katerina as she presses her cheek to mine.

'You feeling better?' she says. She points at the winter rose in my hair. 'A flower in your hair. A new beginning?'

'No, just a little step forward.'

'Good. Mini steps.'

I embrace Tomas and my other friends, and we gather and sit at the table in the warm kitchen. I help Alexi lay out the plates of moussaka, dolmadakia and grilled feta, while Anna slices bread and pours out last year's wine.

Tomas, sitting opposite me and next to Hermann, says to me, 'You're looking good, today. It's that rose in your hair. Don't you think, Alexi?'

'Mmm, sure,' he says, smiling with a hint of a blush.

We fill our plates with food and slice up roast pork as succulent as velvet butter. I soon clear my plate and go to fill it up again when Tomas says, 'Marina, do you remember when Dimitri was very ill?'

On hearing Dimitri's name, I gulp back a sob. I am not used to social interaction nor talking about my past. I glance at Alexi next to me, and he gives me a reassuring nod and smile and says, 'It's OK. Listen to what Tomas has to say.'

'Sorry, Marina,' Tomas says. 'I guess it's not a good idea to talk about these things, but, well, back then, when Dimitri was so ill, I took some of his blood samples to my lab in Athens. Hermann, here, can vouch for what we found. I retested the samples the other day, this time for coronavirus. We are now able to do DNA sequencing which provides the genetic information about a virus. It appears that Dimitri did have the virus … it's something we suspected all along, him being infected back then by some mutant strain. I gave the samples to Hermann, who has analysed the blood he gets from bats around here, and we think the bats which inhabit those caves have the same strain of virus in their blood. I know it's unimaginable, but we are wondering if Dimitri picked up coronavirus when swimming at the thermal springs.'

I pause eating and say, 'I don't understand what you are talking about. It was his heart. Zina said so.' I hate talking about these things and wish they would stop.

'Sorry.' Tomas hangs his head. 'It's just that scientists all over the world are still trying to get to the bottom of that pandemic ... to understand why it started and where it came from. There was possibly a small outbreak here which, thankfully, was reigned in in time. No one is sure how it happened.'

Andreas, sitting beside Gudrun, says, 'Those immigrants got it first, and in the hospital, and passed it onto Yiannis, Fotis, and then Dimitri, and also to some inmates in the prison.'

'But how did they get it?' I say.

'Eh, lots of those migrants were starving and went up into the mountains to hunt wild animals. They'd trap wild cats, rabbits and birds and cook them on fires in the hills or bring them back to the camp beside the stadium. That's how these mutated viruses take hold, wild animals eat bats and starving humans eat feral food. That's how these things start.' Andreas leans back in his chair and calls over to Ahmed. 'Hey, Ahmed, how did you eat on your trip from Afghanistan all those years ago? In the hills, did you trap wild animals to fill your stomach?'

Ahmed nods. 'Bad days. Bad days.'

A part of me wishes they hadn't brought up those dark times, yet I want to give a bow to Dimitri. I look up at Venus, low and gold, and whisper, 'I'm all right now. I'm happy. Our Melissa's here. We'll never forget you.'

*       *       *

299

We never return to Dimitri's house, our house, with the veranda looking over the sea, the telescope pointing to the sky, the cane divans with the cushions and the green glasses on the low table. Fotis and Andreas live there now and have turned it into an Airbnb.

Melissa and I live up at the farm with Alexi. Alexi and I cook, lay tables, prepare pickles, turn mattresses, bottle wine, harvest vegetables and milk the goats for cheese. We grow together like two vines around a pole.

Two years pass, when one day I lie on the new grass under a warm spring sun, a book by my side and a glass of wine in my hand.

Alexi comes and lies by my side and says 'Let's get married.'

I turn and say, 'Of course. It can't be any other way.'

We embrace and kiss and laugh as he runs his hand through my hair.

Later in spring we stand under the vine outside the kitchen door. Maria crowns us with wreaths of laurel leaves and early roses. A priest, in his black totem hat, sings the wedding vows, and Tomas in the background chants the responses with the women from the village. Melissa, now ten, holds onto my skirt and clutches a bunch of wild oregano with her other hand.

'When is this going to end?' she says.

'Soon,' I say, stroking her hair. 'Then there'll be cakes and drinks.'

Fotis and Andreas prepare the wedding lunch, Maria brings her nuts and wine, Ahmed cooks his spiced pilaf and, from early morning, Dina and Vassilis attend to the roasting of a pig.

'You're shining today, Marina,' Katerina says. 'It's the flowers in your hair. You'll be happy here, won't you?'

I nod.

Maria, ready with the knife, cries, 'The cake, the cake.' And we cut the cake and dance to the sound of the bouzouki and early crickets.

*    *    *

Some months later, Alexi calls from the house, 'Marina, your phone!'

I run inside to the living room and pick up my ringing phone.

'Marina?' a male voice says at the other end.

'Yes.'

'Giorgos Kanaris. How are you?'

'Oh, Giorgos, hello. I'm fine, just fine. It's been a long time.' It had been a long time. I'd seen him in the city sometimes, but we'd only stopped for a passing chat and gone on our way. 'And you, how are you?'

'Good. Look, I'm in town for a few days. Do you feel like coming out to lunch tomorrow? I thought you might like to see the new wing at the hospital. It's finished now. Just opened by the Prime Minister last weekend.'

I pause as the encounter with him on the veranda all those years ago springs to my mind. For some reason I blurt out, 'I'm married now,' as if to switch on a warning light. 'And I have a ten-year-old daughter.'

'Yes, I know, I know. Well, what do you say to lunch? Would you be allowed off the hook?'

'Of course.' I don't want to sound infantile nor like someone not in charge of their own person. 'Where and what time?'

'Let's say midday in the lobby of the hospital.'

'OK. I'll see you there.'

The next day I look at the dresses in my wardrobe and see the pink and sage green dress I wore to the piazza on the day I met Dimitri. I push it to the back of the rack. I hadn't thought about clothes for a long time, but now I am.

301

I walk into the hospital lobby and see the words *Kanaris Wing* etched in stone on an expansive piece of wall and, below it, Kanaris leaning on the Reception Desk.

'Hi,' he says. 'You're looking very beautiful. You always did. That sky blue suits you ... same colour as your eyes.' He kisses me on my cheeks and goes to draw me to him in an embrace, but I do not oblige him. 'You've been through a rough time, but I can see you are over it now.'

'I'll never get over it.'

'No, of course not. Come, I'll show you around.'

The smell of new paint and new everything fills the air. We walk along pristine-clean corridors flanked by wide windows and several indoor gardens where patients can sit in a bower of flowers and green. Kanaris takes me into a ward and then the operating theatres.

'Dimitri would have loved this,' I say. 'So sad he's not here to use it.'

As we stand outside Accident and Emergency—a spaceship compared to what it was before—Zina comes through the door.

'Zina!' I say. 'So, Giorgos here has finally got what this place needed. How is it?'

She looks a new person, bright and alive. 'Marina. Hello. So good to see you. Yes, this place. It's as if night turned to day. We are so grateful. And how are you, Marina?'

'I'm happy enough.'

*     *     *

Later, Kanaris drives me along the seafront in his car. 'Everything has been completed along here ... the promenade is finished, the beach cleaned up and the gardens landscaped.'

I marvel at the transformation and compliment him on a wonderful job.

He steers away from the seafront and heads towards the hill overlooking the town.

'Where are we going?'

'To lunch. I'm taking you up to my art museum.'

'Pardon?'

'My art museum. I tore down my old house and built a museum for my collection. I've been buying all over the world and retrieving some of the Greek treasures stolen from our archaeological sites.'

Kanaris's car winds up the road on the hill until we arrive at the large iron gates. They swing open with an easy hum and no recollection of that night so many years ago when we were all trapped inside.

We walk up the marble staircase and pass through a door with a bronze sign above it which reads: *KANARIS MUSEUM OF ART*. Bars and restaurants on the ground floor look out over manicured lawns, flower beds and what had once been the swimming pool but is now a water feature. Kanaris signals to a waiter in one of the smaller restaurants. He guides us to a table, and Kanaris and I soon lunch on grilled salmon with roasted almonds and *un vino bianco Lugana*.

'Giorgos,' I say, 'I am curious as to how you financed all the building at the hospital? I thought Greece had run out of money?'

'My dear,' he says, patting my hand, 'we don't look to the Europeans or the Americans for money any more. We go straight to the Chinese. They are most eager to finance our projects and complete them in super quick time. I fly over to Shanghai, set up my contacts in shipping over there, and find they are most happy to do deals with us on much better terms than any of the Europeans or New York Jewish banks can offer. Of course, they want some little favours in exchange for their largesse, so the Greek government sold one of the islands in the Cyclades to the head of the Bank of Shanghai. Did a good deal. So now we've got a new wing at the hospital, a new beachfront and some help with my new museum.'

'What happened to the Russians you were so friendly with?'

'Well, I got rid of that little bitch who was my art advisor, and once she was without my money, she and her crew of girls had to hurry back home because they could no longer live the high life.' He takes a sip from his wine glass. 'Anyway, my resort went to shit for a year or so, what with the whole Ukrainian war thing. Trouble was those Russkies couldn't obtain visas to exit their country to come and sun themselves on my beach, so I had to do a bit of a scramble and hustle up some more clients, but the Serbs came good, as did the Bulgarians. There are plenty of cashed-up, thieving politicians in those countries to come and sit on my beach and piss-up on cocktails all night. The Chinese come too, of course, but they won't sit on a beach. I've provided some indoor entertaining for them, you know, gambling and stripshows. You can always adapt.'

Kanaris is on a roll and I cannot stop him.

'Of course, those officials in Brussels don't like us Greeks using Chinese money because we won't agree to sanctioning the Chinese for invading those islands off Taiwan. The Portuguese, like us, have done really well out of Chinese money … their country's really looking up with its new roads, railways and hospitals. They won't have a bar of sanctioning the Chinese. Pity the Germans didn't bail us out all those years ago.'

Kanaris pushes back his chair. 'Had enough? Dessert?'

'No, thanks.'

'Good. Now, let me show you round the museum.'

He gives me a most charming smile, and as we stand, he goes to put his arm round my waist, but I step away.

'Yes, yes. I understand. Come.'

He escorts me up a gently spiralling incline until we reach the next floor.

'An Italian architect designed all this,' he says.

'It's wonderful.'

He seems to derive great joy when showing me his favourites: the Mycenaean bronzes, the Minoan jewellery and some marble busts found at the bottom of the Aegean Sea.

'This is one of the Contemporary Art rooms.' He manoeuvres me round the room, his hand at my elbow. 'I bought all these from auction houses in New York and Dubai. This artist is my absolute favourite, an Argentinian graffiti artist. Died of an overdose at twenty-seven. I paid two point five million for it. Like it?'

'Not much.' I am pleased with myself for being bold enough to not gush compliments about these pieces, for they are as stale and boring as slices of week-old white bread.

We continue with the tour until we reach the last room of the contemporary works. Kanaris guides me to the far wall, upon which hangs a large portrait of himself.

'Do you like this one?'

'Yes, I do.'

In the painting Kanaris is sitting on a wooden chair and holding up a bunch of grapes. The green of the grapes is translucent and the walls behind are watermelon red. Kanaris has picked a grape and is putting it into his mouth. With his slight smile, he is caught in a moment and in motion.

'It's a good likeness, sympathetic.'

'It's done by one of your compatriots. I met him and his wife down the coast one evening. They were eating grilled chicken in a taverna and we started talking. He said he was a painter and showed me photos of his work. He's good, isn't he?'

'Very.'

I lean forward and look at the initialled signature at the bottom of the canvas. *R.D.*

# - Acknowledgements -

I would like to thank the creative writing groups in Queenscliff who have listened with such attention and interest to the unfolding of this story. If it hadn't been for their enthusiasm and encouragement this book would never have started or ended.

I owe a great debt of gratitude to Martin Smith who, on reading my first draft, offered to take on the editing of this book and guide me to its publication. His insightful suggestions and meticulous attention to detail went above and beyond anything I could have hoped for. Without his unwavering belief in my project this book would never have eventuated. Thank you so much Martin.

My thanks also go to Sharon, who was on board from the beginning and whose input was also invaluable in the realisation of this publication. A lovely new friendship!

Thanks to Rosie, Franny and Erica for reading my drafts and helping me with feedback.

Special thanks go to Rod, who loved it from the start, and who was a constant in urging me to get to the finishing line.

Thanks also to my lovely children, Franny and Nicky, for all the fun holidays spent in Greece over the years, in tents and on sand dunes with grilled kotopoulo, feta and fried zucchini.

My heartfelt thanks to all the Greek people we have known and met and to the land of Greece, a beautiful country.

www.ingramcontent.com/pod-product-compliance
Lightning Source LLC
Chambersburg PA
CBHW020333120726
47904CB00002B/398